THE BATTLE OF DOWNING STREET

A

In memory of Charlotte

THE BATTLE OF DOWNING STREET

PETER JENKINS
Political Columnist of The Guardian

CHARLES KNIGHT & CO LTD
LONDON • 1970

A2

CHARLES KNIGHT & CO LTD
11-12 BURY STREET, LONDON, E.C.3.

Printed in Great Britain by
BKT City Print Ltd,
A member of the Brown Knight & Truscott Group

SBN 85314 068 5 (hard cover)
SBN 85314 069 3 (soft cover)

Contents

Introduction

MADAGASCAR, Singapore, Sweden and Great Britain had one thing in common in June 1969 – they were the four countries of the world, the only four, in which Social Democratic Parties were in sole command of the government. I learnt this on a train from Eastbourne to London on the morning of June 18. Until then I had not been very hot on the political situation in Madagascar.

At Victoria Station the newsbills announced "TUC at Number 10" and "Cabinet on standby". At Eastbourne the 11th triennial congress of the Socialist International was in session. In London that morning, although I did not yet realise it as I took the train from Eastbourne, the future of Social Democracy in Britain was in question. Madagascar, Singapore and Sweden would have represented a poor tally for one hundred years of world-wide struggle for Democratic Socialism.

Surveying the world from Eastbourne – a point on the south coast of England from which it is seldom surveyed or even, perhaps, noticed – the prospect for Social Democracy was already a bleak one. Willy Brandt, who had spent until late Monday night in private conversation with Harold Wilson in the Prime Minister's suite at the Grand Hotel, was the leader of what had been once the greatest Social Democratic Party in the world. That he would shortly become the first Social Democratic Chancellor of the Federal German Republic did not then seem very probable. Brandt appeared to be the prisoner of a Grand Coalition. Despairing of ever winning governmental power even on the basis of the moderate, hardly socialistic programme it had adopted at Godesberg in 1959, the SPD had joined with its enemies in 1965 to share the spoils of office it could not capture for itself.

In France the picture could not have been more gloomy. Just two weeks previously, in the first round of the presidential election to replace the fallen General de Gaulle, the democratic left had been routed, humiliated, disgraced. Guy Mollet, a vice-president of the Socialist International, had not shown his discredited face at Eastbourne. A solitary and obscure delegate from the recently formed and still small United Socialist Party said by his presence at the congress all that needed to be said on the sorry plight of Social Democracy in France.

In Italy the picture looked momentarily brighter. The forces of Social Democracy had at last joined hands and a united Socialist Party had re-entered the ruling coalition. But hardly had the veteran battler Pietro Nenni returned from his brief visit to the English seaside than Italy was once more without a government and the democratic socialists were again in their accustomed state – split.

On the fringes of Western Europe only the recent triumph of the Swedish Social Democratic Party relieved the dismal scene. In Norway and Austria, both centres of the social democratic tradition, the left was in opposition; so it was in the Netherlands and in Denmark. In Belgium the socialists were losing ground within a coalition.

Beyond Europe, the world had been made safe neither for socialism nor democracy. In the white Dominions Labour was everywhere in opposition – in Australia, New Zealand and in Canada. Not a single party from the continental mainland of Africa was represented at the Eastbourne Congress. Among the off-shore islands of Africa, in South-East Asia and the Caribbean there were a few small pink spots on the map; but it could hardly be said that the social democratic tradition was among the lasting legacies of the ending of British imperial rule.

As at all gatherings of the Socialist International there were also present the pitiful reminders of the vast dominion of another and undemocratic form of Socialism. The Bulgarian Socialist Party in Exile, the Hungarian Social Democratic Party in Exile, the – especially poignant – Czech Social Democratic Party in Exile. There were Latvians, Lithuanians and Estonians – delegates of non-existent political parties from non-existent countries. These were the true heirs to the First Socialist International founded in London by Karl Marx in 1864. Some of them were represented only by a printed card on a desk before an empty conference seat, for such parties often die with the one forgotten man who from some small backstreet office or lodging room in London, Geneva or Paris acts as custodian of the letter head.

It was against this background, splendid yet sad, solidly based on the workers of the world yet falling apart in all directions, the symbol of a living idealism yet the reminder of a past era, that a great drama of Social Democracy was reaching its climax in London. Harold Wilson's premiership was at risk and so was the continuance of the sole Democratic Socialist Government to hold power in a major country. From dull, respectable and intensely bourgeois Eastbourne, where a fresh breeze tickled the deckchairs on the front, to a sweltering claustrophobic London was a short ride on the train into the world of real politics.

* * * * * *

For the delegates attending the International the most enviable feature of the British Labour Party was its united and strong industrial base. The lucky British were not plagued with competing Communist and non-Communist trade union centres nor was their trade union movement divided on religious lines or occupationally between white and blue collars. To the trade unionists from the continent and around the world the most enviable possession of their British brothers was a political instrument, the Labour Party, created in the trade union image but now capable of winning majority power in a modern welfare and full employment society. Why then was a Labour Prime Minister gambling his precious power base and why were the trade unions risking the destruction of so valuable a political tool? The crisis that week in London was a puzzling spectacle for the foreign visitors to Eastbourne.

Harold Wilson's Government, however, was particularly vulnerable on the trade union question. It was the first Labour Government ever to win a majority in ordinary peace time conditions. His political ambition was to establish the normalcy of Labour Government – to explode the myth that progressive government was the occasional exception to Conservative rule, to break down the inhibitions of the British people and cure his own party of its inferiority complex. His technique was not analysis but the therapy of governing. In 1964 Labour's chief claim to office was that it would "get Britain going again". It was elected on a competence mandate – competence softened by concern. By reforming out-dated institutions and modernising obsolescent industry it would achieve a faster rate of economic growth and thereby pay for its ambitious social programmes. But if ever there was an out-dated institution it was the British trade union movement. The unions were a feature of the obsolescence of British industry. They were one of the obstacles to faster economic growth. They were not even much interested in the social justice which Labour claimed would be the end-product of its materialistic endeavours.

The Labour Party had claimed a special competence for dealing with the trade unions. The historical and sentimental ties and – more than that – the community of interest between the industrial and political wings of the Labour Movement would engage for a Labour Government a positive response from the trade unions, denied to Conservative Governments. "We have the right to ask . . ." asserted Harold Wilson before the election of 1964. And from the industrial side of the family came this version of the relationship – from Frank Cousins, leader of the largest and most powerful of the unions: "Harold Wilson," he said, "is wanting to be part of a team that is going to change the system, and the function of a trade union will change along with a change in political function; it is bound to do so. I would suggest to you that one of the things we should always remember is that when we are putting a government in, as we are intending to do, to help us plan the economy, we have the trust that it is the same kind of economy they are helping to create. Therefore, I hope, on behalf of my union, and I hope every other trade union in this country, we can say to the Labour Party: 'We will support you in your intentions.' "

Both versions of the relationship depended upon an article of faith, on what we might call *the Social Democratic assumption.* As Frank Cousins expressed it "*we have the trust that it is the same kind of economy they are helping to create*". He said "economy" but he presumably meant also "society". This was the assumption – that the two partners working by their different means, the one industrial and the other political, were working towards a common end. In the past the relationship had been expressed as a crude division of labour. In 1947 Arthur Deakin, the then boss of the Transport and General Workers Union said "The question of wages and conditions of employment are questions for the trade unions, and the sooner some of our people on the political side appreciate that and leave the job to the unions, the better for production." In 1953 he said "We have the day-to-day job to do looking after our members. We cannot always accept the theories launched upon us. I have in mind some of the ideas projected in the political movement." Frank Cousins, Deakin's successor, said to the Labour Party conference in 1956 "I told you last year not to tell the unions how to do their job and I am certainly not going to tell the Labour Party how to do its job". Even Hugh Gaitskell, who saw that the Labour Party lacked glamour in a cloth cap pulled over its ears by the unions, steered clear of industrial relations as a political issue. "We can safely leave it to the unions to take the necessary action," he said diplomatically. And in 1969 the general secretary of the Trades Union

Congress, Victor Feather, could still say, "The Labour Party and the trade union movement each has its own responsibilities, and neither side wants to strain the loyalties which exist. One vital point does stand out though. If you look around the world to see where Social Democracy is strongest, there you will find a strong, united trade union movement and a strong, united Social Democratic Party, and the two have a close understanding".

The Labour Government under Harold Wilson was now, in 1969, openly asking the questions begged in all these statements. The partnership between a Social Democratic Party and trade unionism could no longer be based on a demarcation agreement. What should be the nature of a more constructive relationship appropriate to modern conditions? What balance of rights and obligations was involved? For it was obvious enough by now that trade unionism left to its own nineteenth century devices was in no sense working towards the achievement of a modern Social Democracy. The reverse was the case; the trade unions were one of the elements in the insoluble post-war equation in which full employment and free collective bargaining had somehow to be made to produce a satisfactory rate of economic growth. The very achievements of British Social Democracy – full employment and the Welfare State – had rendered obsolescent the foundation of British Social Democracy: the division of labour between a Labour Government and the trade union movement. Full employment had conferred upon the unions an inescapable role, negative or positive, in what since Keynes had been called "the management of the economy". Full employment had made it unavoidable for Government to take an interest in the proceeds of collective bargaining – in wages and prices – and made it inevitable, sooner or later, that Government would interest itself in the process of collective bargaining. Government and trade unions had been drawn since the war into ever closening contact; the task of Social Democracy, if it had not outlived its purpose, was to turn the contact into a constructive partnership.

If the Labour Party, as it had claimed, was specially qualified to tackle this problem it was at the same time specially vulnerable to the consequences of failing to solve it. If it was to establish its credentials as a National Party it could not afford to appear beholden to a single section of the community, however large and powerful. There were not enough trade union votes alone to return a Labour Government. The Labour Party was obliged to compete for votes in the centre ground of politics. It could not purport to be radical about everything else while conservative about the trade unions, it could not claim to be the reformer of institutions yet neglect the crumbling institutions of industrial relations, and it could not pretend to plan while neglecting to plan wages and salaries. What was more, the unions had become increasingly unpopular with the public. Because of its institutional and historical ties with the trade union movement the sins of unofficial strikers were visited upon the Labour Party, even in opposition. Bad industrial relations were bad for a Labour Government politically. But they had also become a serious problem for the country.

The number of strikes taking place in breach of agreed procedures between employers and workpeople was increasing. In terms of the amount of working time lost Britain's strike record continued to compare favourably with many other countries. During the years 1964–66 Britain's record was worse than West Germany's, the Netherlands' and Sweden's but a great deal better than the United States' and Italy's and somewhat better than France's and Japan's. But whereas in other countries the strike problem chiefly took the form of organised conflict between trade unions and employers, in Britain it chiefly took the form of the sudden, short, sharp unofficial downing of tools – the "wildcat strike". Outside the coal mines the number of strikes reported in 1956 was 572, in 1967 it was 1,694. The vast majority were unofficial and the industries most affected were engineering, ship building and the docks. The number of strikes in engineering had trebled in the 1960s.

The direct economic consequences of this near anarchy in key sectors of British industry could be exaggerated. The strike prone industries accounted for about one-third of British export earnings but the working time lost even in these industries was far less than the time lost due to sickness. One expert, Professor H. A. Turner of Cambridge University, estimated the total economic cost of all British strikes at less than one-thousandth of the annual national product. He commented, "An effective anti-influenza serum would probably be of more measurable benefit to the economy than an effective anti-strike law – and perhaps be less difficult and costly to produce".

Lost production, however, was not the only consequence of unofficial strikes. They were becoming increasingly damaging to Britain's commercial reputation in the world. After devaluation of the pound in 1967 British export goods were competitive in price; a renaissance in design and style had brought world-wide renown to many categories of British wares; but foreign customers could less and less rely upon their orders arriving on time. It was not necessary for the customer to have had some unfortunate experience for him to decide to buy, say, German instead of British. For industrial relations in Britain were becoming notorious. From their newspapers and television sets foreigners received a picture of a workforce which behaved with frivolous disregard for a once-great country's now parlous economic position. The downing of tools by men of rival trade unions quarrelling over who should bore the hole or turn the valve was becoming as bad a joke as the fall of governments in Fourth Republic France. The British workman's tea break was as risible a symbol of a nation's prodigality as the Latins' siesta had once seemed to the superior, industrious British. Labour relations were the most visible and remarked upon symptom of the "English sickness".

The foreigner's view may have been exaggerated but the British had to reckon with the existence of it. It not only affected orders for exports but also more general confidence in the country's ability to repair its economy and pay off its vast debts. The bad relations in industry seemed to suggest an absence of the social purpose necessary in a people required to undergo a period of rapid and profound change. Strikes affected financial confidence in Britain. The seamen's strike of 1966 had blown the economy "off course"; a dock strike in 1967 had been one of the factors making devaluation finally inescapable. "Solving the trade union problem" was increasingly seen by the international financial community as the essential condition for solving Britain's other problems. One comment will serve for the many which were made: a 1968 study of the British economy by the Brookings Institution of the United States observed "A combination of alleged laziness, suspiciousness of class and progress, and an atavistic opposition to redundancy is what appears to constitute the syndrome known as bloody-mindedness. And bloody-mindedness is alleged to have prevented the diversion of union bargaining strength into more socially useful channels".

The British too were coming to see themselves in this unconfident fashion. The undisciplined behaviour of trade unionists was increasingly coming to be deplored and not only because of the damage which strikes were believed to inflict upon the economy. The public resented the inconvenience caused by strikes affecting public services, notably commuter rail services. The use by the railwaymen of the relatively new technique of "working-to-rule" was especially resented. This was organised bloody-mindedness. The public also questioned the social morality of strikes in which small numbers of workers inflicted idleness and loss of earnings upon thousands of other workers and their families.

Strikes of this kind were coming to be more and more bitterly resented by the affected workers themselves and still more by their wives. Between the summer of 1964, shortly before the General Election, and the summer of 1969 the proportion of Gallup Poll respondents who considered the trade unions a "good thing" fell from 70 to 57 per cent and the number who considered them a "bad thing" increased from 12 to 26 per cent. In 1966 only 11 per cent of respondents saw strikes as the "most urgent problem" facing trade unionism; by 1968 the proportion was 17 per cent, by 1969 46 per cent. All the opinion polls showed a majority still in favour of trade unionism as such, but a larger majority, and a majority of trade union members themselves, believed that the Government should intervene in unofficial strikes and that the law should be invoked to improve industrial relations.

The political crisis in London in June 1969 was the climax to the attempt by Harold Wilson's Government to prove that Labour was a competent governing party of all the people which could meet the public demand for "something to be done" about the unions and, in the process, establish a new basis for the construction of Social Democracy.

I *Socialism in one ministry*

LET US begin with the entrance of our heroine. One day towards the end of March 1968 Barbara Castle was pacing up and down Harold Wilson's room, bullying him as usual. She was bullying him about socialism.

At the time she was the Minister of Transport. She liked to boast that her Ministry was the most Socialist in the Government and if Socialism was to be measured by the sheer scale of governmental intervention, there was no denying her claim. At that very moment she was piloting through the committee stage of the House of Commons a Transport Bill of Gothic proportion and ramification. It created a new State agency to regulate the passage of goods by road or rail; reorganised the railways; established a new framework for regional and urban transport planning; extended public ownership of the road haulage industry; imposed new charges upon the private lorry operators; and sought to extend the benevolent interest of the Minister even into the lorry driver's cab where a "black box" would record his contribution to the productivity of the industry.

But it was not about the socialisation of transport that Barbara Castle was nagging the Prime Minister. Her theme was the Government's policy for productivity, prices and incomes; her complaint was: "Harold, it's not Socialism." The policy, euphemistically dubbed "the planned growth of incomes" by Frank Cousins in 1963, had deteriorated into a crude exercise in wage restraint. It had become a negative policy when, in her view, it should be a positive instrument of socialist planning; the emphasis needed to be on increasing productivity not on holding back wages. "Barbara", said the Prime Minister when she had at last finished, "you've just talked yourself into a job".

The chief responsibility for the productivity, prices and incomes policy lay with the Department for Economic Affairs, a new department set up amid great heroics on the very day Labour took command of the Government in 1964. It had been created in the image of its first and noisiest incumbent, George Brown, for whose restless presence an ample berth was required other than the Foreign Office, from which he had been barred. George Brown was the deputy leader of the Labour Party. He had been beaten by Harold Wilson in the contest for the leadership of the party which took place in 1963 on the death of Hugh Gaitskell. In 1964 he became, in effect though not in name, the deputy Prime Minister; he went second into dinner and gloried in the title of Her Majesty's First Secretary of State and Minister for Economic Affairs. The DEA under Brown functioned in the fashion of a large and powerful private office, better staffed and equipped than the Prime Minister's own "power house" at Number 10. It provided the First Secretary with a base from which to mount his forays into all the main areas of government business. On every matter of state there was a "Treasury view"; now there was to be also a "DEA view".

That was the second reason for creating a Department of Economic Affairs. Labour had come to blame the Treasury for many of the country's economic misfortunes. The Treasury, it was argued, consistently gave the balance of payments priority over the expansion of the economy; it was preoccupied with orthodox financial probity and economic prudence; it put money before industry and took the short money-man's view as against the planner's longer view. Labour wanted a co-ordinating planning ministry to correct this deficiency of central economic government; the power of the Treasury would be checked by the establishment of a rival pole of economic power. The Minister for Economic Affairs would take first place, the Chancellor second place and that would reflect the priorities of a Government committed to growth policies and determined to plan. The idea for a DEA had been conceived, reputedly, in a London taxi cab – it was born as Harold Wilson returned from Buckingham Palace on October 16, 1964 and, according to a memorable "new frontier" press release, "began work that night". Unfortunately, no sooner was the score opened than it was apparent that the devil had been given all the best tunes. A cavernous deficit on the balance of payments account imposed a severe limitation on the new Government's freedom to pursue policies for economic growth. The collapse of confidence, which was one of the first results of a Labour Government assuming office, also ensured that the Treasury's primacy would continue. Moreover, the Treasury succeeded in retaining its dominion over public expenditure. A "concordat" was drawn up between the temporal and spiritual arms of public finance: the DEAwas permitted to draw lines on graph paper, but the Treasury still controlled the allocation of resources. Consequently the DEA became not so much a rival centre of real economic power as a lobby for economic growth within the Government. This unsatisfactory division of responsibility between Treasury and DEA was known hopefully as "creative tension".

In its early days the DEA was a vigorous and effective lobby. All the hopes and excitements aroused by Labour's return to office after thirteen years found their purest, and certainly their liveliest, expression in George Brown's DEA. Many were the "new frontier" goings on there. On one occasion George Brown suspected that the leaders of industry were conspiring in cabal against his National Plan; he tracked them down to Sunningdale, arrived there unannounced and slapped them into line; on the way back his car broke down so he hitch-hiked to London. Exploits of this kind were in the spirit of those times. But the blows rained down upon the DEA. The most crippling came in July 1966 when a hefty dose of deflation superseded all the hopeful prescriptions for economic growth. The National Plan had to be remaindered. The DEA was never the same again. George Brown shortly departed for the Foreign Office. Michael Stewart, a conscientious but rather colourless schoolmaster, succeeded to the now empty dignity of First Secretary of State and Minister for Economic Affairs. Later still the Prime Minister appointed himself to an overlordship of the DEA and appointed his protégé, Peter Shore, to be Minister there. The DEA was thus further devalued. By the time of Barbara Castle's conversation with the Prime Minister all that remained of its past glory was the responsibility for the prices and incomes policy.

This brave experiment in partnership between Government and industry had engaged a large part of George Brown's boundless energy. A great deal of his time had been spent in prices and incomes diplomacy, for example in preventing a penny increase in the price of the standard loaf. "God bless you" he telegraphed a manufacturer who had reduced a price, one among millions. The policy for productivity, prices and incomes had been conceived as a patient instrument for amending the structures of wage and price determination and the attitudes which underlay them. It was chosen as a preferable long-term alternative to the short-term wages freeze which the trade unions, in the first flush of loyalty to a new Labour Government with a majority of only four, would almost certainly have conceded. A tripartite Declaration of Intent was drawn up and signed with theatrical aplomb by Government, trade unions and employers at Carlton House on December 13, 1964. Elaborate criteria were drawn up for the guidance of the wage bargainers and price fixers. A National Board for Prices and Incomes was established for the purpose of scrutinising the justifications for wage and price movements and advising on ways of increasing productivity. Aubrey Jones, a former Conservative Minister and a Solomon among technocrats, was appointed the custodian and arbiter of the national interest. But the exigencies of the economic crisis soon perverted the original purpose of the policy for prices and incomes. It was increasingly put to short-term use. Premature claims were made for it as a substitute for deflationary policies; international bankers were encouraged to invest their confidence in it; it was expected to produce immediate and effective wage restraint. Consequently at each sterling crisis the clamps were tightened. An originally voluntary experiment became an exercise in state compulsion. A statutory element was introduced into the policy in 1965, only months after it had been launched; less than a year later, after the July crisis of 1966, a total freeze was imposed and backed with state powers to delay wage and price increases. These powers were still in effect when Barbara Castle was complaining to Harold Wilson in 1968.

Harold Wilson's first idea when Barbara Castle had talked herself into a new job was to put her at the DEA. He resented the sneering criticisms of that department and would have liked to revive its importance. For his party the DEA remained, however tarnished, the symbol of Labour's commitment to escape from Treasury orthodoxy. And no doubt he was ready by then to lay down his own overlordship, for one early result of his taking "personal charge" of the economy had been the devaluation of the pound. In any case he wanted to put Barbara Castle in charge of the productivity, prices and incomes policy and that policy resided in the DEA. The Chancellor of the Exchequer, however, was not eager to see new life breathed into the DEA. Roy Jenkins was unenthralled at the prospect of "creative tension" with Barbara Castle. Socialism at the Ministry of Transport was one thing, Socialism next door was another. Nor did he want there to be any messing about with the prices and incomes policy when it had a part to play in the strategy he had devised for making a success of devaluation. On this his political future depended. By achieving his ambition to become Chancellor of the Exchequer he had taken a step which could lead him either from Number 11 Downing Street to that most desirable of all addresses, Number 10 in the same terraced row – or to a place in the crowded pantheon of failed Chancellors. He had just introduced a Budget of unprecedented horror in a speech of unusual elegance and authority. He had promised two years of "hard slog" and incomes restraint was part of it. This was no moment for renewed experiments in divided economic control. The Chancellor and the Prime Minister had established a working partnership in survival, they would succeed together or fail together; two was company in this desperate enterprise (although neither found it convivial); but three would be a crowd. Harold Wilson and Barbara Castle were old political chums from the Prime Minister's half-hearted Bevanite days. Roy Jenkins was the pretender of the House of Gaitskell. And Barbara Castle was a determined lady, capable of giving any man a hard time. She had a habit of getting her way. No, Barbara at the DEA was not a good idea.

So Harold Wilson was obliged to have second thoughts. In order to bring her to the fore without too roughly jostling Roy Jenkins he settled upon the idea of creating a new empire for her. The responsibility for prices and incomes was to be transferred from the DEA to the Ministry of Labour and that department would henceforth be known as the Department of Employment and Productivity. The name had a good expansionist, positive ring about it. And with it went the title First Secretary of State for the First Lady of the Labour Government.

The creation of the Department of Employment and Productivity is the occasion for us to write the obituary of the Ministry of Labour. Of all departments in Whitehall it was most steeped in the tradition of the Labour Movement. An executive department of government it also operated in the manner of an embassy to a foreign power – the working classes. As with embassies, it was never entirely clear whether its first loyalty lay with the power it represented or the power to which it was accredited. To the public it was known chiefly as the ministry for settling industrial disputes but in fact it performed many other functions. It operated the Employment Exchange service; it was responsible for safety in the factories and the pits; it was in charge of industrial training; it collected and published a wide range of manpower statistics; it even dealt out milk coupons; but its most publicised and controversial function was conciliation in labour disputes. The unimpressive portal to the headquarters building in St. James's Square formed the backdrop to the much photographed and televised comings and goings which, up to and beyond the proverbial eleventh hour, preceded a great strike or, more usually, the inflationary settlement of a dispute. A prescribed ritual was followed in these matters. First the two sides to a dispute would be invited to make their positions known separately to the Ministry. Then the Ministry's conciliation officers, men of great humour and stamina (they needed both), and with rougher edges than the typical well cut Oxbridge civil servant of Whitehall, would start their go-between activities. At a carefully chosen point the two sides would be brought into the building together and sat down two or three doors of a corridor away from each other. At a later stage they would be brought to the same table. These comings together were often staged late at night when last trains were nearing, or the pubs about to close. At the crucial stage of a grave dispute the Minister himself would "personally intervene". And every now and again the ace card would be played and the negotiations would shift to Number 10 Downing Street. For example, a visit to Number 10 by tradition became the pre-condition for the settlement of railway disputes. The newspapers chronicled these rituals in carefully chosen clichés. The first threat of strike made for a "crisis"; then it would be something like "Docks – Minister Steps In"; inevitably "peace hopes" would "rise"; there would be a "chink of light at the Ministry of Labour" (known in the trade as "that old Chinaman"); finally there would come salvation from the looming disaster, a "midnight settlement" reached invariably at the "eleventh hour".

From about 1962, it having become the first priority of public policy to discourage inflationary wage settlements and the second priority to prevent disputes, it became less easy to arrange these collusive dramas on the stage of the Ministry of Labour. The Ministry was quietly becoming more of an economic department of government, less of an operator in a specialised aspect of human relations. But with the coming of the Labour Government in 1964 there was a reversion to the older tradition. The Ministry became more active in disputes than ever before; it began also to intervene in a number of unofficial strikes in breach of the convention that to do so was to undermine the established authority of unions and employers. That convention no longer corresponded to reality: where the Government took a hand in resolving unofficial disputes, notably in the docks, the constituted authority of the trade union had long before been undermined by the growth of more responsive, and often more competent, unofficial leadership.

There were two reasons for the more interventionist conciliation policy pursued after 1964. One was the Minister himself, the other was the existence, for the first time, of a coherent wages policy as a framework for conciliation. The Minister of Labour, Ray Gunter, had wanted no other job. With his appointment in October 1964 he reached the limit of his political ambition. After he had been despatched protesting to the Ministry of Power to make way for Barbara Castle he soon resigned from the Government. Like a shepherd's dog he lay down in the snow beside his dead master. Ray Gunter was by instinct a fixer; he had the trade unionist's belief that anything could be settled around a negotiating table given a certain amount of good will and enough time; he had the practical politician's nose for a compromise concocted from a slap on this back, a word in that ear and a pint down the other gullet. To the public he epitomised the trade unionist become Cabinet Minister; to the trade unions he did not. With the snobbishness which in England attaches to either the ownership of land or the performance of menial manual work, Ray Gunter was known to the aristocracy of the TUC General Council as "the ticket collector". His offence was to have been a white collar worker. He had been the president of a union with a poor record for militancy – the railway clerks' union which, as the age of status dawned, had become the Transport and Salaried Staffs' Association.

Nor did Ray Gunter, in spite of so looking and sounding the part of the man whose heart remained amongst the "folk from whence he came", regard the trade union movement with unqualified admiration and favour. Indeed he was exasperated, and even disgusted, by much of what he knew, and was now seeing from the other side of the table. His earthy, sometimes apocalyptic and sometimes sanctimonious reprovals of his brothers won him public popularity but it increased the number of his enemies within the trade unions. So sceptical was his view of human nature in general, and the trade union movement in particular, that he saw precious little chance of an effective prices and incomes policy until the antediluvian structure of the trade union movement was reformed. The theological enthusiasm for order which inspired the Department of Economic Affairs and the National Board for Prices and Incomes did not cause Ray Gunter's heavy heart to beat faster. He performed the traditional functions of a Minister of Labour according to his own sound instincts for what would go and what wouldn't. He worked under the willingly accepted guidance of his permanent officials. He was type cast for his role, he learnt his lines dutifully and could be heard at the back of the stalls.

When it was decided to transfer responsibility for prices and incomes policy from the DEA to the new DEP it was feared by Ray Gunter, as well as by Conservative spokesmen, that the one department would now combine the functions of prosecutor, jury and judge. The human touch which had characterised the Ministry of Labour over the years – even after its conciliators had been required to wriggle to their work in the straitjacket of the incomes policy – would give way to the economism of the DEA. The arrival in St. James's Square of the incomes policy experts from the DEA was likened by an old hand at the Ministry of Labour to "theologians entering a corrupt monastery, bearing texts".

The arrival of the First Lady herself, however, did not at first result in visible change. True an appropriately appointed lady's lavatory had to be arranged in that male preserve where jocular exchanges at the chinas of the gents had also played their part in the settlement of industrial disputes. Otherwise things went on much as before. Barbara Castle busied herself finding her way around a new and perplexing masculine world replete with jargon and Christian names (every other man a Bill) and mouthfuls of initials. Her mission was to convert the unpopular and over-rigid prices and incomes policy into a true instrument of socialist planning. She believed in it and she spent an inordinate amount of her time in incomes policy diplomacy. She personally saw a great many of the delegations which trooped in and out of the department; she spent hour upon hour on cases; her formidable persuasive powers were directed at the protagonists in each microcosmic situation which caught her fancy, for instance the lady sewing-machinists at the Ford Motor Company. She was irritated when one of her officials confronted her with a detailed log of her own activities which showed the disproportionate time she had devoted to day-to-day diplomacy at the expense of strategic forward thinking. Dealing with people was what she was there for, she retorted; cases were the real stuff of a socialist prices and incomes policy; productivity was people.

Her honeymoon was an educative but otherwise unsatisfying experience. She had set out a starry-eyed girl. She had some of the Labour left-wing's sentimentality about the workers and their trade unions. She was one of the very few members of the Wilson Cabinet who continued to address the delegates to the party conference as "comrades". As Minister of Transport she had on the whole been impressed by the cooperative spirit shown by trade union leaders towards her socialist designs. She had developed confidence in her persuasive ability to overcome the trade unionist's instinctive hostility to change. She entertained particularily high hopes of Jack Jones, heir to Frank Cousins at the Transport and General Workers' Union and already a power behind his throne. Jones was a hard-boiled union man, sired by the Liverpool docks and trained in the jungle of Midlands engineering, but he was also a socialist – indeed a former Communist. Barbara Castle knew him also from the National Executive Committee of the Labour Party on which he sat as the representative of the most powerful union in the land and she as the darling of the constituency labour parties. She was impressed by Jones's ideas for the extension of industrial democracy; he had been the chief author of a report on the subject by a Transport House working party. When she arrived at St. James's Square it was Jack this and Jack that and "I'll have a word with Jack". But Barbara Castle soon learnt to her pain that there was another Jack Jones. The professions of socialism made by trade union leaders when wearing their Labour Party hats are a poor guide to their behaviour when they have on their negotiating hats. Jack Jones the busmen's advocate, the implacable opponent of the prices and incomes policy and a rough customer in a negotiating clinch, even with a lady, came as something of a surprise and shock to Barbara Castle the politician and socialist. She made other unpleasant discoveries. The quality of the trade union leaders she encountered was, with few exceptions, abysmal beyond her belief. They were selfish, petty, intensely limited, and in some cases rude or unpleasant. She was forced to ask herself, as Maxim Gorky had asked at the great gathering of underdeveloped peoples at Baku: "Is this the rabble from which we are to build Socialism?"

The trade unions complain that public prejudice against them is the result of ignorance and the distortions of the press. So it may be in part. But it is remarkable how the knowledge gained from intimacy has an exasperating and profoundly disillusioning effect upon its recipients. Barbara Castle was by no means the first Minister at St. James's Square to be appalled at what she found beneath the stones. Nor was she the first reformer to find herself becoming a conciliator. As she grew more and more involved in attempting to settle disputes, she grew more and more interested in the causes of disputes. The policy for productivity, prices and incomes, she discovered, was not the instrument for socialist planning she had thought. Like Ray Gunter before her she came to the conclusion that no prices and incomes policy was likely to get very far, no Social Democratic society likely to be constructed, until something radical was done to reform the structures and attitudes of the British trade unions. It was almost in passing that the Prime Minister had said to her on her appointment, "And, of course, you will have the fascinating job of reforming industrial relations on the basis of the Donovan Report". It was to the 145,000 words of the Report of the Royal Commission on Trade Unions and Employers' Associations that Barbara Castle now turned her eager attention.

2 *Taking minutes and spending years*

The Donovan Commission is a character in our drama rather in the manner of a chorus. The actors seldom heed its off-stage chanting but its voice is never absent from the play. It was appointed by Ray Gunter in April 1965. "Greeting!" said the Queen to her Right Trusty and Trusty Well-beloved Commissioners and went on:

"Whereas We have deemed it expedient that a Commission should forthwith issue, to consider relations between managements and employees and the role of trade unions and employers' associations in promoting the interests of their members and in accelerating the social and economic advance of the nation, with particular reference to the Law affecting the activities of these bodies; and to report:

"Now know ye that We, reposing great trust and confidence in your knowledge and ability, have authorised and appointed, and do by these Presents authorise and appoint you the said Terence Norbert, Baron Donovan (Chairman); Alfred Baron Robens of Woldingham; Edwin Savory; Baron Tangley, Harold Francis, Baron Collison; Sir George Pollock; George Woodcock; Hugh Armstrong Clegg; Mary Green; Otto Kahn-Freund; Andrew Akiba Shonfield; John Thomson and Eric Leonard Wigham to be Our Commissioners for the purpose of the said inquiry."

The idea for an inquiry into the law affecting the trade unions originated from the Conservative administration in its dying days. The Conservatives were not prepared simply to restore the full immunity from suits for damages which until the judgment of the Law Lords in the case of Rookes v. Barnard everybody had believed the 1906 Trade Disputes Act to confer upon the unions. The TUC demanded a short sharp Act of Parliament to restore the status quo before it would consider co-operating in any inquiry. The deadlock between the

Government and the trade unions on this matter persisted until the election of 1964 at which a Labour Government was returned. The Labour Party had promised a short Bill and it was quickly enacted. On the strength of that an inquiry of a more general kind became open. Harold Wilson was originally not enamoured of the idea; he told the pre-election Congress that a Royal Commission would "take minutes and spend years". Any necessary changes in the field of collective bargaining could be discussed on an informal and friendly basis between the TUC and the Government, he suggested. The TUC general secretary, George Woodcock, on the other hand, offered to a Labour Government what the TUC had denied to a Conservative Government. Provided its purpose was not to put the unions in the dock, a Labour Government could have an inquiry. Woodcock, indeed, for some while had actually wanted an inquiry, although he would not have one on Tory terms. He wanted it because ever since he had succeeded to the general secretaryship to the TUC in 1960 he had been looking for a catalyst for trade union reform. Gravely introspective, radical in thought but cautious (some alleged plain lazy) when it came to action, Woodcock in 1963 had asked his famous rhetorical question of the trade union movement. "What are we here for?" he had mused. He had come to the general secretaryship of the TUC late – too late. He was fifty-five when he took over in 1960, not an age at which ambitious men have finished their life work but an advanced age for starting upon it. For Woodcock had waited thirteen years for dead man's shoes, serving through all that time as assistant to a man for whom he had no love or admiration whatsoever. By then he was also deracinated, sick in his heart it sometimes seemed for having been so long and far removed from the Lancashire weaving town of Bamber Bridge where as a youth he had worked at the trade until a scholarship took him to Oxford. His life in suburban Epsom apparently contained no joys for him; his abilities and sense of purpose – which could have taken him to the very top in any chosen career – atrophied in waiting. He had earlier sat at the feet of Walter Citrine, the TUC's first professional bureaucrat whose achievement was to lead the trade union movement out of Trafalgar Square and into the corridors of power in Whitehall. Citrine had rehabilitated the trade union movement from the disaster of the General Strike and, on the strength of a mutually fruitful wartime collaboration, had left it a close and trusted partner of government. Woodock in 1960 undertook a similar mission: he was the first to see clearly that unless the trade union movement acted to put its house in order, government would seek to do it for it; therefore his task was to equip the TUC to perform the functions which Government would otherwise take upon itself.

He saw clearly what this involved; the problem of wages (the bargaining strength of trade unions in full employment conditions) had to be grasped or Government would either seek to impose legal curbs on collective bargaining or allow unemployment to rise, or both. In order that the wages problem be grasped the central authority and influence of the TUC would need to be increased at the expense of the jealously preserved sovereignty of individual unions; the TUC needed to speak to Government with full authority, to bargain with Government on behalf of the unions, and it could only make bargains if it was in a position to keep them. For this to be possible, and also because it was necessary in itself, the structure of the movement must be reformed – there were too many unions (Woodcock would have liked to have set industrial trade unionism as the target – one trade union per industry) and their procedures, particularly their relationship with shop floor organisations, were inadequate for the modern tasks. George Woodcock thought all this, said it eloquently in his speeches, and said it again and again to reporters who printed it in their papers. But he could never see quite how to bring it about and therefore looked outside the trade union movement, and outside himself, for the energy to which he could harness his purpose. Thus he rejoiced in the creation of the National Economic Development Council even though it coincided with the hated Selwyn Lloyd pay pause. By participating in planning for economic growth the trade union movement, he hoped, would be forced to face up to its own responsibilities in the matter. He welcomed the prospect of a Labour Government in 1964 and the challenge of the prices and incomes policy which would then be presented to the TUC, and he did so for the same reasons – external pressure was the one hope for internal reform. And it was for this reason that he also favoured a Royal Commission.

The type of inquiry he wanted, however, was very different from the usual form of Royal Commission. He certainly did not want a panel of experts and lawyers to sit down to decide how the unions should go about their business. His conception of the inquiry was pedagogic, almost as if its chief function would be to think aloud – an activity which Woodcock himself found congenial, especially in the presence of journalists. It would be designed to educate the unions, the public and the Government. For the unions the experience of producing evidence,

Woodcock hoped, might prove revelatory; somewhere in Congress House, concealed perhaps in a musty file, the lost soul of the trade union movement might be rediscovered. The existential question he had posed might find its answer. For these reasons it was essential to George Woodcock's purpose that he should be a leading member of the Royal Commission. There was nobody on the General Council, for most of whose members he felt a disdain tempered only by charity, who could be trusted to argue the true philosophy of trade unionism from within. Membership of the Commission would not prevent him from presiding over the preparation of the TUC's evidence to it. And by this Socratic device of giving evidence to himself George Woodcock might glimpse the Platonic patterns laid out in the heavens.

Ray Gunter did not see matters in quite the same way. He was not content to appoint a Commission in the form of a seminar to suit George Woodcock, he was interested in finding answers to some practical problems and meeting the concern of the public; he was not greatly interested in existentialism. He did not think that Woodcock should be a member. He thought an eminent judge would be the most appropriate chairman. He drew up terms of reference which mentioned specifically some of the problems of industrial relations – such as productivity and restrictive practices. The TUC quarrelled with the Government over both the terms of reference and the membership and George Woodcock quarrelled personally with Ray Gunter. Woodcock preferred dealing with George Brown, whom he liked, than with Ray Gunter whom he did not. He did not like Ministers of Labour very much, whoever they were, and resented the idea that they formed the chief channel of communication between Congress House and Whitehall. He liked to go where the power was, to Chancellors of the Exchequer direct. In George Brown he found a powerful and stimulating opposite number; to Ray Gunter he said, in an outburst which embarrassed the General Council who were dining with the Prime Minister at Downing Street, "We've had nothing but snot from you". Gunter got his judge but George Woodcock, at his own and the General Council's insistence, was appointed to the Royal Commission, and its terms of reference were unpejorative.

But Woodcock had lost a good deal of his enthusiasm for the inquiry by the time it came to be set up, not because of his bad relations with Gunter but because he now thought he saw a better way of serving his purpose. That was George Brown's prices and incomes policy which became his chosen instrument for the education of the trade unions in the facts of twentieth century life.

For the Government the Commission served the useful purpose of doing something about an awkward problem without actually doing it now. As A. P. Herbert said long ago in a speech to the Commons, "A Royal Commission is generally appointed not so much for digging up the truth, as for digging it in: and a Government department appointing a Royal Commission is like a dog burying a bone, except that a dog does eventually return to the bone". With a majority of only four the Government felt obliged to bury this particular bone and to bury it in a spot largely selected by the unions themselves. Thus, as Harold Wilson had predicted it would, the Royal Commission on Trade Unions and Employers' Associations sat down to "take minutes and spend years". But after more than three years the dog on this occasion returned to the bone and Barbara Castle found it – Ray Gunter's bone – on her desk at the Department of Employment and Productivity.

Lord Donovan's Commission produced a very British report. Ask the British why they go about things in a certain way and they will examine themselves in great detail, search down into the roots of their long modern experience, and arrive at the conclusion that they do things a certain way because they have always done them that way. The tried is nearly always preferred to the untried, time is much honoured; the British pay visits to the past and discover that it works. That is not to say that they are excessively conservative, no more so than Americans or Frenchmen, but that change, even when, as recently, it may be quite rapid and radical, is usually accomplished by a sleight of hand. Tradition is viewed not as inimical to change but as the sound basis for change. Sometimes a superficially radical theory conceals a cautious plan for continuous evolution, sometimes a very traditional analysis disguises the extent and speed of changes taking place; but seldom does radical theory accompany radical action. Often the public orthodoxy lags behind the reality and inquirers may find that by the time they have caught up with what was already happening something else is happening. This, to some extent, was the fate of the Royal Commission on Trade Unions and Employers' Associations. Its report belongs to the tradition of British empiricism: by bringing the description of reality up to date it was radical when set against the myth but not so radical when set against the likely future. What would have been unorthodox ten years before, eye-opening to many even when the Commissioners first sat in 1965, was by 1968 becoming too orthodox – already new theory was lagging behind new practice. The sheer effort of description, unless guided by theory, creates a prejudice in favour of the present. Andrew Shonfield, a German schoolman – so to speak – fallen among British empiricists, was the sole member of the Commission to reach out for an over-arching theory of trade unionism in modern capitalist society. The opening words of his brilliant "Note of Reservation" were: "The main report addresses itself to the immediate situation in British industrial relations and proposes a number of remedies which I heartily support. But it barely concerns itself with the long-term problem of accommodating bodies with the kind of concentrated power which is possessed by trade unions to the changing future needs of an advanced industrial society."

The empirical foundations of the Donovan Report were laid by what we may call the Oxford or Nuffield school of industrial relations. Hugh Clegg, formerly of Nuffield College, Oxford, now professor at Warwick University, was the author-in-chief of a descriptive chapter from which all else flowed. Not far behind his pen was Allan Flanders, senior lecturer in industrial relations at Oxford and one of the most influential witnesses to the Commission. Clegg and Flanders were the academic doyens of the all dominant "voluntary school" of industrial relations. The "Clegg Chapter" of the Donovan Report began: "Britain has two systems of industrial relations. The one is the formal system embodied in the official institutions. The other is the informal system created by the actual behaviour of trade unions and employers' associations, of managers, shop stewards and workers". And it concluded its analysis as follows:

> "The formal system assumes industry-wide organisations capable of imposing their decisions on their members. The informal system rests on the wide autonomy of managers in individual companies and factories, and the power of industrial work groups.
>
> "The formal system assumes that most if not all matters appropriate to collective bargaining can be covered in industry-wide agreements. In the informal system bargaining in the factory is of equal or greater importance.
>
> "The formal system restricts collective bargaining to a narrow range of issues. The range in the informal system is far wider, including discipline, recruitment, redundancy and work practices.
>
> "The formal system assumes that pay is determined by industry-wide agreements. In the informal system many important decisions governing pay are taken within the factory.

"The formal system assumes that collective bargaining is a matter of reaching written agreements. The informal system consists largely in tacit arrangements and understandings, and in custom and practice.

"For the formal system the business of industrial relations in the factory is joint consultation and the interpretation of collective agreements. In the informal system the difference between joint consultation and collective bargaining is blurred, as is the distinction between disputes over interpretation and disputes over new concessions; and the business of industrial relations in the factory is as much a matter of collective bargaining as it is at industry level.

"The formal and informal systems are in conflict. The informal system undermines the regulative effect of industry-wide agreements. The gap between industry-wide agreed rates and actual earnings continues to grow. Procedure agreements fail to cope adequately with disputes arising within factories. Nevertheless, the assumptions of the formal system still exert a powerful influence over men's minds and prevent the informal system from developing into an effective and orderly method of regulation. The assumption that industry-wide agreements control industrial relations leads many companies to neglect their responsibility for their own personnel policies. Factory bargaining remains informal and fragmented, with many issues left to custom and practice. The unreality of industry-wide pay agreements leads to the use of incentive schemes and overtime payments for purposes quite different from those they were designed to serve.

"Any suggestion that conflict between the two systems can be resolved by forcing the informal system to comply with the assumptions of the formal system should be set aside. Reality cannot be forced to comply with pretences."

This theme, "pretence and reality", runs right through the Report. The logic behind all the Commission's recommendations, and behind its rejection of most of the proposals put to it for changes in the law or other radical departures, is summed up in the following paragraph:

". . . recent changes offer some guidance as to the direction which a reform of our system of industrial relations might take. Its central defect is the disorder in factory and workshop relations and pay structures promoted by the conflict between the formal and the informal system. Consequently the remedy must seek to introduce greater order into factory and workshop relations. This cannot be accomplished by employers' associations and trade unions working at industry level, or by means of industry-wide agreements."

From the diagnosis that the ills of the system are to be found on the shop floor and therefore must be treated at the shop floor, a point which the academics had been making for years, flowed the platitude that "both sides are to blame" and the more emphatic conclusion that the chief responsibility for reform belonged to on-the-spot management. The "reality" of the situation on the shop floor is given as the reason for rejecting all departures from the voluntary system of industrial relations; until the two sides of industry have sorted themselves out at the workplace the State's role must remain minimal, the role of the law cannot be extended, industrial trade unionism is not a practical proposition, the powers of the TUC are for the most part adequate. The argument is in fact circular: because the system, the "real" system at the shop floor, is autonomous it must right itself autonomously; because industrial conflict takes the form of conflict between management and men it must be removed by management and men. The other conflict, the conflict between the system itself and the requirements of society as a whole, is hardly considered by the Commission. Society must wait for the "two sides of industry". Hence:

"By far the most important part in remedying the problem of unofficial strikes and other forms of unofficial action will be played by reforming the institutions of whose defect they are symptoms."

"This lack of intention to make legally binding collective agreements, or, better perhaps, this intention and policy that collective bargaining and collective agreements should remain outside the law, is one of the characteristic features of our system of industrial relations which distinguishes it from other comparable systems. It is deeply rooted in its structure."

"Any attempt to deal with unofficial and unconstitutional strikes in isolation must be deprecated. This applies to the legal enforcement of procedure agreements as much to the proposal to eradicate these strikes by imposing an overall obligation to give notice before resorting to a stoppage or to similar action such as go-slow, work-to-rule or overtime bans. None of these measures promises any success in the sense of improving our industrial relations as long as the underlying causes of the strike have not been removed."

"We do . . . not . . . think that the law could not in any circumstances assist in the reduction of unofficial strikes. It cannot do so in this country today – this is the point. To take steps in this direction today would be not only useless but harmful, and they would undo a great deal of the good we hope to see done through the reform of the collective bargaining system which we recommend."

"The British system of industrial relations is based on voluntarily agreed rules which, as a matter of principle, are not enforced by law."

These statements, perhaps sound enough in themselves but undeniably static, served as the recommendations of the Donovan Commission, the chief of which, and the one which governed all others, was for the rationalisation of industrial relations on the shop floor. The chosen means were almost wholly voluntary, the task of the State persuasion and the role of the law silence.

However, these conclusions were reached not without dissension within the twelve-member Commission. Inevitably the hard men were dubbed "hawks" and the soft men "doves". The hawks throughout were looking for legal penalties to back up the reform of what, they agreed, would remain an essentially voluntary system of industrial relations. The doves were against penalties of any kind which, they believed, would hinder rather than assist a solution to the underlying problem; their faith was in persuasion. The chosen instrument for prodding the system to self-reform was to be a new State agency, a Commission for Industrial Relations. This was the brain child of Allan Flanders. Of course he conceived it on voluntary lines. The first round of the battle was fought in July 1967. The Commission had repaired for a week-end think-in at the National Coal Board's Staff College at Chalfont St. Giles and there the Flanders plan for an independent body to promote reform was accepted in principle. The first battle for voluntaryism was won. The second battle concerned the powers, if any, to support the persuasions of the CIR. By the beginning of 1968 it looked as if the hawks were ahead. A majority of the Commission seemed persuaded of the need for some reinforcing penalties. Then Hugh Clegg confronted the Commission with the powerful restatement of the voluntary case which he had been privately drafting. It was put forward for discussion but it threatened to develop into a minority report and Woodcock threatened to sign it. The Clegg draft was worked up to become the foundation chapter of the final report and the CIR was to be without teeth. The doves had scored again. Then the hawks staged a surprise attack. Woodcock was absent one Tuesday from the weekly meeting of the Commission which took place in a dreary government building in the Theobald's Road. He was taking part in the TV budget show. At the instigation of Lord Robens, Minister of Labour in the Attlee Government and now chairman of the National Coal Board, proposals for withdrawing financial benefits from unofficial strikers were reinserted in the draft. Woodcock was livid. For the first time the doves organised themselves into a cabal. Woodcock and Clegg, Otto Kahn-Freund, another member of the Oxford gang, Eric Wigham, the doyen of the Fleet Street industrial correspondents, and Harold Collison, ennobled pillar of the TUC establishment, together succeeded in winning Donovan back on to their side. With Donovan came the floating vote, the less expert, earnestly moderate middle-of-the-road members of the Commission – Mary Green, the headmistress, John Thomson, the banker. The hawks fluttered a few times more. As the report neared completion in May they tried anew to introduce financial sanctions; at the very end they attempted to reopen the question of powers for the CIR. Their only victory was a modest one. A majority of the Commission favoured the withdrawal of legal immunity from actions for tort from unofficial groups and their leaders; the doves put their dissent on the record. The final report made many recommendations but the ones which concern us for the purposes of our story are the proposal for a Commission for Industrial Relations to work by voluntary means to create order on the shop floor and the negative recommendations against the use of legal penalties of any description to promote reform or prevent industrial disputes.

Every member of the Commission signed the main body of the report. Donovan all along had worked for a unanimous commission. Above all he had worked to keep George Woodcock with the majority. As he saw it a minority report carrying Woodcock's signature would wreck the influence and authority of the Commission's long labours. In this he succeeded but at a high price: the final report had an air of extravagant compromise and culminated in an orgy of addenda, doubting notes and reservations. Donovan himself, once a Labour Member of Parliament, a mild, patient and public spirited man – now nearing seventy – himself wrote an agnostic and melancholy "addendum". He recognised the force of the argument that the root cause of unofficial strikes was the absence in many parts of industry of satisfactory procedures for the peaceful settlement of disputes but he also recognised that the improvement of these procedures was likely to be a slow business. "In the circumstances", he went on, "I have been reluctant to trust entirely to the expected effect of better procedure agreements, and have sought some interim remedy which would be both workable and just. I have found it very elusive".

A "Supplementary Note" by Lord Tangley, the solicitor who had presided over the public inquiry which had led to the reorganisation of local government in London, argued the case for powers for the CIR. He feared that otherwise it would become "yet another voice crying in the wilderness". Tangley urged that the Secretary for Employment should be given the power to order compliance with CIR recommendations in cases where persuasion had failed.

Lord Robens, Sir George Pollock (former employers' leader and make-weight for Woodcock on the Royal Commission) and John Thomson the banker, added a further "Supplementary Note" in which they supported another of Tangley's proposals. This was to give the CIR the power to deregister a union or employers' association which failed to comply with its own rules or which frequently or gravely breached its registered agreements. The effect of deregistration would be to remove legal immunities and open the offending organisation to civil actions for damages.

Finally, Andrew Shonfield, entered a longer and carefully argued "Note of Reservation". Although agreeing with most of the Commission's recommendations he challenged its whole underlying analysis. "It is no longer possible to accept the traditional notion of the individual workplace as a separate and largely autonomous estate, where employers and employees are able to conduct their quarrels with little or no regard to the effects of what they do on other workplaces". Shonfield considered the balance of "rights" and "obligations" in a wider context than the rest of the Commission. One of the obligations upon trade unions, as he saw it, was "to conduct their industrial relations in such a way as not to hold back improvements in the standard of living of the community as a whole". He was unable to envisage a modern society for ever leaving its trade unions outside the law. He foresaw movement towards a "regulated system" of industrial relations. The nineteenth century doctrine of trade unions as "licensed conspiracy" had outlived its social usefulness. Shonfield adopted a far more positive attitude towards the role of the State and its laws. He noted the several recent incursions by the State into many areas of industrial life – redundancy payments, industrial training, contracts of employment. "But all the while", he commented, "the myth that the act of regulation is a falling from grace and that each case is to be treated as a regrettable exception, which must not in any circumstance be generalised, continues to influence powerfully the judgement of many of those concerned with industrial relations. (His fellow Commissioners?) Since my own view differs profoundly from this received opinion, it is necessary to say something briefly on the general topic of the place of law in an industrial system. I start from the proposition that the deliberate abstention of the law from the activities of mighty subjects tends to diminish the liberty of the ordinary citizen and to place his welfare at risk".

On the strength of this analysis – in essence a counter-stroke against the whole orthodoxy of the Donovan report, in effect a minority report though not in name – Shonfield recommended increased protection under the criminal law against damage to persons or property caused by strikes; powers of intervention backed by monetary penalties for the CIR to deal with inter-union disputes; an independent judicial function for the CIR (instead of waiting, as the main body of the report had recommended, for references from the DEP); power for it to order the parties, under pain of financial penalties, to bargain to extend the scope of their agreements where these were inadequate and conciliation had failed; similar powers in respect of restrictive practices; and, finally a change in the bias of the law so that collective agreements took on the character of normal undertakings in which each party has a claim for redress if the other fails to keep its side of the bargain. In short, Shonfield, alone among the Commissioners looked forward to a legal framework for industrial relations and urged immediate and quite radical steps in that direction.

Donovan's labours were not enthusiastically received. They had taken too long. It had been hoped that the Commission would spend eighteen months to two years but it had taken more than three years. During that time much had happened. The incomes policy had developed through several stages of State intervention and, although unpopular and not very successful, was accustoming the public to the notion that the State had a responsibility for regulating the conduct of collective bargaining. Hence Donovan's emphasis on the evolutionary reform of workplace practices ran counter to a growing public mood. It also seemed to many to miss an important point. This was that modern industrial society contained a public conflict no less troublesome than the private conflict between the "two sides of industry". The public conflict was between governments, charged with managing the economy so as to produce rapidly rising prosperity, and wage and salary earners, whose dissatisfactions seemed to grow rather than diminish with prosperity and which were finding a more and more disorderly expression. The Donovan Report had little to say on the incomes policy which had hardly begun when it embarked upon its inquiries. It had little to say about the interests and responsibilities of the State which, under the pressure of public opinion, could hardly be expected to sit back and wait for the academics to complete their worthy experiments in the social laboratories of the shop floors. Nor did Donovan have much to say on the subject of citizens' rights. The settlement of disputes was no longer a matter purely of utility in which all that counted was to resume efficient production and restore the best possible relations between the management and men concerned. Others were also concerned – the general public and the managements and men indirectly affected, in particular the many workers who might suffer injury as the result of the actions of the few in a far away factory of which they knew little. There was a case to be made for more vigorously asserting the rights of these victims even at the expense of the functioning of "the system" and of the national economy. True the arguments against each suggested legal device were formidably rehearsed and nobody after reading the report could be confident about the effectiveness of a pet scheme for the use of legal penalties. But the Commission's underlying analysis of the legal problem was static: employers made it their practice not to sue *ergo* they would not do so in the future, collective agreements were not intended to serve as contracts *ergo* they would remain informal and voluntary, the miners of Kent in 1941 had made a laughing stock of the law *ergo* workers in the future would not consent to pay fines. The possibility that what was most wrong with British industrial relations and the trade unions was a deficient sense of public accountability which derived from their being largely ignored by the law did not seem to have been deeply considered. Certainly there was a *prima facie* case to be made that Britain's unique problems were connected with the unique legal status of her trade unions and employers' associations. Furthermore, the Commission did not look far into the future. For example it dismissed industrial trade unionism on the grounds of practicability, when there would have been no harm in the first wide-ranging Royal Commission on the subject of industrial relations since the 1890s attempting to map out desirable objectives for the 1990s and beyond. It would be surprising indeed if the functions of trade unions and their relationship with society did not undergo far-reaching changes under the pressures of technological and social change but the Commission hardly attempted to analyse current problems in terms of possible long-range future requirements.

The Donovan Commission's 145,000 word report was the result of considering evidence from 450 organisations and persons, of 128 sittings and £113,500 of the taxpayer's money. Ian Macleod, the sharp-tongued Tory "Shadow" Chancellor, could not recall a worse report. He called it "a blueprint for inaction". Allan Flanders, predictably, hailed it as "a victory of realism over pretence, of knowledge over ignorance". (It was, of course, also a victory for Allan Flanders.) "Complacent" said the *Daily Telegraph*, "Donovan Funks The Issue" complained the *Sunday Times*. It did not receive, on the whole, a good press.

However, the Donovan Report has to be considered not only as an expert inquiry into industrial relations but also as a political document of the times. It was no good it recommending actions which it knew or believed the Government would not consider; it was no good it antagonising unions or employers to the point where their cooperation in reform would be lost; it was no good pretending that public opinion was not a factor in the situation. The Commission appeared to have finely judged the tone of its report and the force of its recommendations in the light of these three factors. What to do about the unions was already a live political issue, for the Conservatives had anticipated its report with their own plans for industrial reform which included making collective agreements enforceable at law.

The political judgement implicit in the Donovan Report may have been accurate but it did not suit the Government which had been in very close touch with what was going on inside the Royal Commission. Ray Gunter and his officials at the Ministry of Labour had been hoping for a more radical report. It would have suited the Government best to have been able to do rather less than a "hawkish" Commission had recommended. That would have left it room for manoeuvre with the TUC. Now it was faced with a situation in which, as a result of the Opposition's pre-emptive bid, and under the pressure of public opinion, it would have to do something rather more than Donovan had recommended. That promised a row with the trade unions and, perhaps, party difficulties. In particular the Government was disappointed at the failure to discover the elusive galvaniser for which Lord Donovan himself had racked his brains and conscience. Even if the analysis of the Report was accepted, practical politicians running a government needed some means of getting from A to B – something more credible than a Commission for Industrial Relations without powers, some more reliable devices of policy than persuasion and pious hope. The Royal Commission after more than three years had failed to provide it. The buried bone was now laid at the doorstep of the Labour Government.

3 *In place of Donovan*

BARBARA CASTLE has a little book in which she has collected the thoughts of Aneurin Bevan. In it is recorded a remark which Bevan made at a meeting of the National Executive Committee of the Labour Party in the aftermath of the humiliating third-in-a-row defeat at the 1959 election. "The trade unionist", said the great guru of the left, "has voted at the polls against the consequences of his own anarchy". The First Secretary of State for Employment and Productivity discovered ample evidence in support of this view during her early days at her new department. She had arrived there, it will be recalled, with strong ideas of her own on the subject of productivity, prices and incomes and a certain starry-eyed innocence concerning the sons of toil with whom she now had to deal at closer quarters than ever before; but she apparently had no preconceived notions on the subject of industrial relations. On first reading the Donovan Report she was not very impressed with it. It was an admirable enough exposition of the strengths and weaknesses of the British system of industrial relations but, to the taste of her orderly mind, lacked theory. Where was the philosophy behind it? What *was* the role of trade unions in a democratic society beyond the pursuit of their sectional interests?

As she became more distressed by her encounters with the unions in situations where their sectional interests were involved so she began to think about the words of her hero Nye. Nobody could say that Nye Bevan was anti-union. Why it was he who was always stressing the need for more working class trade union people in Parliament and fewer middle class intellectuals. Bevan wanted a strong proud trade union movement. But why then was he always quarrelling with the trade unions? Because he was disappointed in them, frustrated by them; in their existing state they were not the stuff of the Democratic Socialist

Society but one of the chief impediments to its construction. "The trade unionist votes at the polls against the consequences of his own anarchy". That in a nutshell, she began to realise, was the social democratic dilemma in Britain.

She began to suspect that the trade unions were chiefly interested in the Labour Party as a cover for their own inadequacies. They were opposed to any legislation which touched upon their traditional activities but they were for ever crying out for legislation to do the things they could not do for themselves. Their attitude to equal pay for women gave the game away. What had the unions ever done about it at the bargaining tables since the TUC passed its pious resolution in 1888? Now they wanted a Labour Government to do it for them – by law. She sat there listening to requests for the Labour Government to do things for the unions, but what were the unions prepared to do for a Labour Government? Ruin it with inflation and ludicrously irresponsible strikes and then vote at the polls against the consequences of their own anarchy?

For Barbara Castle the beginning of action is theory. "We've got to get away from this bloody pragmatism of Harold's" you can hear her saying. That was what was wrong with the Donovan Report – it contained no coherent philosophy of the rights and obligations of the trade unions in a modern democracy. And what a depressing picture it painted! It was a picture of stagnation, of a trade union movement failing to extend its organisation into new industries and among new categories of workers, failing to raise its sights to new targets, stuck with the defensive, defeatist attitudes which belonged to the age of the "licensed conspiracy", not over powerful but the reverse, fragmented and feeble, lacking status and authority. The problem, therefore, was not merely to repair and strengthen the higgledy-piggledy system which had grown out of economic and social conditions which no longer applied, but to strike a new balance of rights and obligations. The union movement must be made stronger in order to become a fit partner for a Labour Government engaged in the task of constructing a Social Democracy. No easy task – the balance between social organisation and political democracy was a delicate one. The Great Nye had said that without industrial democracy political democracy was a charade. That also meant a stronger trade union movement. Basic trade union rights – the right to join a trade union, the right to bargain, the right of redress against arbitrary dismissal – these had to be secured. But there were also some basic obligations, one of which was to honour bargains freely entered into. The fundamental right to strike was likely to be challenged before long unless the unions were prepared to answer some of the public criticisms of their behaviour. And surely the trade union movement existed for something more than the aggregation of the sectional interests of the individual unions. Was not this why they had created a Labour Party? And if so was there not some obligation to assist it in the planning of the economy as a whole and in serving the interests of all?

It was in this ambitious spirit, and by something like this process of reasoning, that Barbara Castle embarked upon her experiment in practical Social Democracy. The major legislation which she would have to bring forward following the Royal Commission's inquiry must be based upon a "coherent philosophy". She would aim for something which would last for as long as the 1906 Act. Her contribution to the statute book would ensure her place in the history books. The Castle Act would lay the foundations for the new social democratic order of the future. The task of the philosopher, Marx said, was to change the world. In place of Donovan and in place of strife there should be Socialism. Thus spoke Barbara Castle.

Harold Wilson was shown an early outline of Barbara Castle's plan which was eventually published as the White Paper *In Place of Strife – A Policy for Industrial Relations* in January 1969. Barbara Castle was after a package which, on the one hand, would strengthen the trade unions – for example, give them the legal right to organise and negotiate – and on the other hand, require additional obligations of them, for example to act constitutionally in the conduct of industrial disputes.

Until she communicated her "philosophy" and an outline of her proposals to the Prime Minister there is no evidence to suggest that he had any very clear ideas of his own on the subject. In the autumn of 1968 he had been mainly preoccupied with Rhodesia. That summer he had determined to have one more meeting with Ian Smith, one more attempt to reach a settlement with the rebel regime consistent with Britain's honour and obligations. Either he would bring off a surprise diplomatic coup or he would effectively seal the question off in domestic British politics. So for a great part of the time between the publication of the Donovan Report and the fruitless meeting with Ian Smith in the second week of October, Rhodesia was chiefly occupying Harold Wilson's mind. Harold Wilson was a Prime Minister who liked to worry one bone at a time. When he did take up an issue he tended to become obsessively involved in it. The seamen's strike of 1966 was one such; the application to join the European Common Market another; Rhodesia on at least two occasions became his overriding interest. Industrial relations would shortly come to obsess him more than any issue before.

That is not to say that Harold Wilson had not thought at all about the trade union problem. Like Barbara Castle he had drawn some hard lessons from his experiences with industrial disputes. The seamen's strike in May and June 1966 remained in his view the chief reason why the Government had been "blown off course" in July of that year. And that had been the start of Harold Wilson's troubles, the rudest possible awakening from the tired but contented state in which his spectacular triumph at the polls in March had left him. Also engraved upon his memory was the all night vigil at the Adelphi Hotel, Liverpool in November 1967. There he had struggled desperately to end an unofficial dock strike which was having a crippling effect on the struggling British economy and a disastrous psychological impact overseas. It helped to make inevitable the devaluation of the pound which he had so long and obstinately resisted. In his shattered state following the forced devaluation of November 16, 1967 the Prime Minister attributed a part of the humiliation brought upon him to the chaos and bloody-mindedness which ruled the industrial relations of the Mersey waterfront.

There were earlier memories too. In the 1964 campaign, and during the long pre-election period in which the thirteen-year-old Conservative administration was staggering to its end, Wilson entertained no doubt that strikes were seriously damaging to the reputation of the Labour Party. He had intervened cheekily but successfully in the strike of television technicians which was about to black out the screens in the homes of millions of voters. He had played it fast and loose when electricity supplies were threatened, breaking the convention that the Opposition refrains from jogging the elbow of the Government when a serious industrial dispute is under negotiation. During the campaign itself he lived in dread of embarrassingly irresponsible unofficial strikes which could undermine Labour's claim to be specially qualified to modernise the country. One of its chief claims to office was the co-operation it had the right to demand, and which it expected to receive, from the trade union movement. Wilson's nervousness about strikes explains his rash and unsupported allegation that an unofficial strike at a Midlands motor accessory firm, Hardy Spicer, had been deliberately provoked by friends of the Conservative Party. Only a gift from the heavens in the form of Herbert Hill, the Hardy Spicer boss, had got him off that particular hook. Herbert Hill became a figure of ridicule and contempt, when he described the strikers as "poor dears" of "not very high intelligence". Was this the attitude of British management towards the workers?

Harold Wilson drew upon all these experiences when he began in the autumn of 1968 to give his close attention to the trade union problem. In political terms the line he needed to adopt was fairly obvious. In March of that year the Conservative Party had anticipated the Donovan Report by publishing its own proposals for the reform of industrial relations. These proposals went far beyond the subsequent recommendations of the Donovan Commission. The Tories promised that they would make all contracts between trade unions and employers enforceable at law except where the parties to the contract clearly indicated that this was not their intention. The Conservative policy statement *Fair Deal at Work* included proposals for confining registration of trade unions to those whose rules conformed to certain basic principles. Measures of a somewhat vague nature were promised against restrictive labour practices on the same principle as governed restrictive trading practices. The law would be changed to require secret ballots before strike action was taken. Whatever the practicality of some of these measures, and the weight of the Donovan Commission was against them, there was every likelihood that they would catch the public mood. The Tories' proclaimed readiness to reform industrial relations drew attention to the fact that the Government had so far done nothing. As Harold Wilson was later to admit, the Donovan Commission had occupied three years in which nothing had been achieved. Now the public demand for action was becoming more insistent. He had to "do something about the unions". And in order to hold the centre ground of British politics he now had to aim higher than Donovan while lower than the Tories.

The "philosophy" outlined to the Prime Minister by Barbara Castle and the draft proposals she laid before him, appeared to meet his need. The shape of her plan – measures to help and strengthen the trade unions balanced by measures against unofficial strikes which were likely to receive widespread public approval – exactly fitted the political hole which had to be plugged. He could steal some of Edward Heath's clothes on the recommendation of a political friend whose judgement he respected and whose Socialist intentions it was not for him to doubt. What is more Harold Wilson was genuinely convinced that Barbara Castle's proposals were what were needed for the reform of British industrial relations. He was becoming increasingly exasperated himself by certain kinds of unofficial strikes which threatened to sabotage the recovery of the British economy each time it appeared to be in the offing.

The strike at the Girling brake factory in Cheshire which began on November 11 confirmed the Prime Minister's opinion that measures of the kind proposed by Barbara Castle were needed. Here was a truly deplorable state of affairs. The factory, which supplied an important section of the motor industry with essential components, had experienced fifty-seven disputes in eighteen months. When twenty-two machine setters came out on strike on November 11 more than 5,000 car workers were laid off at other plants. The machine shop had been the scene of thirty-three of the fifty-seven disputes and of these thirty-three only eight had been taken through the constitutional procedure for settling grievances. The latest strike was of the very kind which most exasperated the public and caused foreign financiers to despair of Britain ever solving her economic problems.

It had begun with the member of one union turning on an oil supply valve which was held to be the property of members of another union. The members of the offended union declared the machinery "black"; they were suspended by the management and the strike began in consequence. In fact the dispute was not quite so trivial as it seemed. The objection to the foreman turning the valve was that he was a recently recruited member of the Association of Supervisory, Technical and Management Staffs, the most militant and fastest expanding of the white collar technicians' trade unions. The machine setters, who were skilled members of the Amalgamated Engineering and Foundry Workers' Union, alleged that ASTMA had been poaching members at the plant. The dispute thus was an inter-union dispute but not simple a "who-does-what?" dispute. But whatever the rights and wrongs of the case (the facts were set out in the report of a committee of inquiry under Professor Donald Robertson published on December 9) it was perfectly clear that labour relations at the plant were in a chronic state, that strikes were taking place in complete disregard for the constitutional procedure for settling disputes, and that large numbers of other workers were suffering loss of employment and wages as a result of the action of a handful of men. What was more the strike illustrated clearly how an important device of the voluntary system of industrial relations in Britain had ceased to be effective. Until recently the appointment by the Minister of a Court or Committee of Inquiry into an industrial dispute had almost invariably resulted in a return to work pending the findings of the inquiry. In the Girling case – and cases of the kind were becoming increasingly common in industry – the men persisted with their strike until the Committee had reported. The Girling brake factory reopened on Monday, December 9, the day on which Professor Robertson's report was published but more than two weeks after his inquiry had begun. The Girling affair reinforced the case for some new device for bringing about a resumption of work pending an inquiry or a negotiated settlement of a dispute.

The strike at Girling's was also of symbolic importance. It coincided with a period of extreme instability in British politics which on Friday December 6, exploded into hysterical outburst. A fortnight previously, on return from a crisis meeting of the "Group of Ten" Finance Ministers in Bonn, Roy Jenkins had introduced his third "Budget" of the year. In spite of the massively deflationary Budget in March he had been obliged twice again to check the growth of domestic demand. Following the failure of the Bonn meeting to bring about a revaluation of the Deutschmark officials at the Treasury seriously feared that the pound sterling might be forced off parity in the week beginning November 21. In fact funds flowed back into London and the crisis seemed for a while to have passed. But the clumsy diplomacy of the British Government during the crisis, coupled with the sense of economic mismanagement communicated by the Chancellor's two bites at home demand in a period of only two months, added to the public's doubts about the competence of the Wilson government. On Friday, December 6, there was suddenly a panicky flow of funds out of London. The run was based entirely on rumours, none of which were in the least plausible and all of which could have been shown to be false by routine inquiry. The rumours began abroad. One version had it that Wilson was at Buckingham Palace tendering his resignation to the Queen. Another version was that the Chancellor of the Exchequer had resigned and that the pound would be devalued again that week-end. In fact Harold Wilson spent most of the "Black Friday" on railway trains; in the morning he was travelling back to London from the west country and in the afternoon he set off for the north to keep a speaking engagement. Roy Jenkins also left for the north that afternoon to keep a long previously arranged speaking engagement. Nobody went near Buckingham Palace.

Contrasting conclusions were drawn from the costly behaviour of the City of London on that Friday. Ministers were shaken to discover the degree of irrationality they had to contend with. *The Times* and the

Daily Mirror concluded that the Wilson Government was no longer able to govern the country and called for Coalition. The opinion polls were showing a dramatic relapse in the Government's popularity, convalescent since the summer. An Opinion Research Centre poll published in the London *Evening Standard* on December 4 had put the Conservatives 27 per cent in the lead over Labour. Wilson's personal popularity had plummetted 10 per cent in a month. On December 13 a Gallup Poll published in the *Daily Telegraph* confirmed these findings. Support for Labour had fallen below 30 per cent of the electorate which meant that fewer than one hundred Labour Members would be returned to Parliament in a General Election. Only 17 per cent of Gallup respondents expressed approval of the government's record, only 18 per cent expected its post-devaluation economic policy to succeed, only 15 per cent saw prospect for success in the prices and incomes policy. There was no denying that confidence in the Wilson Government was at an extremely low ebb – and when *The Times*' editorial lumped all the nation's fears and grievances together, mentioning among others the Girling strikers and the football rowdies, it may have accurately sensed the national mood, although the Printing House Square plan for coalition was received with ridicule at Westminster.

Thus the formative period of Barbara Castle's White Paper *In Place of Strife* coincided with this period in which everything was going badly for the Government, in which its authority was being challenged on all sides and in which unofficial strikes were erected as one of the chief symbols of the alleged national malaise. Moreover, the strike wave continued. A dispute involving one woman cleaner caused 2,400 motor industry lay offs; at a Midlands engineering works sixty supervisors walked out after one of their number had been sacked for parking his car in front of a director's. The problem of doing something about industrial relations became intertwined with Harold Wilson's problem of how to restore the authority of his government and his own authority as Prime Minister.

There was one controversial proposal in Barbara Castle's White Paper which bore the imprimatur of the Prime Minister himself. This was the proposal for compulsory ballots before strikes could be called. The Donovan Commission had rejected the arguments in favour of this reform. It could find no evidence to suggest that workers would be less ready to vote for strike action than their leaders. A vote in favour of a strike could limit the freedom of action of trade union leaders in negotiating a settlement to the dispute. According to the Commission the decision whether or not to ballot was best left to union leaders. Barbara Castle and her expert advisors were impressed by Donovan's arguments on this point but the Prime Minister had become strongly attached to the idea of ballots. The reason for this was the situation which had arisen when a national engineering strike had been threatened that October. The strike had been called by the Amalgamated Engineering and Foundry Workers' Union, now under the new militant leadership of Hugh Scanlon. Scanlon was a former Communist Party member and had received Communist support in the election to succeed Lord (previously Sir William and before that plain Bill) Carron. Hugh Scanlon, who had long shop steward and local officer experience behind him, was new to national negotiations; he was out to prove himself and he was of strongly militant persuasion. It was open to grave doubt whether Scanlon's million plus members shared his readiness to embark upon strike action. According to Gallup 48 per cent of AEF members were against the strike and 43 per cent in favour. Two other unions with large interests in engineering balloted their members and discovered substantial majorities against. The AEF refused to conduct a ballot. The strike was in the end averted and the details need not concern us. The significance of the incident was its effect on the thinking of Harold Wilson. Had it taken place the strike would have wrecked the Government's endeavours to swing into balance of payments surplus on the basis of a devalued pound. This appalling damage to the economy could have been done against the wishes of the members of the chief union concerned. And was it not also morally wrong for men to be called upon to forsake earnings and inflict suffering on their families without their wishes being first discovered? For these reasons Harold Wilson pressed strongly for compulsory strike ballots to feature prominently in Barbara Castle's White Paper.

Thus the three most controversial proposals contained in *In Place of Strife* related to actual situations which had occurred that autumn. First was the proposal for the twenty-eight day "conciliation pause". The Minister would have the power to order a resumption of work pending inquiry and negotiation. At the same time an order would be made for the status quo to apply. For example, the man peremptorily dismissed for parking in front of the director's car would be reinstated. The scheme was designed to meet not only the unconstitutional behaviour of workers but equally the feudal arbitrariness of bad managements. Second there was the plan for dealing with inter-union disputes. In cases where neither the Commission for Industrial Relations nor the TUC succeeded in sorting out quarrels between unions the Minister would have power to impose a settlement. The Girling dispute might have been dealt with either by ordering a "conciliation" pause or by an order as to who was to turn the valve or which union was to organise the supervisors. Third, there was the proposed power to order a strike ballot in certain circumstances. That could have applied to the case of the threatened engineering strike. In each case the Government's orders would be made under pain of fines levelled not by the ordinary courts of law but by Industrial Boards. The White Paper contained many other proposals, as we shall see, but it was these – three out of altogether twenty-five – which were the cause of one of the greatest and most fascinating controversies in recent British politics.

Harold Wilson and Barbara Castle were of a single mind as they set out on their perilous course. They adopted a most irregular and unusual procedure for steering their proposals through the machinery of government. What they did was to by-pass the established procedures of Cabinet Government. In setting out to deal with unconstitutional behaviour in the conduct of industrial relations they themselves behaved in the manner of unofficial strikers or arbitrary managements and instead of patiently negotiating their case through procedure they prepared to confront the Cabinet with a *fait accompli.*

The usual procedure for preparing controversial legislation is to process it first through a committee of Ministers. Ad hoc committees of the Cabinet are constituted for this purpose. Each cabinet committee has its carbon copy in a committee of officials. A lot of the detailed diplomacy between departments is conducted by the civil servants on the official committees which, in effect, prepare the agenda for their ministerial committee. Cabinet committees are normally composed of the Ministers whose departmental interests are in one way or another affected by the subject in hand. Questions which cannot be settled among interested Ministers in committee are eventually referred up to the Cabinet. A Minister who loses an argument in committee can "reserve his position" and reopen the question in Cabinet. The Cabinet can reverse or alter the decisions of its committees but this seldom happens when the Ministers most directly concerned with a problem have solved it to their satisfaction. As John Mackintosh puts it in his standard work *The British Cabinet** the Cabinet is the "Court of Appeal" for the committee system.

There is nothing to oblige a Prime Minister to observe the normal

*2nd edition, Stevens. 1968.

procedure but it is more often than not in his interest to do so. Genuine practical difficulties have to be worked out at expert level between departments. Political differences if not ironed out in committee have to be settled in full Cabinet. Ministers excluded from the decision-making process are invited to disclaim collective responsibility for the decisions reached without them. In the case of industrial relations an ad hoc committee of the Cabinet had been reconstituted in 1967 for the express purpose of preparing Government action on the Donovan Report when it was received. But Harold Wilson and Barbara Castle decided to by-pass it. Their reason was a very simple one: they feared that they would not get their proposals through the machine if they proceeded in the conventional manner. Instead of taking her plan to the industrial relations committee of the Cabinet Barbara Castle prepared her White Paper in a much smaller expert committee.

By so doing she and the Prime Minister excluded the Home Secretary, James Callaghan, from the discussions, and it was their deliberate intention to do so. Once she has made up her mind Barbara Castle is not a lady to waste time on argument. Elaborate position work had been undertaken in her own department for whose officials she had the highest regard. A long list of possibilities had been set before her ranging from the most hawkish to the most dovelike devices for introducing greater order into industrial relations. She had pored over historical papers on the subject of the trade unions and industrial relations; she had involved outside experts in the studies and the arguments. When she had convinced herself of the correct policy she had without difficulty convinced the Prime Minister. Moreover, she and he had taken the precaution of acquiring one powerful ally, the Chancellor of the Exchequer, Roy Jenkins. He, to his subsequent regret, promised full support for her plan. On the strength of her own convictions and with these allies Barbara Castle, in whose character the authoritarian streak is strong, saw no reason to invite Callaghan to make a nuisance of himself. For it was held certain that Callaghan would oppose a strong line towards the unions. He had been busily at work making friends among their leaders. In May 1968 the former Chancellor, now the Home Secretary, had broken ranks with the Cabinet and declared his opposition to the continuation of legal restraints on wages on the grounds that they were causing "great strains between the various parts of our movement". That was just after his successor at the Treasury had presented his hard slog Budget. Then on the eve of the Labour Party conference in October he had pressed in the national executive committee of the Party for Barbara Castle to give the conference an undertaking that the penal incomes policy powers would not be renewed on their natural expiry the next year. The executive split twelve-twelve and the Government was spared grave embarrassment only by the casting vote of the party chairman, Aneurin Bevan's widow Jennie Lee. In these ways Callaghan had pushed himself forward as the unions' friend. Harold Wilson and Barbara Castle not only expected him to oppose their plans for industrial reform but suspected that he might disclose their schemes prematurely to his trade union friends.

For these reasons the Prime Minister, Barbara Castle and Roy Jenkins formed a powerful triple alliance against Jim Callaghan. It was a mistake. Not only did it ensure Callaghan's determined opposition to their policy at each subsequent stage but it angered other members of the Cabinet who were also excluded from the formative stages of policy-making. And it resulted in the Government's policy for reforming industrial relations being personally and very closely identified with Harold Wilson and Barbara Castle. Barbara Castle's second great error was more understandable. With the Prime Minister's consent she decided to consult the General Council of the TUC before she took her package to the Cabinet. She did so on the advice of George Woodcock. Woodcock had been called to the DEP to be given private sight of her proposals in their draft form. To the astonishment and delight of the DEP officials, who knew his grumpiness well and would not have been surprised by a tantrum, Woodcock responded favourably to the plan. He looked up at Barbara Castle and said calmly in his usual *sotto voce*, "I don't think there is anything in this to which the unions can fundamentally object". But he strongly advised her to demonstrate her trust in the General Council of the TUC by allowing him to place the proposals in confidence before them. Barbara Castle agreed. George Woodcock's positive reaction to the draft White Paper was considered so important that it was worth taking risks to retain his good will. The risk in consulting the TUC General Council before the Cabinet lay in the Cabinet objecting that it was being confronted with a *fait accompli.* There would almost certainly be leaks from the General Council and Ministers would complain that they had been reduced to informing themselves of Government policy, even on so important a matter, from the newspapers. But the risks of going to Cabinet first seemed to Barbara Castle equally great. The proposals were just as likely to leak out and then the TUC, ever sensitive on the subject of prior consultation, would feel that *it* was being presented with the *fait accompli.* It was a delicately balanced choice, but George Woodcock's positive first response to the draft White Paper convinced her that she should take the risk of going to the TUC first.

Sure enough Barbara Castle's way of going about things sparked off a great row in the Cabinet when it was allowed at last to discuss the proposals contained in the White Paper. That was more than a week after she had discussed them at meetings with leaders of the TUC and the Confederation of British Industry. The newspapers were already full of them. Richard Crossman accused her of constitutional impropriety; smarting under his own exclusion from the policy-making process, he suggested that they might soon reach the stage when the Cabinet was not consulted at all. Barbara Castle had committed the Government to highly controversial policies which probably would not work. The interests of departments, including his own Ministry of Social Security and Health which would be involved in her schemes, had not been consulted and consequently her proposals were inadequately worked out. Jim Callaghan, as was to be expected, was fundamentally opposed to the Castle-Wilson scheme. He did not believe that either the conciliation pause or the strike ballot would work. It was folly for a Government as unpopular as this one and with the economy in its existing condition to risk further incurring the ill-will of the trade unions. Callaghan was the treasurer of the Labour Party. How could the trade unions be expected to cough up a million pounds for the next election, he demanded, if the Government went on beating them over the head? Richard Marsh, the Minister of Transport, joined the opposition. He was suspicious of Barbara Castle's elaborate schemes through having inherited her Transport Bill. Marsh had been a trade union official; he did not believe her proposals would work; he believed they would irritate the unions without making much impact on industrial relations.

Roy Mason, a former coal miner and the only *bona fide* manual worker in the Cabinet, took a similar line. Judith Hart, recently promoted to Cabinet rank, circulated a paper criticising Barbara Castle's proposals on grounds of principle and warning against their political consequences. They were criticised from a different angle by Anthony Crosland, the President of the Board of Trade. He had been especially impressed by Andrew Shonfield's minority report. Crosland believed that the Government should either accept the majority verdict of the Donovan Commission or do what Shonfield urged and give independent powers to the Commission for Industrial Relations. He favoured the latter course.

No less than six meetings of the Cabinet were required to secure support for the White Paper. Barbara Castle was punished for her behaviour by being made to do now the work she should have done in Cabinet committee. The series of long Cabinet meetings began the moment the Commonwealth Prime Ministers' Conference came to an end on January 8. The final meeting of the Cabinet lasted three-and-a-half hours and finished at 10 p.m. on January 14. The White Paper was published on January 18 which shows that printing arrangements must have reached an advanced state while the debate in Cabinet was still continuing. In the end the White Paper was agreed. But no final decision was reached on legislation. It was assumed there would be a Bill in the next session of Parliament but in the meanwhile there would be consultation with the parties.

The opening sentence of *In Place of Strife* was written by Barbara Castle, a member of the National Union of Journalists. It said "There are necessarily conflicts of interest in industry". The remainder of the document bore the hall mark of her personality: its tone was boldy interventionist. It stated that radical changes were needed in the system of industrial relations to meet the needs of a period of rapid technical and industrial change. Until action was taken to remedy the defects of the system, conflict in British industry would often be damaging and anti-social. The Government's proposals for containing the destructive expression of industrial conflict were based on its belief that the efforts of employers, unions and employees to reform collective bargaining needed "the active support and intervention of Government." There followed an historical analysis to show how the State had never been disinterested in industrial relations and how its involvement had grown in recent years to take account of changed circumstances. "The need for State intervention and involvement, in association with both sides of industry, is now admitted by almost everyone", the White Paper claimed, adding: "The question that remains is, what form should it take at the present time?"

Next came a list of the defects of the existing system of industrial relations, with special reference made to the problem of strikes. The right to strike was re-affirmed as "one of the essential freedoms in a democracy" but strikes by groups in key positions could these days damage the interests of other people so seriously – including the interests of other trade unionists – "that they should only be resorted to when other alternatives have failed". Four objectives were set for remedying the defects of the system:

(i) the reform of collective bargaining;
(ii) the extension of the role and rights of trade unions;
(iii) new aids to those who are involved in collective bargaining; and
(iv) new safeguards for the community and individuals.

On the reform of collective bargaining the White Paper stuck closely to the Donovan Commission's basic analysis. It accepted the doctrine of the "two systems", stressed the prime need for comprehensive, mutually agreed procedures and laid at the door of management "the major responsibility for solving the problem". Without reform of procedures there could be "no fundamental solution to the problem of unofficial strikes". The Donovan recommendation for a Commission on Industrial Relations was accepted and, in accordance with Donovan, it was to be given no powers of its own. It was seen by the Government as "a disseminator of good practice and a focus for reform by example". The various proposals for enforcing collective agreements were all rejected. The White Paper recognised that "employees may well be justified in striking in breach of procedure, in defence of their interests, if the procedure is slow and clumsy and protects an employer who has taken unilateral action such as victimisation". Penal powers for dealing with restrictive practices were also ruled out. To help strengthen the unions the Industrial Relations Bill which the Government intended to bring before Parliament would contain a provision to enable unions to obtain from employers certain sorts of management information needed for negotiations. This went beyond Donovan. So did the promise to support experiments in worker representation on company boards of directors.

Under the head "The Extension of Collective Bargaining" the Government proposed to legislate the right of every employee to belong to a trade union. Disputes between unions and managements over recognition or over the failure of an employer to engage in genuine negotiations would be referred to the CIR. Where an employer refused to accept the CIR's recommendation the Government would have the power to make an Order. If the Order was not observed the union would have the unilateral right to take the case to arbitration before the Industrial Court and the court's finding would be legally binding. Inter-union disputes about recognition would be referred to the TUC in the first instance and subsequently to the CIR if necessary. On the recommendation of the CIR, the Minister would have the power to make an Order imposing a solution. It would be "a reserve power in the last resort". Failure by employer, union or union members to comply with the Order would render them liable to financial penalties. The penalties would be imposed by a new Industrial Board which would consist of employer and employee representatives sitting under an independent chairman. The White Paper promised "There will be no liability to imprisonment in default of payment or on account of failure to obey an Order". It hinted that the most likely procedure would be the attachment of earnings, that is to say the deduction of fines from pay packets.

Under the head of "Aids to Collective Bargaining" the chief proposal, and a novel one, was for public grants and loans to trade unions and the TUC. These would be administered by the CIR and would be for assisting mergers between unions, training union officers including shop stewards, and the development of union research facilities.

But the most controversial of the White Paper's proposals for legislation came under the fourth head – "New Safeguards". The section began by echoing Donovan: "The fundamental solution lies in the re-structuring of our present system of collective bargaining when it is disordered or defective . . . In many circumstances at present the use of the strike weapon is understandable, and in some it is justified". But, it went on, the reforms which the Government intended to initiate and encourage would inevitably take time. Britain's special problem was strikes which took place before adequate negotiation or discussion of the problem had taken place. Society urgently neededa means of ensuring that the processes of conciliation were followed before the resort to damaging strikes.

Therefore the Government proposed to reinforce the machinery of conciliation by a "discretionary reserve power" to secure a "conciliation pause" in unconstitutional strikes. It would be used only when the effects of a strike were likely to be serious and where normal conciliation methods by the Department of Employment and Productivity had been tried and had failed. When all else had failed the Secretary of State would have the power to order a return to work for a period of twenty-eight days while attempts were made to negotiate a settlement to the dispute or, if appropriate, an inquiry took place. During that time the *status quo ante* would be preserved. For example if the cause of the dispute had been a dismissal the employer would be obliged to reinstate the dismissed employee. It was no denial of the right to strike, the White Paper contended, for "the community to require that groups of employees shall not take precipitate strike action, which seriously damages the economy and their fellow workers, before they have used the machinery of discussion to which they themselves have agreed or which may be made available by the Government".

The proposal to give the Secretary of State discretionary power to order a strike ballot was justified on similar grounds. "It is a matter of concern that at present it is possible for a major official strike to be called when the support of those involved may be in doubt". The Government also intended to legislate safeguards for employees against unfair dismissal and it promised to give sympathetic consideration to changes in the law which denied unemployment benefit to workers laid off as the result of a dispute at their factory in which they were taking no part. The White Paper contained a number of other proposals some of which, although of a more minor or technical kind, were helpful to trade unions. Altogether it contained twenty-five proposals to serve as the basis for further consultation on what was clearly going to be a huge piece of legislation. The final paragraph of *In Place of Strife* said:

"These are the major actions and policies which the Government proposes to strengthen and improve industrial relations in this country and which it will further discuss with the trade union movement and managements. They are intended to retain the best aspects of our traditional system – its freedom, flexibility, tolerance and general sense of reasonable compromise, while at the same time enabling us to grapple with what is wrong. They are designed to build on the initiatives already being taken by management and unions and to reinforce, not weaken, their responsibility. They are an opportunity and a challenge. The Government proposes a joint effort with all those involved to remake and improve the relationships of people at work."

That was *In Place of Strife*. Barbara Castle was often to complain later that the critics of her White Paper had not read it. As she saw it, it was based on a "coherent philosophy" and a philosophy which was essentially Socialist. At one of the many union conferences she attended to expound and defend her policy she said, "I have not come here as a siren holding out a poison package but as a Socialist arguing a coherent philosophy. I have come here in my true colours today" – and indeed she was wearing a bright red coat. Her package contained both rights and obligations but its total effect, she firmly believed, would be a strengthening of the trade union movement. The powers she sought would be safe in her hands but if a Labour Government did not act on the union question the unions might find themselves in the less tender grasp of a Conservative Government with far more extensive powers at its disposal. She was saving the trade unions from themselves, public opinion and the Tories. The conciliation pause could, in the last resort, mean the fining of trade unionists but it also gave the unions something they had been seeking for nearly fifty years – the preservation of the *status quo* during the negotiation of a dispute caused by management action. She contended that her proposals were realistic and took full account of Donovan's underlying analysis. She was not saying that all strikes were bad, she was not expecting the law to achieve what could only be achieved by fundamental reform. An ardent believer in the power of reason, a dirigiste by instinct, a benevolent authoritarian by temperament, and above all a tireless enthusiast for whatever she set her passionate heart on, Barbara Castle was proud of her White Paper. Unfortunately for her, and for Harold Wilson – feeling comfortable in some of Edward Heath's clothes – it was to cause nothing but trouble and strife.

4 *All kinds of rebels*

DURING the next two months the explosions of the future were being quietly compressed beneath the surface. The trade unions seemed almost to be going out of their way to demonstrate their incapacity to tackle the problems to which *In Place of Strife* purported to have the answer. The Parliamentary Labour Party was allowed to drift rudderless, or rather whipless, into a state of chronic indiscipline and low morale. The Government made some Grand Military Bungles. Positions on industrial reform hardened all round – the Prime Minister's, Barbara Castle's, James Callaghan's, the TUC's and the rebels' – in the Parliamentary Labour Party.

But the very first reactions to *In Place of Strife* gave some encouragement to Barbara Castle's belief that reason would prevail. She was right: therefore, she confidently assumed, others would come to see that she was right. She and her officials had expected the TUC General Council to kick up, but by the time the legislation was on the statute book – which would not be until some time in 1970 – the election would be near, the ranks would close and the TUC once more would "reluctantly acquiesce" in the actions of the Labour Government. The left-wing of the Parliamentary Labour Party would be in a stew, but that would be nothing to write home about: the Government had grown accustomed to a state of affairs in which mutterings in the pit were the best indication that the sound of its voice was carrying to the back of the stalls. Divisions in the Cabinet had become no less *de rigeur*. The party of the left had long ago learnt to rationalise its internal quarrels as the authentic sign of its purposiveness in government; for Wilson, Castle and Jenkins there was no surer sign that they were striking somewhere near the mark than the sound of Callaghan's pain.

Meanwhile – and it was a very important fact for them – public opinion appeared to be on their side. *In Place of Strife* received a good press. The editorial writers were not wildly enthusiastic about its proposals but few saw in them cause for great *angst* by the trade unions or the Labour Party. And the opinion polls revealed a firm basis of public support for a government that would "do something about the unions". *The Times* was typical of the tone struck. "Mrs. Castle and her colleagues", it commented, "have accepted the view of the Donovan Commission that the voluntary nature of our collective bargaining system, which has been its special characteristic, should be retained, but she has gone further in providing for legal restraints than the majority of the Commission wished". And the editorial went on to say, "The unions would be foolish indeed if they try to work up resistance to the White Paper proposals. The compulsory measures are the least that any government could put forward in the present climate of public opinion. They are certainly far less than the Conservatives propose. It is unlikely that any of them will be much used and they never need be if the unions put their own house in order. The outcry from some Labour backbenchers is little short of ridiculous". The reaction from the Labour Correspondent of *The Times* was also revealing, for he had been a member of the Donovan Commission. Eric Wigham warned Barbara Castle that she was proposing "enough Government intervention to risk antagonising the trade unions but not enough to have any major impact on the country's main industrial problem". He went on, "The proposals will not provide the restrictions on unions and strikers which the Confederation of British Industry wants. They will be an ineffective irritant to the unions". Wigham remained convinced that Donovan's answer was the correct one. But he acquitted Barbara Castle of allegations that she had joined the "strait jacket school" and his final word was, "I wish Mrs. Castle would forget some of her proposals. But if she has to make some concession to public clamour the unions can afford to ignore them. They don't matter much".

For the public's attitude we must rely chiefly on Dr. Gallup's door steppers. They conducted their soundings before Barbara Castle's proposals were published but after they had been well leaked in the newspapers. According to the poll published in the *Daily Telegraph* on January 16, 73 per cent were in favour of government intervention in unofficial strikes. The attitude to the government's chief proposals was as follows: fines – 69 per cent in favour; secret ballot – 63 per cent; "cooling off period" (the popular name for the conciliation pause) – 61 per cent; compulsory recognition of unions – 43 per cent; and financial aid to unions – 23 per cent. Labour had lost its lead as the party able to "best handle" the unions. In October 1968 it led the Tories 33 to 30 per cent; by January it was in arrears 25 to 33 per cent. It seemed that the Government had only to talk about a subject in order to impair confidence in its ability actually to deal with it. On the other hand, 21 per cent said they would be more likely to vote Labour if the Government made it more difficult for workers to go on strike and 22 per cent of the deserters who had voted Labour in 1966 (the floating vote that Harold Wilson was after) indicated their willingness to be impressed by Government action on industrial relations. This poll, broadly supported by others, indicated not a sudden lust for governmental action towards the unions but a remarkable stability in public opinion which had long believed that something must be done and continued over the next months to hold unwaveringly to this view.

Opinion in the Labour Party, among trade unionists, and among trade unionist MPs was more polarised, as was to be expected; nevertheless a majority appeared to be in favour of Government action. A poll conducted for *The Sunday Times* by the Opinion Research Centre found that 57 per cent of trade union sponsored Labour MPs approved of the conciliation pause while 36 per cent were against it. A Marplan Survey published in *The Times* gave 51 per cent of Labour voters in favour of legal limitations on the right to strike compared with 61 per cent of Conservative voters and 55 per cent of all voters. And an impressionistic account of the mood in the Labour grassroots by Hugh Noyes of *The Times* endorsed the pollsters' findings. "Indeed", wrote Noyes, "one of the most resounding votes of confidence came for Mrs. Castle's proposals. Although details were not known at the time there was not a single voice raised in protest at what she was doing". He quoted as a typical attitude "This is something that has got to be faced up to and Barbara, rather late in the day, is facing up to it". A Yorkshire miner told him, "It is something that has to be done. The trade unions have dragged their heels for too long and we are getting into the state, as at Girling, where the country is held to ransom by a few people without any valid reason for striking".

The first reaction from the trade union group of Labour MPs was calm and moderate. Barbara Castle was misled by the slaps on the back she received from people who were later to spit in her eyes.

The backbenchers were the very last to be consulted – after the TUC and the CBI and even after the Cabinet. Two hours before publication of the White Paper the First Secretary attended a thin meeting of the trade union group. It was still the Christmas recess and only twenty seven members of the 130 strong group turned up. They were less alarmed by her policy as she expounded it than by the advance publicity in the newspapers. Four days later seventy three members of the group attended a second meeting and on this occasion only two speakers out of twelve supported her. But taking account of who they were and of the private reactions which were reaching her, Barbara Castle at this stage saw no cause for great alarm.

From Congress House the news was no worse than had been expected, if anything slightly more encouraging. George Woodcock had seen to it that the General Council's response was at least constructive in tone. He had given Barbara Castle his personal opinion: "I don't think there is anything in this to which the unions can fundamentally object". His chief concern was that the Commission for Industrial Relations, Donovan's chief recommendation, should be set up on a voluntary basis and this the Government had agreed. He was eager to become its first chairman on these terms. Barbara Castle had overcome her early reluctance to appoint him and the job was in the bag by the time the TUC was called upon to strike an attitude towards the White Paper.

Woodcock's position was never simple when it could be tortured and complicated. Throughout his career as general secretary of the TUC, the career of which he was now tiring, he had passionately upheld the voluntary principle. He believed that there was no substitute for will: the State could not succeed in and should not undertake tasks which required the voluntary compliance of workpeople. This had been his attitude towards the statutory reinforcement of the incomes policy. He had advised the General Council against its "reluctant acquiescence" in penal powers to back up the 1966 wages standstill. But his position had always been complicated by his belief, on the one hand, that State interventions of this kind were wrong and, on the other hand, that they were impracticable and therefore largely irrelevant. The use of law was mistaken and wrong if it presumed to take the main burden, it was tolerable when given a very minor supporting role on the fringes. In this case he satisfied himself that the essence of Barbara Castle's approach was voluntary. The conciliation pause and the compulsory strike ballot were discretionary powers for rare use, at worst minor and irrelevant idiocies. The Government's proposed powers in inter-union disputes were again only for the last resort and could be used only after full consultation with the TUC and the CIR, of which he was to be the boss. Thus in George Woodcock's sophisticated view no great principle was here at stake.

In any case he was always against the TUC striking negative attitudes, a firm believer after Citrine in always giving the General Council a constructive document to chew over. By the time of the emergency meeting of the General Council, which had been called when its senior committee – the finance and general purposes committee – known usually as the "inner cabinet" – was given private sight of the Government's draft proposals, Woodcock's staff had prepared a carefully worded statement. This was carried in the General Council on January 7 – before the proposals began their rough passage through Cabinet – and was published on January 17 at the same time as the White Paper. The Woodcock document forestalled an attempt by Frank Cousins to have the General Council reject the whole Castle package on grounds of principle. Thus by the time the Cabinet met Barabara Castle could report that the General Council had put down what in parliamentary terms would be called "a reasoned amendment" – that was nothing to be alarmed by.

Some of her proposals, the TUC recognised, "could in principle help to improve industrial relations and to promote trade union objectives". The General Council was "opposed to", or at least had "reservations about", the other proposals and wished to leave the Government "in no doubt about the nature of those reservations and the strength of their objections". But it was the General Council's aim "to reach agreement with the Government on ways of improving industrial relations and of strengthening voluntary collective bargaining". The General Council did not exclude the possibility that the Government might add its weight to recommendations by the CIR but was convinced that financial penalties would "militate against finding a genuine solution of this problem". The General Council was "by no means enthusiastic" about the offer of financial aid to trade unions. But it welcomed the Government's acceptance of the Donovan view on enforcing collective agreements. Compulsory strike ballots it regarded as "completely misguided and quite unacceptable". The conciliation pause was "neither practicable nor desirable". The General Council hoped that the Government would reconsider.

This was not exactly fighting talk. And the muted reaction of the

TUC was thrown into sharper relief by the contrary reaction of the employers. John Davies, the director-general of the CBI, angrily accused the Government of "taking a nut cracker to crack a cannon ball". The Conservative Party's reaction also contributed to the generally torpid atmosphere which at first built up around *In Place of Strife*. The Conservatives, of course, did not find Barbara Castle's plan convincing, but they were careful not to knock it at this stage. The technicalities of industrial relations were hard to put over to the public, but undoubtedly there was political mileage in "doing something about the unions" – as the Tories had been the first to recognise. Some of their leaders privately feared that Wilson was on to a winner. Public opinion research in depth which was being conducted for the Conservative Central Office showed that trade union reform had rocketed up the charts into the Top Ten of issues which concerned the public. Thus the "Shadow" Cabinet decided on a cautious line. It was enough at this stage to point out quietly how the Socialists had moved along a path mapped out by the Conservatives while reminding people that it was the Conservatives who were prepared to travel the distance. Edward Heath noted that both parties were agreed now on the need for action; here then was "an historic opportunity" which it would be tragic to throw away. The Tory spokesman on labour matters, Robert Carr, said that the Government had put on some of the Conservatives' outer garments but had left off many of the important foundation garments. He complained that there was to be no legal framework for collective bargaining; that the conciliation pause was too short at twenty-eight days; that too much power was being given to the Minister – the power to order the conciliation pause should be vested in the Commission on Industrial Relations.

The Prime Minister must have himself believed he was on to a winner for he lost no time in putting money on it. On January 20, two days after the publication of *In Place of Strife*, he appeared on the BBC television programme Panorama. He identified himself closely with Barbara Castle's proposals, announcing that he and she had worked on them together for months. He rejoiced in the Government's ability to be tough and its readiness to be unpopular. He said, "I have never tried to get a compromise policy out of the Cabinet . . . I have always said we must get the answer right, however unpopular, and I have lost colleagues in the course of it. I am prepared to do that whenever it becomes necessary". He repeated: "I have said we have got to do what is right and go on regardless of popularity".

But the Government had fundamentally misjudged the situation and, with the benefit of hindsight, we may begin to see why. Politicians often fall into the error of which they accuse political writers – of taking too short a view. They too can be suckers for the instant reaction and they were on this occasion. A half-hearted first huff from the TUC, a bit of favourable press comment and a hopeful trend in the public opinion polls was enough to buck them up no end. Barbara Castle seized upon these straws to reinforce her arguments in Cabinet, for on this unusual occasion opinion was able to form around her policies before they had been agreed in the Government. The Ministers who warned that her policies would do more political harm than industrial good in a pre-election year were brushed aside as faint-hearts and Jonahs. What she and her supporters had not realised was that the Government no longer had the strength or authority for bold experiments, was too far gone in its troublesome term of office to embark upon long-range institutional reforms of a controversial nature. Her proposals provided no quick answers to the industrial problem; she herself emphasised the philosophy underlying her plan. In other words, it represented a few modest steps in a brave new direction; under the pressure of the State's intrusion into the private grief of the workplace, new attitudes would eventually emerge, new procedures and practices grow up and a new, more balanced, relationship between Government and the two sides of industry would evolve. But that would take time and a Government needs a full stock of authority if it is to shift the whole weight of tradition in a society and point it in a new direction. This Government no longer had that authority.

On paper (and they existed only on paper at this stage – a White Paper) her actual proposals may have seemed moderate and sensible enough. But the Government failed to perceive their symbolic potential. The trade unions for some while had stomached the Government's incomes policy powers, but a restriction on the *proceeds* of collective bargaining, necessarily temporary, was one thing, while a permanent restriction on the *process* of collective bargaining was another. The Labour Party quickly sensed that the new policy involved some fundamental reappraisal of the historical and traditional basis of the "Labour Movement", that unquestioned alliance of interests between socialists, co-operators and trade unionists.

In Place of Strife suffered the common defect of carrot and stick policies – the carrot is all you are going to get while the stick is the thin end of a wedge. Two or three years previously there might have been enough trust in the Government but by now there had been too many false departures and dead ends and slippery slopes. The most slippery slope was the incomes policy. Now once again the Government was trying to undersell a policy to the interested parties and oversell it to the general public. On the one hand it was saying quietly to the trade unions, "Look, you go along with this and we can settle the union question in such a way that your enemies the Tories will not be able to reopen it. These modest powers will be safe in our hands and we hope we shall seldom if ever have cause to use them. Trust in us". But on the other hand it was saying noisily to the public, "Look how tough we are. See how radical we can be. Strikes are crippling the economy. We are doing something about them. We are not afraid, not even of our friends the trade unions".

Governments need rhetoric in which to clothe their deeds but rhetoric dressed up as action tends either to be alarming or unconvincing. The trade unions and the Labour Party were by early 1969 in no mood for new philosophies and the public, impatient as ever, was in the mood for quickly effective measures. Between rhetoric and action lay the credibility gap, and over the next two months it opened gapingly before the Government's startled eyes.

The General Council of the TUC is a predictable creature. It moves slowly on all fours, usually forwards and seldom backwards. It has extremely regular habits and does not adapt readily to a changed environment or variations in diet. A peculiar feature are the eyes, like those of an insect which hazily perceive obstacles in their path but see little to either side. Although the jungle is its natural habitat the TUC thrives in a domestic environment provided it is sufficiently petted and is fed on the proprietary foods to which it has grown accustomed. Great patience is required to teach it new tricks.

As the only central organ of the trade union movement, and as the unchallenged spokesman to Government on behalf of work people and their unions, the TUC is favourably placed to exert leadership. At the same time it has virtually no powers of formal control over its affiliates. It is the leader of the trade union movement but at the same time its servant. In its evidence to the Royal Commission the TUC said, "Except for the extreme powers of suspension and then exclusion the TUC has no sanctions that it can impose on unions".

Over the years attempts had been made to enlarge the authority of the TUC at the expense of autonomous unions in three areas: the structure of the trade union movement; the conduct of unions in dispute; and wages. In each case the unions showed themselves intensely jealous of their autonomy and little progress was made towards centralisation. In fifty years there had been three attempts to rationalise the structure of the trade union movement and in each case the impetus for reform came from those who wished to move towards industrial trade unionism – one union per industry instead of, in some cases, a couple of dozen. But in each case the vested interests of the craft and general unions proved too strong and the General Council, which itself reflected the divisions within the movement, was able to do no more than use its good offices to assist with mergers and joint working agreements. In the case of disputes between unions a code of good conduct in the form of the Bridlington Principles of 1939 had been drawn up. The authority of the TUC to rule in the inter-union quarrels brought before it was universally accepted but its role was that of an appeal court not a law enforcer. In disputes between unions and managements it had no powers. Where the action of one or more unions affected the interests of other unions they could seek the TUC's assistance, but the TUC could do no more than convene meetings and try to knock heads together. In the matter of wages all attempts to move towards a national wages policy, even on the basis purely of consultation between unions and the TUC on bargaining strategy, foundered on the rock of union autonomy. In no area was this more jealously asserted than in wage bargaining. It was only when the State intervened with a statutory policy for prices and incomes in 1965 that the unions consented to report their claims to the TUC and permit it to express opinions upon them. It could only express opinions, it still had no powers. For the unions this was a revolutionary step, for the State after twenty years of worrying about the wages problem it was another case of too little too late.

The classical doctrine was neatly expounded by Sir Tom O'Brien on behalf of the General Council at the 1960 Congress: "There are many things which the General Council can do and many things which the General Council cannot do, but it has no authority to order unions around. Each union is a sovereign body; each union has its own executive authority and its national delegate conference in one form or another, and the General Council cannot super-impose its own authority upon individual unions". In spite of the progress made since then on the wages question, and in spite of the gradual change in attitudes which was perhaps taking place, that remained the reality of the situation in 1969.

The leaders of the trade union movement were not blind to the need for change. They realised the considerable impotence of their position as they conducted, on the one hand, high diplomacy with the Government on behalf of the whole trade union movement while, on the other hand, they struggled with constituents over whom they had little control. They purported to be the authoritative representatives of the unions but they knew that they were seldom in a position to enter into a firm bargain on their behalf. Many of them would have liked nothing better than to gain some effective authority over trouble-makers and unofficial strikers or to extend the TUC's authority so as to assist the weak and poorly paid at the expense, if necessary, of the strong and better paid. But each man who reached the General Council of the TUC, usually when well into his fifties, was a child of the trade union movement. The broadening out into a trade union statesman was expected to come at the end of a long narrow experience as a trade union officer. It was hard for them to see things in the wider context of society's needs after having considered them for so long not merely in the narrower context of the trade union movement but, for the most part, in the microcosm of a single trade, a single district or even a single factory. Thus the measure of change which they applied bore small relation to the movement of the world around them. What might appear to outsiders a pitifully slow pace of internal trade union development seemed remarkable to these insiders. Changes had taken place which a few years previously they would never have believed feasible. Who would have dreamt that the TUC would be taking a hand in wage bargaining? They resented the impatience of outsiders for change: outsiders were ignorant, they did not know the facts and "the problems".

Their limited experience made them great respecters of practical knowledge. A long trade union life had taught them that what went in one industry did not necessarily go in another. Respect for skill was one of the dignities of labour which trade unions existed to preserve and defend. One craftsman did not tell another how to do his job, one union did not interfere with another and the TUC did not try to tell experienced and expert unions and their officers how to suck eggs. Everything they knew warned against generalisation; their instinct was to particularise their experience rather than to aggregate it into a theory or a coherent framework of policy. In this way they were defensive and introverted; people who came along with schemes were suspected of not knowing what they were talking about. This conservatism was a form of social nostalgia; having mastered one piece of machinery in all its detail they preferred it to any new model. Knowledge of how something works often produces the belief that it works reasonably well. Most members of the General Council were old enough to have some adolescent recollection of the thirties, and for many the troubles of that period were their formative adult experience. The thirties are the starting point of contemporary folk memory. The achievements of trade unionism since then appeared to the trade union Establishment far more remarkable than its non-achievements, the penalties of regression seemed greater than the prizes of progress. "What are we here for?" George Woodcock had asked them. A typical intellectual's question! "We're here because we're here because we're here".

These attitudes had come out when the General Council's representatives gave oral evidence to the Donovan Commission. That had been an embarrassing occasion and George Woodcock had had to blush. Asked if he was entirely satisfied about relations between unions and shop stewards, Victor Feather, the assistant general secretary, had answered, "In general, yes". In reply to legal probings by Lord Donovan, Sidney Greene, general secretary of the National Union of Railwaymen, said, "I would be much happier, with great respect to you my Lord, if we didn't have anything to do with the law at all". Asked about the Government's role in collective bargaining Feather said, "We don't think there should be a third party in collective bargaining. Collective bargaining is between employers and trade unions". Greene asked Donovan, "Why do you want to raise all these problems when we've got enough problems as it is?"

That had been in November 1966. Now if any further evidence was needed that something had to be done about the state of British industrial relations and that the TUC was unlikely to do it, the months of February and March 1969 produced it. During these months the TUC was presented with a classic test case of its competence to resolve disputes between unions and the export economy was hit badly by a shutdown of the Ford Motor Company.

The inter-union dispute for several weeks threatened a serious strike in the recently nationalised steel industry. The issue concerned which of the unions should be recognised by the British Steel Corporation for the purposes of negotiating pay and conditions of non-manual workers. The dispute had been smouldering away since the industry had been nationalised in 1967. In that year the Corporation decided to restrict recognition to the unions already established in the industry. This gave the Iron and Steel Trades Confederation a virtual monopoly in the organisation of white collar workers. The decision was resisted by the Association of Scientific, Technical and Managerial Staffs and by the Clerical and Administrative Workers' Union. Both of them were eager to organise the workers who before nationalisation had belonged to the company staff unions. They called a strike in the steel industry which had little effect. Then they threatened to withdraw their members from the motor car industry. Here was a dangerous and unusual development: in order to achieve their ends in one industry unions were resorting to industrial action in another; so as to put pressure on a public corporation, and on the Government, the unions were threatening strikes in the most vulnerable part of the private sector. Barbara Castle decided to reopen the question of which unions should be recognised. She appointed a Court of Inquiry under Lord Pearson. It recommended that the ASTMS and CAWU should be recognised. The ISTC, which had refused to cooperate with the Court of Inquiry, now in its turn called a strike. The TUC next tried its hand at sorting out the confusion. It ruled in favour of the established unions. The sixteen manual workers' unions recognised on Vesting Day should have the field to themselves and the white collar unions should be excluded. On the strength of this the British Steel Corporation turned turtle again. It reverted to its original position, which was now the TUC's, and rejected the independent findings of the Pearson inquiry.

The incident invited the comment that the TUC remained dominated by the big battalions of the horny handed, the manual workers' unions, and lacked the impartiality necessary for the adjudication of inter-union disputes. This seemed to strengthen the case for the reserve powers which the Government was proposing to take for dealing with inter-union disputes. The affair also suggested that for all its tough talk the Government was not prepared to face strikes which could cause serious damage to the economy. The British Steel Corporation and the Government caved in to superior power. With more than 100,000 manual workers in membership the ISTC was in a position to stop the steel industry; the aspiring white collar unions were not.

The dispute at the Ford Motor Company was an altogether more serious affair. The whole principle of keeping to bargains was at the centre of the dispute. It served as a test of the feasibility of using penalties against unconstitutional strikers. It resulted in an important legal precedent being set in the High Court. It revealed the weaknesses of the union negotiating structure. It brought the union leaders into bad repute. It revealed the impotence of the TUC in cases where the most powerful of the affiliated unions were involved. It heightened the whole atmosphere surrounding *In Place of Strife*. It had a powerful effect on the mind of Barbara Castle.

The incident began when the Ford management offered to improve the pay and conditions of its 46,000 employees in exchange for their undertaking not to engage in unoffiicial strikes. The "no strike clause" is a common feature of trade union contracts in the United States but rare in Britain except in the form of a very general, and in practice meaningless, undertaking to behave constitutionally. In the agreement now proposed the improved benefits could be withdrawn from workers who had taken part in unconstitutional stoppages of work. The agreement was attractive to the official union negotiators in spite of these conditions. In addition to a basic pay increase of from 7 to 10 per cent the annual holiday bonus was to be increased by £20 and workers who were laid off as a result of strikes or supply difficulties at other factories would be guaranteed two-thirds of their average earnings for up to ten working days.

This last provision represented a substantial addition to the security of the car workers. The plague of the motor industry is its over-inter-dependence. A dispute or a production bottleneck at one factory can quickly affect the employment and earnings of workers at another. The industry is especially vulnerable also to trade recessions and seasonal fluctuations in demand. There was a rough justice in the offer to protect workers from the consequences of unofficial strikes by others in exchange for their not themselves engaging in unofficial action. Moreover, the package would not have conformed to the conditions of the Government's prices and incomes policy unless it could be shown that by reducing the number of unofficial strikes the productivity of the company would substantially increase.

For these reasons the unions on February 11 voted seven–five in favour of accepting the terms. The Ford Motor Company's national joint industrial council consisted of fifteen unions. Each wielded one vote regardless of membership. The Amalgamated Engineering and Foundry Workers' Union represented 15,000 of the 46,000 workers but its vote against the agreement carried the same weight as the others. The Transport and General Workers' Union represented 17,000 of the workers. In the first instance it voted for acceptance but later repudiated the agreement. Between them these two unions thus represented nearly 70 per cent of the Ford workers. No sooner had the agreement been officially accepted by majority decision of the fifteen unions than shop stewards from twenty-one of the twenty-three Ford plants in Britain rejected it. For more than two months shop stewards had been whipping up opposition to the agreement which threatened to devalue their own chief weapon – the unofficial strike. On February 21 members of the TGWU and AEF at Halewood, Merseywide, came out on unofficial strike. On February 26 the AEF declared the strike official. The company's main plant at Dagenham was now entirely stopped. That day the negotiating council voted by nine unions to six to uphold the agreement. But the TGWU changed sides and was now demanding that the agreement be suspended and re-examined. On February 27 the TGWU declared the strike official on the grounds that the company refused to reopen negotiations. So now a majority of the company's employees were on *official* strike against an agreement reached between the management and the unions' constitutional negotiating body.

The next day the Ford Motor Company did a most unusual thing. It went to the courts for an injunction against the two unions acting in breach of agreement. It was, admittedly, in a most unusual position for the employees' side of the negotiating council was demanding payment of the new rates from March 1 while the two biggest unions were on strike against the agreement. The High Court hearing would at least determine whether the company was bound to pay or not. Companies in Britain very seldom resort to the courts in connection with industrial disputes. Employers are entitled at law to sue their employees as individuals for breaches of their individual contracts of employment. They generally do not do so because their objective is to quickly restore good relations not exacerbate bad relations. This was the most common argument against removing the unions' immunity from civil actions. In this case the company was seeking injunctions not against its employees but against two trade unions. The Trade Union Act of 1871 prohibited legal contracts between employers' associations and trade unions. The Ford Motor Company was an employer not an employers' association. Nothing in the 1871 Act would seem to prevent an employer and trade union agreeing a legally enforceable contract. The question was whether the negotiators in this case intended to enter into such a contract. The Trades Disputes Act of 1906 indemnified trade union officials against actions for damages arising out of trade disputes but it was silent on the subject of injunctions.

Ford was granted a temporary injunction. The unions paid no heed to it and the strike continued and spread. The case came to trial on March 4 after the defendant unions had obtained a week's adjournment. On the first day of the case the judge, Mr. Justice Geoffrey Lane said: "I sigh and sigh only because the whole matter is not a simple matter of law. It is complicated by what people will inevitably do regardless of what the law says is correct. Unfortunately, I am sitting as a judge, not as an arbitrator. The thing is coloured by a relationship of management and labour".

The case turned on the intentions of the parties in reaching their agreement. Had they intended to make a legally enforceable agreement which the company would expect the Court to uphold by injunction? The onus of proof was on Ford. The counsel for the unions argued that all the precedents, including the opinion of the Donovan Commission, were against collective contracts being enforceable in the courts. To this the Judge said:

"You are saying that I have to decide in the climate of opinion against which these particular negotiations, to use a neutral term, were carried out. One has to do that in every case, although in most cases it does not need more than a split second's thought. For instance, an ordinary commercial contract for the supply of steel is plainly enforceable. The ordinary contract to take someone out to dinner is not enforceable. Those are matters one can decide against one's own background of commonsense, judicial knowledge or what you like. But where one has a negotiation carried out in a sphere with which most of us unhappily are not immediately familiar, one has to look at what one can in the way of contemporary documents, reports and so on in order to discover the background which in ordinary cases would be obvious. So you say when one looks at the extra-judicial authorities the background is perfectly plain. The parties did not intend to create a contract." The counsel agreed that this was exactly his submission.

Later in the case the efficacy of an injunction was queried. The counsel for the unions pointed out that the injunctions had been in force for several days without making any difference to the actual position. The strike was continued. This emphasised the point often made that in industrial disputes the courts were the wrong forum. Often the unfortunate effect of court proceedings was that the parties took stands which were more hostile than they might take round the negotiating table. The judge replied that he had been troubled considerably by this. "Assuming that the plaintiffs (Ford) are right in everything they say," he went on, "it is difficult to see what the result of mandatory injunctions will be. I am not sufficiently experienced in industrial relations to be able to forecast; but one wonders if the difficulty of enforcing a matter like this by ordinary legal action has any bearing on the more pressing problem of legal enforceability".

Judgment was given on March 6. Mr. Justice Lane agreed that there was nothing in law to prevent employers and unions entering into legally binding agreements but concluded that this was not the intention of the parties in this case. He read out the relevant passages of the Donovan Report. The parties had obviously been aware of this and of other documents which showed the climate of opinion to be overwhelmingly in favour of collective agreements carrying no legal obligation. The agreements between Ford and the unions were composed largely of optimistic aspirations, presenting grave problems, and had been reached against a background of opinion adverse to enforceability. They were not, therefore, in his Lordship's opinion, contracts in the legal sense. "Without clear and express provisions making them amenable to legal action they remain in the realm of undertakings binding in honour only".

This important case was naturally confused with the issues which, by coincidence, were debated in Parliament on March 3. The Commons then for the first time discussed Barbara Castle's White Paper. In fact that Ford case had very little bearing on the political issue. It was extremely rare for unions to act officially in breach of contract. *In Place of Strife* was concerned with unconstitutional behaviour by union members. But the incident contained a number of lessons none the less. It gave support to the opinion of the Donovan Commission that collective agreements in the form in which they normally were drawn up were not suitable documents for enforcement at law. It drew attention to the pressing need to reform the procedures and relationships in industry. It suggested that in spite of the public support for Barbara Castle's "penal clauses", including among rank-and-file trade unionists, groups of workers would resist the application of penalties to themselves. It showed dramatically how a court order could be totally ignored by strikers with their blood up. Would an order by the Government have any greater effect? It gave support to the Donovan view that recourse to the courts made industrial disputes more difficult to solve. The DEP conciliators had been prohibited from trying to settle the dispute during the ten days in which it was *sub judice*. Thus the litigation helped to prolong a dispute which was said to be costing £1 million worth of exports a day.

The strike – which continued for another ten days before a compromise was reached – took place in a highly charged political atmosphere. On February 26 Ford's managing director Bill Batty alleged on BBC Radio "Our employees, their wives and families and my company are now being forced to foot the bill in a struggle caused by one union's opposition to the Government's prices and incomes policy and its labour relations White Paper". He asked, "How can industry and our nation fight for a place in the world with labour relations like these?" The "one union" he had in mind was the AEF. Its representative on the Ford negotiating council was Reg Birch, a far leftist who had been expelled from the British Communist Party for adopting a Maoist position. Nevertheless, it is very doubtful whether the AEF's motives in declaring the strike official were overtly political or connected with that union's opposition to Barbara Castle's policy. The AEF had quietly entered into similar conditional bargains in other parts of the engineering industry. The president, Hugh Scanlon, was in Australia when the Ford dispute broke out. Had he been in command the strike might not have been declared official in such precipitous fashion. Nor is there any evidence that Jack Jones of the TGWU was moved by political considerations in following suit. When one major union is on strike it is hard for another to pursue a contrary policy. A suspicion of political motivation was aroused by the fact that the TGWU's representative on the Ford council, Les Kealey, was a supporter of the Castle White Paper. He was sacked by his union for acting against instructions in upholding the decision of the Ford council. Both Jack Jones and Hugh Scanlon stumbled into a situation brought about by their unions' inadequate control over their negotiators, inadequate authority over their stewards, inadequate communication with and control over their members, and the unrealistic system whereby one union cast one vote regardless of its membership strength.

Nevertheless, the furore aroused by the penal clauses at Ford became connected, in many people's minds, with the Government's proposals for penalising unofficial strikers. Some of the shop floor militants saw themselves engaged in a political struggle. And leaders of the other unions, who were angered by the AEF's and TGWU's repudiation of the agreement, joined in alleging some kind of conspiracy. On the day of the judgment in the High Court, TGWU shop stewards proclaimed a "victory" in the campaign which was building up against *In Place of Strife*. The Communist Party organ, the *Morning Star*, the next morning carried the headline "First Round Won – Now for the K.O." "Ford's penal clauses are similar in essence to the anti-union measures in Mrs. Castle's White Paper", it claimed.

The muddle, the double-dealing, the bitter recriminations and the opportunism which caused and prolonged the Ford dispute finally disillusioned Barbara Castle of any remaining hope that the unions might succeed in putting their house in order. She saw their conduct at close quarters and thought it disgraceful. The TUC had been impotent throughout. She became doubly determined that the Government must act. The Ford affair also provoked the Prime Minister into the most bitter public condemnation of the unions he had yet made. Speaking in his own Merseyside constituency on March 14 he recalled all that the Government had done to bring industry and employment to that area. In 1968 alone Merseyside had received £58 millions of public development money. "And the response?", he asked; "Strike after strike frustrating the effort of Government, signalling the question mark to those industrialists who are attracted by the inducements the Government provide and who are considering establishing themselves here". Wilson went on to cite the Girling strike and another which was going on at the Vauxhall Motors' plant at Ellesmere Port where ten platers had virtually stopped the company's operations and thrown 13,000 out of work.

The Prime Minister then referred to *In Place of Strife* and declared: "I want it to be clearly understood that the Government means business about these proposals. All that has happened in the last three weeks provides powerful support for the measures we shall be introducing in Parliament". And he added a few words of warning to the Labour Party, recalling his final words to the previous year's party conference: nothing could stand in the way of the success of the Labour Movement, he had asserted – misquoting Franklin Delano Roosevelt – except the Labour Movement itself.

His speech enraged left-wingers and some of the trade union MPs. This was no way for a Labour Prime Minister to go around talking about the trade unions, as if they were to blame for everything.

The political wing of the Labour Movement lived in a chronic state of disappointment. Nothing the Government did seemed to work. Time and again the dispirited MPs had swallowed the nasty medicine prescribed by their Government only to see Ministers reappearing at the Despatch Box proferring still larger spoonfuls. So many hopes had been dashed. Policies for economic expansion had given way to policies of economic restriction. Devaluation of the pound had been forced upon the Government in humilating circumstances but even now, fifteen months afterwards, there was no sure sign of economic recovery. Cherished policies and principles had been put to the knife – prescription charges reintroduced, the raising of the school-leaving age postponed, and the Asians of East Africa who held British passports barred from entering the country at will. Budget followed Budget – three doses of taxation in 1968. Attempts to bring the rebel regime in Rhodesia to account had failed, so had the attempt to gain entry to the European Common Market. The party was rotting at the grass roots; Labour-held town halls had become rare oases in a Tory desert. The Government's standing was unprecedentedly low: an election would mean a Conservative avalanche; the Prime Minister was the most unpopular since Neville Chamberlain. The Parliamentary Labour Party did not present a happy spectacle.

On the left of the PLP a group of from twenty to forty MPs persistently opposed most of the Government's important policies. They were opposed to the post-devaluation economic strategy no less than they had been opposed to the policies deployed to save the pound. They were opposed to the level of expenditure on defence, although reduced, and opposed to all restrictions on the growth of social expenditure, although it had been considerably enlarged. Most of them were opposed to joining the Common Market. They were opposed to the incomes policy. They were in favour of "Socialism". Huddled together below the gangway of the House of Commons the hard core of the left looked more like a party of opposition than a part of the party in government. They walked with impunity into the division lobbies against the Government and freely abstained from supporting it against the Tories. Ministers at the Despatch Box spent as much time debating over their right shoulders as in addressing the Conservative Opposition across the floor of the House. The Socialist Opposition had no leader. Its members comprised the Tribune Group, thus called because of its associations with the left-wing weekly founded by Aneurin Bevan. The leadership of the left and the mantle of Bevan would undoubtedly have fallen upon Michael Foot, his hagiographer and heir to his constituency at Ebbw Vale. But Foot remained the inveterate loner – the prima donna who would not lend his voice to any organised chorus. The now ageing baby of a famous political family, he was the outstanding parliamentary rhetorician of his day. He was opposed not only to the policies of this Government but also, or so it often seemed, to Government itself. Were the Socialist millenium to dawn Foot would be there, on the plinth in Trafalgar Square, leading the protest. The Socialist Opposition was the party of protest. Its members seldom consented to contribute to the legislative committee work of the House of Commons but they signed many motions. Sentimentally, they clung to the lingering belief that Harold Wilson was in his secret heart a man of the Left who had strayed but might one day be brought back to the true path of virtue. The Left lived in its own world.

On the right of the party was a smaller group, if group it can be called, whose chief complaint against the Government was the way in which it was led. This handful of MPs consisted chiefly of young men from the universities, some of them dons, others of them journalists or professional men, who had won seats in the Labour landslide of 1966. Many of their seats would be lost unless the Government could stage a spectacular recovery, and they faced returning to interrupted careers in highly competitive fields. Some of them were disappointed in hopes of office. Some found the life of an ordinary backbench MP an insufficient outlet for their abilities. Several of them sat at the feet of the dashing intellectual members of the Cabinet – Roy Jenkins, Tony Crosland, Denis Healey. They thought of themselves as the "radical right", radical in their willingness to rethink the traditional assumptions of socialism, radical in their attitude to income distribution and the balance of private and public expenditure, radical in their response to libertarian questions. They were moved more by bureaucratic than technocratic considerations; they were interested in the machinery of government but not much in the machinery of computers; they were arts graduates for the most part, not scientists. They tended to be elitists. The book they had all read was Crosland's *The Future of Socialism*, the standard text of revisionism. They could be called "Gaitskellites", except the expression no longer meant very much; in Gaitskell's battles they would have been on his side, save in the case of the Common Market. Harold Wilson had taken the Labour Party further along the path of Gaitskellism than Hugh Gaitskell had dared to contemplate but in Roy Jenkins some of them saw a better and more shining leader than Harold Wilson.

Between the flapping wings of the party was its great gangling body. Out of about 350 Labour MPs (by-elections affected the exact total) the trade union group accounted for about 130. The vast majority of the union MPs belonged to the centre of the party although about a dozen sat below the gangway with the Left and one or two had links with the "radical right". There were ninety members of the House of

Commons – Ministers, Junior Ministers and Whips – on the "pay roll vote" which left 240 backbenchers. Of these only about fifty could be clearly identified with either wing of the party. Thus the "centre" was large (about 190 MPs) and amorphous. The great majority of these MPs were unknown beyond the confines of Westminster and their constituencies. They were the Government's stable lobby fodder. They seldom signed motions, joined inner party factions or issued statements to the press. They were not invited to appear on television or discuss the state of the nation on "The World at One". They were not often consulted by the Lobby Correspondents of the national newspapers. They inhabited the members-only tea room. They were what Iain Macleod unkindly called the "blancmange" of the Parliamentary Labour Party. Their job was to support the Government, most of them entertained no hopes of office, and they sullenly resented the antics of the left and the arrogance of the intellectual young right. They were the most important section of the party.

The occupational and educational composition of the party had not changed as much as many people thought. Ray Gunter urged that it should become "once again the party of our people and not a party of middle class intellectuals". The 1966 intake had given the impression of a middle class invasion. Of the seventy-two new MPs only fourteen were workers. But the change between the party of 1951 and the party of 1966 was less dramatic. In 1951 35 per cent of Labour MPs were professional men and women, in 1966 they accounted for 43 per cent. The proportion of workers had fallen from 37 to 30 per cent. The proportion of MPs who had received university education had increased from 41 to 51 per cent. It was not true that the Labour Party in Attlee's day was predominantly a working class party, it was not true that the Labour Party under Harold Wilson had lost its solid working class base. Of 363 Labour members elected in 1966 the first or formative occupation of 109 was at manual trades or on the railways. There were forty-seven skilled workers, thirty-two coal miners, twenty-one semi and unskilled workers and nine railway clerks. In addition to the 109 there were twenty-two miscellaneous "white collar" workers. There were 132 MPs sponsored by twenty-seven different trade unions. Not all of these were workers for some of the unions had taken to sponsoring professional men, for examples, Jeremy Bray, an automation consultant, was a TGWU member of Parliament and Jack Ashley, sponsored by the GMWU, was a BBC television producer. There were forty trade union officials among the trade union MPs although some of them had long been away from their unions, for examples, George Brown and Robert Mellish, both TGWU officers on secondment but both by now professional politicians of long standing. The non-industrial section of the party in 1966 included thirty-six barristers, eighteen solicitors, twenty-four university teachers, fifteen adult education teachers and thirty-three school teachers (teachers accounted for 20 per cent of the party!) and there were twenty-nine journalists. Across the whole party 186 MPs had attended university, sixty-six a public school. Command of the centre was the key to the management of the Parliamentary Labour Party. The left was a containable nuisance, the radical right a mere irritant. The rebels on the left did not like entering the division lobby with the Tories and very rarely did so. Negative votes when the Conservatives were abstaining or carefully controlled abstentions when the Conservatives were dividing the House could do no serious harm to a Government with a majority of seventy-five, for as long as the centre held. On none of the issues which had so far divided the party – East of Suez, defence expenditure, cuts in social spending, prices and incomes policy, Vietnam and the Common Market – had the rebellions spread far beyond the contagious wings of the party into its sound body. But now, in early 1969, there was a rebellion with a difference. The revolt against the Parliament Bill to reform the House of Lords found support on both sides of the House and in all sections of the Labour Party. It was a novel expression of what, after the blacks and the students, was soon dubbed "backbench power". Discipline in the party was already at a low ebb. At the best of times the Labour Party is not a very orderly crew. It contains a lot of argumentative and strongly committed people without whom it would not be a party of the left. From the earliest days the Standing Orders contained a "conscience clause", first provided to enable Keir Hardie to vote for women's suffrage. Throughout the Attlee Government, which had a majority of 146, the Standing Orders were suspended, which meant that a vote against the Government did not have to result in the withdrawal of the Whip. A Labour MP who loses the Whip is reported to the National Executive Committee of the party which is bound to refuse the offender endorsement at the next election. A candidate without an official party ticket stands virtually no chance of winning. Thus the punishment is severe. The Standing Orders were reimposed while Labour was in opposition and applied from November 1964 through to the election in March 1966. With a majority never higher than four the party behaved itself; the only significant revolt was when two maverick right-wing MPs –

Desmond Donnelly and Woodrow Wyatt – rebelled against the plan to nationalise the steel industry. After the 1966 election the Standing Orders were suspended once more. Labour then began with a majority of ninety-seven and what became known as the "liberal regime" was introduced. This gave ample scope for MPs to vote according to conscience provided they supported the Government on votes of confidence.

From 1966 the Parliamentary Labour Party became much more difficult to manage than it had been under Attlee's premiership. There were substantial backbench revolts in the 1945–51 period but they were very largely confined to questions of foreign affairs and defence. The Government's policy at home was loyally supported throughout and the leadership never became a question among backbench MPs. After 1966 there were revolts on both home and foreign issues and the Government was challenged on policies which were central to its programme. For example, the Government's East of Suez policy was challenged from both wings of the party in June 1966. In July there were twenty-seven left-wing abstentions on the Prices and Incomes Bill in spite of the state of economic emergency in which it was introduced. In February 1967 there were sixty-three abstentions on the annual defence White Paper. In January 1968 twenty-five MPs abstained on a motion of confidence in the Government and on various cuts in public expenditure which were made in consequence of the devaluation of the pound. In January 1968 the "liberal regime" was modified. The Chief Whip was empowered to reprimand rebels and to suspend them from attendance at party meetings before invoking the supreme penalty of withdrawing the whip. Temporary exclusion from party meetings was not a sufficient punishment for it to have any deterrent effect.

By early 1969 an increasing body of MPs were fed up not with the "liberal regime" as such but with the manner of its operation by the Government Chief Whip, John Silkin. Silkin was a young and inexperienced man for this key job. More usually a Government Chief Whip is a senior and experienced MP and often he is a powerful political force in his own right. He attends Cabinet, although not a member of it, and in times of difficulty may play in it an important independent role. At the same time, however, the Chief Whip needs to have a close personal relationship with the Prime Minister, whose agent he is. He is the Prime Minister's eyes and ears and his leading adviser on party matters. But it is also his duty to inform the Prime Minister of bad news and facts however unpleasant. In that sense he has to be a double agent. For example, the Conservative Chief Whip, William Whitelaw, saw it as his duty in 1965 to inform Sir Alec Douglas Home that he no longer enjoyed the support of his party. John Silkin was not this kind of Chief Whip. He had entered Parliament only in 1963; when appointed in 1966 he was forty-three. His only obvious claim to the office was his success as pairing whip; with a majority of four or fewer this had been a crucial task and in eighteen months Silkin had not made a single mistake in his arithmetic. He was held to be on the left of centre – his wife, the actress Rosamund John, had been associated with the Campaign for Nuclear Disarmament. His father was Minister of Town and Country Planning in the Attlee Government and now a life peer.

John Silkin was his master's servant and his master was Harold Wilson. He owed his position entirely to the Prime Minister. This was one of the chief complaints against him; MPs suspected that the Prime Minister sometimes received over-optimistic accounts of the state of the party and that messages from the Party to Number 10 were not getting through as loud and clear as the messages in the other direction. He was also accused of capriciousness. Occasional offenders felt that he was tougher with them than with the hardened recidivists on the left. A bottle of wine with Stan Orme was not what the party loyalists called discipline. But the most serious complaint was that the easy-going Silkin sometimes did not appear to care whether people voted or not. For example, one MP who abstained on a not very crucial vote, but only then after much wrestling with his loyal conscience, passed the Chief Whip in the corridor the next day to be cheerfully greeted as if nothing had happened. "If that's all my vote is worth", he said later, "I shan't bother the next time." It was frustrating for those who supported the Government, often with misgivings, to see those who consistently failed to support it none-the-less retaining the Chief Whip's favour. Tolerance of slack pairing undermined the discipline of those who still took the trouble to pair – why bother to forsake a good dinner table for a two line whip? The solid centre of the party felt its sense of loyalty being cheapened. The liberal regime, as administered by John Silkin, suited some of the more sophisticated younger members and accommodated the unruly behaviour of the Left; but supporting the Government was psychologically important to many MPs, particularly the older inhabitants of the centre – what else were they there for? –and they felt increasingly unhappy in the permissive, casual and bitchy atmosphere which grew up at Westminister. And as John Silkin's unpopularity grew so his arithmetic began to deteriorate.

On March 3 *In Place of Strife* was debated in the Commons and fifty-three Labour MPs voted against the Government and an estimated forty more abstained. The revolt was more serious than the party managers had anticipated. The next night the by now usual protest against the annual defence White Paper was staged with around thirty Labour MPs deliberately abstaining. But more serious for the Government was the humiliation it was experiencing with its scheme for the reform of the House of Lords, which its chief author, Richard Crossman, had neglected to call *In Place of Ermine*. Here was no mere demonstration: a determined body of back-benchers from both sides of the House were set upon wrecking or defeating the measure.

The conditions for such a rebellion were unusually favourable. Because the bill concerned Parliament the committee stage was being taken on the floor of the House. Most Bills are sent to committee in smaller rooms upstairs. The party authorities select the members of the committees. If the rate of progress is unreasonable the Government can use its majority in the Chamber to impose a timetable or "guillotine." Unless the proposed legislation has aroused great controversy between the parties the Opposition usually cooperates with the Government in following an informally agreed timetable. On this occasion the committee was the whole House. That meant that every minute spent in committee ate into the Government's legislative timetable. The opponents of the Bill, who would have been under-represented on a hand-picked committee upstairs, were free to use every procedural device to delay its passage. The Opposition was not cooperating with the Government – the "usual channels" had broken down. It was not the custom to impose a "guillotine" on a constitutional measure. In any case, the Conservatives would undoubtedly oppose a "guillotine" motion and there was no guaranteeing that enough Labour back-benchers would support it. For once the legislature had the executive on the run.

The Parliament Bill was the brain child of Richard Crossman. There was no more fertile brain in the Government and it left behind it a trail of progeny, legitimate and illegitimate. Crossman was the archetypal left-wing intellectual – Wykehamist, Oxford don, political journalist and pamphleteer, MP since 1945. He had collected the nicknames "Tricky Dick" and "Double Crossman". It was not that he was innately disloyal as a man – the charm of Dick Crossman was great – but that he had grown up in the convention of "brutal frankness" which ruled among the English upper class intelligentsia of his generation – a happy family life consisted in one long ferocious controversy. H. A. L. Fisher, the Liberal historian, had packed him off from New College into politics. Attlee – who knew his father – treated him as a lively sixth former who was better not trusted in the prefect's room. Crossman held no office from 1945–51. His first job in the Wilson administration was as Minister of Housing and Local Government. But the author of "Plato Today" embarked upon his Syracuse period when in 1966 he became Lord President of the Council and Leader of the House of Commons. The constitution-making could now begin. Crossman, who is interested in most things, had for some while been excited on the subject of parliamentary reform. In 1963 he set out some thoughts on the subject in a long introduction to Bagehot's *The English Constitution*. His thesis was that behind the lingering appearance of Cabinet Government the reality was "Prime Ministerial Government". The transformation of the system was now complete; Parliament and the Cabinet were now, in Bagehot's terminology, among the "dignified" parts of the Constitution; Prime Ministerial Government had become its "efficient secret". The power of the Prime Minister rested upon his undisputed control of a highly centralised political machine (party) and an equally centralised and vastly more powerful administrative machine (the Civil Service). But Crossman hoped to be overtaken by events as Bagehot had been. He wrote: "In theory – but also in practice – the British people retains the power not merely to choose between two Prime Ministers, and two parties, but to throw off its deferential attitude and reshape the political system, making the parties instruments of popular control, and even insisting that the House of Commons should once again provide the popular check on the executive. It is my hope and belief that this will happen".

From 1966 Crossman embarked on a programme of parliamentary reform. Various procedural changes were made to improve the efficiency of the House of Commons. One of them, which made it easier for MPs to obtain emergency debates, helped to revive the Commons as a debating society but hardly contributed to its capacity to check the executive. The others for the most part helped the Government to get its business through and could be said therefore to increase the power of the executive. The most notable reform was the experiment in specialised committees. These gave the keener MPs something more useful to do but they were denied the powers which would have made them real instruments of parliamentary control. Nevertheless,

Crossman's reforms were in the right spirit and were generally welcomed, especially by the younger, more ambitious and restless MPs who had recently arrived to liven up the historic monument at Westminster. But when Crossman turned to the House of Lords he made enemies of the very MPs who had approved of his Commons reforms.

On the question of the House of Lords he was an apostate. Crossman changes his mind like other men change their socks. His attitude towards the Upper House had hitherto been the standard left-wing attitude which was that it should be abolished and the hereditary peerage along with it. Now he decided that far from being abolished, or even downgraded, it should be reformed and strengthened. One argument he used was that the reform of the Commons would be assisted if the Lords could be equipped to handle a larger share of the Parliamentary business. Another was that if the Government did not do something about the delaying powers of the Upper House it might find itself in trouble during the last two years of its term. Under the Parliament Act of 1948 the Lords could delay a measure for thirteen months plus the time it took for the Commons to re-read the Bill. Coming from the Ministry of Housing and Local Government where he had appointed a Royal Commission on local government, Crossman anticipated possible trouble over parliamentary boundaries. The suspensory veto of the Lords applied to a Distribution of Seats Bill could conceivably cost Labour the election. He convinced himself that nothing could be done about the powers of the Lords unless its composition was also reformed. And he convinced himself that the only practical way to reform the Second Chamber constructively was by consensus among the parties. That could not produce the most satisfactory answer but the Government would be able to shelter from its backbench critics behind the need for all party agreement.

His enthusiasm for House of Lords reform, we may suspect, had also something to do with the fun he expected to have. Working out a new composition for the Upper House so as to remove the hereditary Conservative majority, which had remained since the time of George III, would be a fascinating brain teaser, better than a New Statesman competition. Reaching an agreement with the Tories would be an exciting test of his political skill, for many of his colleagues doubted the possibility of agreeing anything acceptable to the Labour Party. And the whole affair would be rich with historical associations and intellectual enjoyments.

Crossman's chief allies in this enterprise were the Prime Minister, who had seen in it something to cheer the troops, and Roy Jenkins, then the Home Secretary, who was perhaps especially attracted to the idea of settling the Lords question as a result of his deep interest as an historian in the earlier controversies surrounding it. But there was strong opposition in the Cabinet even at the beginning. George Brown and Jim Callaghan were both against; their instincts told them that the dangers would be greater than the rewards. What if the deal with the Tories came unstuck? There was a lot to be said, they thought, for Herbert Morrison's attitude which was that "The very irrationality of the composition of the House of Lords and its quaintness are safeguards for our modern democracy". Barbara Castle was bitterly opposed to her friend Dick's scheme. She did not believe he would be able to reach an acceptable agreement with the Tories, he was being too clever by half as usual. And her democratic spirit rose up against the extension of Prime Ministerial patronage which would be involved in the creation of an appointed Second Chamber.

Crossman did pull off an agreement with the Conservatives and Liberals but on the very day in June 1968 on which he circulated it Harold Wilson lost his temper with the Tories and announced rashly that the Government was breaking off the all party talks and would bring in its own measure. That was provoked by the refusal of the Tory peers to make a Government Order imposing further economic sanctions against Rhodesia. Their action may have been intolerable (the sanctions had been approved by a unanimous resolution in the Security Council of the United Nations) but it was effectively only a gesture. However, the Government's precipitate response enabled the Conservative Party, which was discovering that the opposition on its backbenches to the agreed reforms was stronger than had been expected, to absolve itself of responsibility for the Crossman plan. Without all-party agreement Crossman's strategy collapsed. But he persisted nevertheless and again managed to carry the Cabinet. The Prime Minister had committed himself to a Bill. Crossman tried without success to patch matters up with the Opposition. Eventually he was obliged to bring forward the plan as agreed between the representatives at the all-party conference but no longer agreed between the parties officially. This he did on November 19 and this was the beginning of the trouble.

The essence of the scheme was to give the government of the day a majority in the Upper House by converting it from a hereditary chamber into a nominated one. Whichever party formed the government would have a small majority over all peers taking a party whip. But "crossbench" peers, that is to say non-party peers, of whom there would be about thirty with voting rights, would hold the balance. If they used their votes to defeat a government measure it would be delayed for six months from the point of disagreement. The effective power of delay would be further reduced by allowing Governments to carry over Bills between sessions, that is to say a Bill delayed by the Lords would no longer have to be begun all over again in the Commons because a summer recess had intervened. The hereditary principle was to be destroyed by the introduction of a "two tier system". All peers entitled to vote would be appointed by the Prime Minister. The voting peers would be required to give at least one-third of their time to the House of Lords. The original plan provided for salaries. Other peers, including the existing peers of succession for the remainder of their life times, would be entitled to attend and speak but not vote. Hereditary peers would be eligible for appointment as life peers with the right to vote and it was anticipated that the bulk of new creations necessary would be made from the ranks of the hereditary peerage. Other interests were to be protected. For example sixteen out of twenty-six of the Lords Spiritual (the bishops) would be given voting rights and so would the Law Lords, in their case regardless of attendance. The Law Lords were also to be exempted from the retirement age which for voting peers was to be set at a sprightly seventy-two. Non-voting but speaking peers could remain to die with their mouths open.

Objections were levelled against practically every feature of the scheme. It was attacked for being impracticable, undesirable or both. It reeked of the Establishment. It perpetuated the mumbo-jumbo of titles and Lords Spiritual and Temporal. A hereditary peerage would remain in existence. The reformed Second Chamber would not look a very modern chamber. The scheme was undemocratic. The patronage power of the Prime Minister would be dangerously increased. The delaying function of the Lords would be reduced on paper but increased in practice, for a reformed Chamber would feel free to use its powers whereas an unreformed one seldom dared to do so for fear of provoking a constitutional crisis. The "cross benchers" would wield undue power. Either they would be the creatures of the Prime Minister's patronage or, alternatively, creatures of the Establishment. It was unrealistic to suppose they would be completely neuter – as Enoch Powell put it "neither flesh nor fowl nor good red herring" – and what use would they be if they were? These and other objections came from all sides of the House of Commons.

A thoroughly unholy alliance formed against what one member called "the Mafia of the front benches". Some backbenchers wanted a weaker House of Lords, some wanted a stronger one; some wanted to abolish it, some wanted to leave it as it was; some wanted a regionally elected Second Chamber, some wanted no second Chamber. The romantic right joined hands with the romantic left; the old joined forces with young; Sir Harry Legge-Bourke went into the lobby with Willie Hamilton. The rebels agreed among themselves on one score only – that Richard Crossman's White Paper stank. In a two-day debate only two backbenchers spoke with any enthusiasm for the scheme. The House had been asked only to "take note" of the proposals but 159 MPs voted for Willie Hamilton's amendment which called for its summary rejection. An unprecedented backbench revolt was taking place.

Second Reading was given to the Parliament Bill on February 3. The size of the revolt had somewhat diminished. The Government had the whips on although the Conservatives and Liberals allowed a free vote. A concession had been made to backbench opinion and it was no longer proposed to pay peers a salary. Labour backbenchers had been more ready to defy the Government on a White Paper than on an actual Bill. Nevertheless, twenty-seven Labour MPs joined 105 Conservatives and three Liberals in the "Noe" lobby. The real war began, however, when the guerrillas took over. Taking advantage of the greater procedural freedoms available on the floor of the House, and of the breakdown in the "usual channels", a determined body of parliamentary fighters set out to destroy the Bill, clause by clause, line by line, word by word. The Ché Guevara of this campaign was Robert Sheldon who on one day occupied the House for three hours and fifty-one minutes with time-wasting procedural questions. The next day the Committee sat from 10 a.m. but a further hour-and-a-half was spent on points of order. For hour upon precious hour of parliamentary time the Bill progressed by not a line. During one such session the Liberal Chief Whip, Eric Lubbock, announced that he had "heard nothing but piss and wind all the time I have been here". So it went on, through February, March and into April. Passage of the Bill against the organised efforts of this small enthusiastic army of some seventy backbenchers from both sides of the House was not assisted by a situation in which the Ministers chiefly responsible lacked enthusiasm for their work. The Home Secretary, James Callaghan, was in charge of piloting the Bill through Committee yet he was to be seen in the tea room nodding in agreement with its opponents. John Silkin, the Government Chief Whip, had never been a supporter of the plan. Its original proponents – Richard Crossman as Leader of the House and Roy Jenkins as Home Secretary – had both departed for other fields.

By April the drama had become a farce. On April 2 Silkin was obliged to report that he could no longer guarantee the Government a majority. Dispirited MPs were drifting off for the Easter holidays like a crowd leaving early from a poor football match on a nasty winter's afternoon. The Government was looking silly in the extreme. Something had to be done to restore its authority. The rebellious backbenchers might be having some fun, and were perhaps striking a blow for parliamentary freedom at the same time, but their activities had become extremely damaging to the Government's reputation for competence. A monstrous muddle was on display. The Prime Minister was urged by some of his colleagues to stop the rot before it was too late. If the backbenchers were allowed to taste blood on this occasion they would be baying for it on others. The Government's credibility must be restored. Harold Wilson was advised to read the riot act, impose a "guillotine" on the Bill and be prepared to withdraw the whip from MPs who refused to support the Government in its crisis. Among those urging this stern course was Barbara Castle. She had in no way changed her opinion of the Bill but she believed that Governments should see their policies through. But the Prime Minister was not willing to make an issue of the Parliament Bill. He did not wish to use a "guillotine" on a controversial constitutional question. He was advised by Silkin that the party would probably not support the Government even on a procedural motion.

The rebel backbenchers thus defeated the Parliament Bill and humilitated the Government. In the process, as we shall see, they finished the career of John Silkin as Chief Whip. There was rejoicing at the arrival of "back bench power". Parliament was by no means as powerless as the pundits had asserted. Richard Crossman had looked forward to the day when the House of Commons would "once again provide the popular check on the executive" and that day, it seemed to some, had now arrived – over the dead body of his own Parliament Bill. The guerrillas had shown how a Government could be beaten by the use of procedure without arriving at the confrontation of a confidence vote. They had invented a form of limited warfare which could be put to future parliamentary use.

Harold Wilson having declined to do battle on the Parliament Bill was left to find some other way of restoring his tattered authority.

5 *The Keeper of the Cloth Cap*

AT Transport House, Smith Square, on the last Wednesday of each month the national executive committee of the Labour Party meets. On the last Wednesday of March its meeting became headline news. Harold Wilson's authority was openly challenged by a senior colleague.

The Labour Party shares its dim headquarters with the Transport and General Workers' Union, another reminder of the intimate, taken-for-granted, interlock between the industrial and political wings of the Labour Movement. The relationship is reflected in the composition of the twenty-eight member national executive committee. The Leader of the Party and the Deputy Leader of the Party, who are elected by MPs, sit on it *ex officio*. So does the Treasurer of the Labour Party who is elected by the party conference. There are twelve representatives of the trade unions who are elected at each annual conference by the trade union votes alone; there are seven representatives of constituency parties, who are elected by the local parties alone, one representative elected by Co-operative societies, and five representatives of women who are elected by the whole of conference, men and women. Voting at the conference is according to the affiliated membership of organisations. Thus the Transport and General Workers' Union has 1,250,000 votes, which are always delivered *en bloc* as a single vote, while a small constituency party has only one vote. As a consequence of this system the unions command about 80 per cent of the voting strength at the Labour Conference. And this means that apart from sending their own twelve representatives to the NEC they can if they wish call the tune also in the election of the five women representatives and the Treasurer. In practice therefore they can elect eighteen out of the twenty-five member executive.

The constitutional position of the NEC is a matter of tired controversy. The position as defined by Clement Attlee and many times endorsed since is that whereas the NEC, and the conference which instructs it, does not have any right to instruct a Labour Government it *does* have the constitutional right to decide the party programme. Exactly what happens when the party decides one programme and the Labour Government pursues another has never been resolved. The Labour Party's constitution only works when not too many questions are asked about it. The constitutional contradiction is smoothed over by the assumption that the tactical freedom allowed to a Labour Government is consistent with the ultimate achievement of the programme. Previously when Labour had held office the tensions between party and Government were easily enough contained within this doctrine. The most serious split between the parliamentary party and the extra-parliamentary party occurred when Labour was in opposition; that was in 1960 when, in defiance of Hugh Gaitskell's leadership, the conference adopted a policy of unilateral nuclear disarmament. This led to renewed controversy about the constitutional position of the conference and the NEC. The then general secretary Morgan Phillips summed up the political realities behind the constitutional appearances when he said that although the conference clearly could not dictate to the parliamentary party the two could not for very long remain at loggerheads. Gaitskell himself doubted if he could remain leader if defeated a second time.

Differences between the conference and the Government had arisen on two major questions and a number of minor ones since 1966. The conference since 1967 had been in declared opposition to the prices and incomes policy and it had called upon the Government to dissociate itself from the United States bombing of North Vietnam. Harold Wilson's attitude to a conference defeat was clear enough: after the unfavourable vote in 1967 he instructed his press officer, "If anybody asks 'what is the government going to do now?' simply say 'govern'." This was essentially the Attlee doctrine restated. But it begged a number of vital questions. In the case of the prices and incomes policy it could be argued that the Government and the conference were in conflict about the temporary, and necessarily unpopular, means of achieving an agreed end, full employment, economic growth, "the planned growth of wages" etc. In the case of Vietnam, it could be argued that it was appropriate, or at least did no great harm, for the rank-and-file to demonstrate its horror at the war in an emotional fashion. Everybody was in favour of peace, the Government was trying to use its influence –

by diplomacy not by declarations – to promote an end to the bombing and to the war, and therefore there was no great gulf of principle. These arguments stretched the facts a little, perhaps, but were sound in principle. For at none of the conferences since 1964 was the tone of the proceedings generally hostile to the Government. None of the divisions over questions of policy had been made into questions of fundamental principle; therefore they had given rise to no constitutional crisis within the Labour Movement.

But what would be the situation if the government imposed legal penalties on the trade unions without the support of the party? As the opposition to *In Place of Strife* mounted steadily during March and April 1969 this question awkwardly presented itself. Was the issue of such a fundamental kind that a repudiation of Government by party could not be brushed aside with the assertion that "The government must govern"? A number of practical problems were also involved. The ultimate deterrent for maintaining party discipline at Westminster would cease to be credible when the party in Parliament and the party in the country were at loggerheads. For how could the supreme body of the party, the NEC, refuse endorsement at an election to somebody who had lost the whip as a consequence of supporting conference policy on so fundamental a question? If a majority on the NEC itself was opposed to Government policy and in agreement with conference policy there could be no question of it refusing endorsement on these grounds.

Another problem concerned the Labour Party's manifesto. The constitution gave to the NEC the right to approve the party programme at elections, although the programme itself was drawn up in consultation with the leaders of the Parliamentary Party. Suppose then that the Prime Minister asked for a dissolution of Parliament in order to go to the country on the issue of trade union reform but the party refused to campaign on these grounds. It would mean disaster at the polls: some candidates would be running in defiance of their leader's policy, others in defiance of party policy; the voters would not know which way to turn. This meant, as we shall see, that the threat of dissolution lacked all credibility as a means of closing the ranks behind the Government on the trade union question.

Finally there was the position of MPs sponsored by the trade unions. The accepted convention was that trade union MPs were the representatives at Westminster of the constituents who had elected them, not of the unions which paid them allowances or contributed to their campaign funds. Attempts to instruct their voting behaviour could be construed as breaches of parliamentary privilege. On the other hand there was nothing to stop trade unions if they so wished deciding at the time of an election to withdraw their sponsorship from one candidate in favour of another. It had been their practice not to do this but there would be much stronger grounds for pulling the rug from under the feet of an MP who had failed to support his sponsoring union's policy in Parliament when that policy was also the official party policy democratically decided by the party conference.

These considerations ceased to be academic on March 26 when the national executive committee repudiated *In Place of Strife*. The decision of the executive was somewhat fudged by the procedural wrangling which had taken place. Joe Gormley began by moving a resolution which stated that the NEC could not accept "any legislation based on all" the proposals in *In Place of Strife*. Gormley represented the miners; in normal times he was a stalwart Labour loyalist. After some discussion Jim Callaghan suggested that the word "any" be removed. Some members of the executive thought that he was trying to be helpful but that was not Barbara Castle's opinion. By slightly softening Gormley's hostile resolution Callaghan was nevertheless siding with it. Tony Greenwood passed Barbara Castle a note on which he had pencilled out an alternative amendment. She proposed that the Gormley resolution be dropped and that instead the executive should simply "welcome" the Government's readiness to consult further about the proposals in *In Place of Strife*. Callaghan now supported her but her amendment was defeated by fifteen votes to seven. So Gormley's resolution, as amended by Callaghan, was put to the vote and carried by sixteen votes to five. Callaghan voted with Gormley against Castle. Thus the executive declared itself unwilling to accept "legislation based on all" the proposals in the White Paper and this decision was underlined by its refusal to "welcome" the Government's readiness to consult. It was perfectly clear what this meant. The executive would not accept legislation which included penal clauses and was not even prepared to consult with the Government as far as the penal clauses were concerned. And it was perfectly clear too that Callaghan was deliberately pitting himself with the party against the policy of the Government for which he shared collective responsibility as a Cabinet Minister.

Barbara Castle was furious. Callaghan had ratted on her. She interpreted his behaviour as a gratuitously hostile act. Moreover she had been beaten by a margin of more than three to one in the supreme policy-making organ of the party. A humiliating defeat at conference was now inevitable. For the policy in which she so firmly believed, and which she was convinced was based on sound Socialist philosophy, to be repudiated by the NEC was a bitter experience. During the years of opposition when Barbara had been the darling of the constituency parties – on several occasions topping the poll in the annual elections to the NEC – she had been one of the champions of inner party democracy. She had defended the decisions of conference and asserted the importance of the NEC. When she had found herself with the minority, which was more often than not, it was a left-wing minority confident in its claim to be the guardian of the Socialist tablets. Now she found herself defeated by an alliance between the right and her old comrades of the left. Friends like Tom Driberg, an old Bevanite crony, had joined forces with the men who had in the past ruthlessly used their block votes to put down the Bevanites.

But the most infuriating aspect of the affair was the behaviour of colleague James Callaghan. He was not the only offender. There were ten Ministers on the executive and one parliamentary private secretary. Jennie Lee had also voted for the Gormley resolution and so had Tom Bradley, a trade union MP, but also Roy Jenkins's PPS. Two other Ministers had abstained – Arthur Skeffington and Eirene White. But Callaghan was a senior member of the Cabinet. He had declared his opposition to Government policy and he might just as well have done so in public. The proceedings of the NEC seldom remain secret for very long. It quickly became known that having lost the battle in Cabinet he had carried it into the forum of the party. Not only had he been a party to the collective decision of the Cabinet, from which he had made no move to resign, but he had also voted in the Commons to "take note" of the White Paper, indeed his name had appeared on the Order Paper as one of the sponsors of the motion. The NEC had no standing whatsoever as a revise chamber for Cabinet decisions. Callaghan could argue, on the other hand, that the Cabinet had not decided upon industrial legislation but only to publish a White Paper. The purpose of a White Paper was to serve as the basis for discussion and consultation. It was therefore perfectly proper to argue that legislation should not contain "all" the White Paper's proposals. It was not unprecedented for Ministers to dissent from Government policy in the fraternal privacy of the executive. For example, at the home policy sub-committee in January Arthur Skeffington and Jennie Lee had supported a left-wing motion against the Government's incomes policy. However, none of these constitutional explanations could alter the fact that Callaghan had spoken out against the penal clauses, which were an essential part of Barbara Castle's policy, and had joined in a vote aimed unmistakably against them.

It is not certain whether he arrived at Transport House that morning intending to carry his opposition into a new phase. In the opinion of someone sitting near to him he did no more than react spontaneously to the situation which developed within the executive. In the opinion of Barbara Castle he was taking a calculated stand. What is certain, however, is that he perfectly understood the significance of what he had done after he had done it. He realised that he had thrown his hat into the ring and he took no steps subsequently to retrieve it. That is not to say that he intended to stage a coup against Harold Wilson. But he was letting it be known that if for any reason a vacancy should occur in the leadership he stood ready to fill it. Some comment at the time suggested that he had come to the conclusion that a Labour defeat at the next election was inevitable and was preparing to be the salvage man. But that was not what he was about. True, he had decided that Labour stood little chance of victory under Harold Wilson's leadership: but he thought there was still a chance of victory under his own. For victory to be possible, he believed, the Government had to stop antagonising its own people and win back the support of the working people organised in trade unions. He was nailing his personal standard to this policy; Wilson was committed to the contrary policy of trying to recapture the centre ground even at the risk of jeopardising his traditional territorial base.

In other words Callaghan was challenging the leadership on a clear issue, he was identifying himself with an alternative strategy; he was offering a different style of leadership. For these reasons he had no intention of resigning. He correctly believed that the battle was by no means over. His situation in the Cabinet was somewhat embarrassing but it would be folly to relinquish his position within the Government while things might go his own way. If Wilson wanted to make an issue of it at this stage he would have to sack him. The Home Secretary was fairly confident that he would not be sacked. That was how Jim Callaghan saw his circumstances after the sensational meeting of the national executive committee on Wednesday, March 26.

His had been a most remarkable political recovery. After the traumatic experience of devaluation in November 1967, less than eighteen months previously, he had come to the verge of breakdown. He had put in three gruelling years at the Treasury. His Chancellorship rates as probably the least successful of modern times. His first intention at the time of devaluation was to resign from the Government. A letter was in the Prime Minister's hands. But had been persuaded by political friends, and even more strongly by the political life force within himself, to alter his decision. Within barely twenty-four hours of devaluation a telephone call to Number 10 Downing Street had withdrawn the letter of resignation. His decision to stay, and his request to move to the Home Office, had opened the door of the Treasury to Roy Jenkins. Had Callaghan quitted the Government Anthony Crosland might have been preferred as Chancellor; when Callaghan decided on the Home Office Harold Wilson had no further excuse for denying Roy Jenkins his dearest ambition. The Home Office represented a demotion for Callaghan: his position in the pecking order fell from number three to number seven. Politically, he was on the slide. From Home Office via Treasury to Downing Street was a blazed trail; from Treasury to Home Office to Downing Street was like travelling from Birmingham to London via Newcastle-upon-Tyne.

Jim Callaghan arrived at the Home Office and took up farming. A hobby farm engaged his enthusiasm about equally with his new department; at least that was the impression he gave, one of enjoying a deserved semi-retirement. It was easy enough to imagine him in Wellington boots leaning upon rustic gates indulging from time to time in home-spun philosophy. But he had also a strong streak of bitterness to keep him going. He had been handed an outsize can to carry. His responsibility for the humiliation of forced devaluation was at worst equal with the Prime Minister's. It had been the Prime Minister who had declared the word unmentionable, had even put to the flame the position papers on the subject by the Government's economic advisors. Callaghan had momentarily been persuaded of the case for floating the pound in July 1966 as an alternative to the harshly deflationary measures taken to defend its parity. In the late autumn of 1967 he had clambered out of the last ditch at about the same time as the Prime Minister, perhaps a moment or two before him.

In his successor at the Treasury he saw all that was effete, middle class, Oxford and effortlessly superior triumphing over all that was plain, unprivileged, self-made and rudely practical in his own political make up. Jenkins was going up, he was going down – that was hard to take. Underneath the thick political hide of the former Chancellor lived a man far more vulnerable than he appeared. The anti-intellectualism in him derived, so it was said, from a sense of educational inferiority. When he would begin sentences "You know, some of us old fuddy-duddies . . ." there was more to it than jovial self-deprecation – there was a strong hint of resentment at the arrogant sureness of the highly educated. Behind the glad-hand charm, behind the beaming visage of Sunny Jim, concealed within the somewhat lumbering appearance, there were – so his enemies insisted – qualities of resentfulness and cat-like speed of claw.

He was a politician whom it was all too easy to under-estimate – as his amazing recovery showed. His manner and his spectacular failure at the Treasury gave rise to a good deal of silly snobbery. There had been sneers before the 1964 election when it became known that the prospective Chancellor was taking economic lessons at Oxford at the week-ends. But why not? As Chancellor of the Exchequer he soon learnt to hold his own with all comers, especially on the complicated subject of international finance. His officials at the Treasury were under no illusion that he was a fool. He combined political shrewdness with a natural ability to master facts quickly and expound them clearly – a fair substitute for an original or creative political intelligence. He was a powerful platform speaker. "God bless my soul", he would say – epitomising plain sense; "Now, you know me . . .", he would say, inviting trust in Honest Jim. He might have made a successful Tattersalls bookmaker. He was a formidable parliamentary performer, equally effective at question time and in debate. His political judgement was usually sound – for example, about House of Lords reform. He was perhaps the last remaining member of Harold Wilson's Cabinet with a real feel for the Labour Movement. The Wilson Government had sadly lacked an Ernest Bevin. George Brown, the fur salesman, and Ray Gunter, the ticket collector, had gone; Jim Callaghan, the tax collector, was left.

Now he was the Keeper of the Cloth Cap.

As he began his recovery at the Home Office he showed how a skilful politician can make the best of the cards which are dealt him. The Home Office is no longer quite the great Department of State it once was, but it keeps a man in the news and touches closely upon the concerns of ordinary people. When Alan Watkins of the *New Statesman* applied the word "populist" to Callaghan he seized upon it with delighted approval – that was just what he was, a man of the people. His policies at the Home Office were more popular in the country than with the left and liberal wings of his own party at Westminster. When he repudiated the Wootton Report on the drug cannabis Callaghan was saving the nation not only from pot but from experts. It required his sort of genius to invent a distinction between "hard games" and "soft games" and thereby erect a standard whereby bingo was a harmless flutter while chemin-de-fer was wicked gambling. Another Home Secretary might have found more important things to do than appear after question time with a statement on football rowdyism, but James Callaghan knew on which side his career was buttered. From his new base in the Home Office he projected a clear colourful image of himself. Everybody knew where *he* stood, everybody knew Jim – tough on immigration but soft on race relations, tough on crime but soft on capital punishment, tough on drugs but soft on children; the note was exactly right: the British admixture of virtue and hypocrisy, tolerance and prejudice was epitomised in Sunny Jim, Grim Jim and Honest Jim Callaghan.

His election to the treasureship of the Labour Party in 1967 was an important consolidation and broadening of his political base. The treasurership of the party is an office of no intrinsic importance but it carries with it a safe *ex officio* seat on the national executive committee. An elected representative of the constituency labour parties, as Callaghan was, risked being thrown off at their left-wing whim but the treasurer was elected by the whole conference, which meant in effect by the unions, and the unions seldom used their block votes to create redundancies. The office was of no political significance until Gaitskell and Bevan fought over it in 1953 as a preliminary trial of strength for the leadership contest two years later. The treasurer does not actually keep the books, someone does that for him; but he acts as a front man for fund-raising. That throws him into close contact with the trade union leaders who provide more than 80 per cent of the funds. Callaghan became party treasurer while he was still Chancellor but when he left the Treasury the office provided a useful cover for shifting his ground on key questions of policy. As Chancellor he had stood firmly behind the incomes policy but by the spring of 1967 he was letting it be known publicly that he favoured dropping it because of the strains it was causing within the Labour Movement. Now he was using the same argument in connection with the reform of industrial relations – how could the unions be expected to dig into their pockets while the Government was beating them with a big stick?

Callaghan's behaviour in the national executive committee on March 26 had the effect of a smouldering match flicked casually into dry tinder. Within days the flames were leaping up around the Government. It was one of those weeks in which everything went wrong. On the

Monday there was a sharpening of the TUC's opposition to the Government. There has been growing pressure in the General Council for an emergency summoning of the Congress and in order to resist this Victor Feather requested an urgent meeting with the Prime Minister. On Wednesday the Post Master General, John Stonehouse, was reported to have said in a speech, "We have to admit that devaluation has not been as successful as we hoped it would be". This statement of the obvious caused a ruction within the Government, so tender was the state of its nerves; Stonehouse was solemnly carpeted. On Thursday the significance of Callaghan's stand in the party executive began to sink in and the newspapers speculated about his intentions – was he preparing a bid for the leadership? That night the results of three by-elections came through. Labour had done lamentably. Walthamstow East had gone down. The Tories won two of their own seats in a canter. There had again been a massive Labour abstention. The swing to the Conservatives in the three contests was 16 per cent. In twenty-six by-elections since 1966 the Government had lost twelve seats. Attlee's Government had not lost a single Labour seat. A bad week ended with the Prime Minister setting off on a peace mission to Nigeria which was already doomed to failure. In preparing for his trip he had missed the meeting of the party executive. His authority had been semi-openly challenged by Callaghan and everybody was waiting for his reply. Would he sack him, as Roy Jenkins and Barbara Castle were urging? The answer would have to wait for his return. Meanwhile, the Parliament Bill had become a grave embarrassment. Morale in the party was at a new low. Talk of a leadership crisis was starting again. It was no time for a weakened Prime Minister to turn his back.

The problems which occupied Harold Wilson's mind as HMS *Fearless* swung round the buoy in Lagos Harbour were these: how was he to restore the authority of his government? How was he to escape the embarrassment of the Parliament Bill? What was he to do about James Callaghan? The three problems were intertwined. He had been urged to put his foot down on the Parliament Bill, to make a confidence issue of a "guillotine" motion and to reimpose some discipline in the party. Before leaving London he had rejected this course. John Silkin, his Chief Whip, had warned him of the determination of the Parliament Bill's opponents. So, instead, his senior colleagues had begun urging him to stake his authority on the industrial relations question by bringing forward a short, sharp, urgent measure in the current session of the Parliament.

It was not the first time he had been urged to do so. Roy Jenkins had been in favour of this tactic from the start and had argued it at the January meetings of the Cabinet. His chief argument was that if the Government was going to act on strikes it should do so quickly and decisively. If it was saying that unconstitutional strikes were an urgent problem then it could not afford to wait until 1970 before legislating. In the meanwhile there would be the danger of a snowballing opposition within the Labour Movement. The trade unions would spend the summer firing hostile resolutions at the Government from their seaside conferences. The annual TUC in September and the Labour Party Conference in October would probably register massive protests against the Government and that would make the parliamentary situation difficult in the next session. There was thus the risk of a great parliamentary battle in the months before the General Election. The Government would present a damaging spectacle of disunity – better to get it over with. In addition, the Chancellor already in January anticipated that the Government would have to relax the incomes policy. Nevertheless, he wanted something to put in its place. It was important to maintain a show of strength on the wages front. Bankers and the International Monetary Fund, from which new credits would be required, would be more ready to accept a relaxation of incomes policy if at the same time the Government was showing determination to deal with the "English sickness" – unofficial strikes.

Barbara Castle had argued strongly and successfully against this approach. In the first place she believed she could convince the trade unions of the rightness of her policy and of its advantages for them. She was not afraid of the union conferences; she would fight on the beaches. Secondly, she was determined to find her place in the history books as the architect of a comprehensive Act of Parliament to reform industrial relations; she was not interested in going down as the author of half measures. In particular she was violently opposed to the idea of legislating the penal clauses first and separately – that would destroy the whole balance of her package and undermine its philosophy. Thirdly, there were strong departmental arguments. Complicated legislation was involved and it needed careful drafting; there would have to be consultations; even a "short Bill" would contain fifty or more clauses and her department could not be expected to produce it in a hurry.

But by the time the Prime Minister left for Lagos the Jenkins case had gained great strength. It was becoming clear – to those who had ever doubted it – that Barbara Castle was not going to succeed in persuading the unions to acquiesce in *In Place of Strife*. The agendas for the union conferences were beginning to appear and their message was clear. The TUC was proceeding in a most leisurely fashion to act on the Donovan Report. During the Ford dispute it had stood impotently on the sidelines. By the end of that affair Barbara Castle herself had come to two conclusions: one was that the only language the TUC seemed to understand was the language of a pistol pointed to its head; the other was that the trade union movement, and increasingly the Parliamentary Labour Party, were in a state of hysteria in which her sweet reason was unlikely to prevail. But she was still reluctant to present an interim Bill in the current session of the Parliament.

However, the voice of Richard Crossman was now raised powerfully in support of Roy Jenkins. Crossman had lost faith in his Parliament Bill. Its opponents were like Parnell's Irish Home Rulers and were calling the tune in the Commons. He had offered to help Callaghan to fight the Bill through committee but the Home Secretary had repulsed his helping hand, perhaps because he thought that if he had Dick Crossman for a friend he would not need enemies. The Prime Minister was not willing to make his stand on the Parliament Bill. Crossman was the author of the Parliament Bill and had been its most eager proponent; he had been opposed to *In Place of Strife* and was among its most severe critics: now he reversed his enthusiasms and argued strongly for jettisoning the Parliament Bill and hurrying with legislation against strikes. As he now saw it the Government's authority was at stake and it must be restored by taking a determined line on industrial relations. He was at one with Roy Jenkins in believing that the damage within the Labour Movement would be less if the Government acted quickly than if it permitted the row to continue into election year.

If the Prime Minister was still unconvinced by the Jenkins–Crossman case the Callaghan affair finally won him over. The Cabinet had so far taken no decision on legislation; it had decided only to publish a statement of its policy in the form of a White Paper. A decision to legislate in the current session would oblige Callaghan to resign from the Government or bow to the Prime Minister's authority. That was preferable to having to sack him, as Jenkins and Castle had been urging. Harold Wilson did not like sacking people. But he could not let the Home Secretary get away with what he had done. By the time he returned to London the Prime Minister's mind was all but made up in favour of early legislation on industrial relations in place of the Parliament Bill. He returned to find that his senior colleagues had got together in his absence and settled upon the same conclusion. An informal "inner cabinet" had formed itself. It consisted of Roy Jenkins, Barbara Castle, Richard Crossman, Michael Stewart, Denis Healey and Fred Peart. They had agreed among themselves that urgent steps must be taken to restore the Government's authority, that the Parliament Bill would have to be abandoned and that there seemed no alternative to bringing forward a short Industrial Relations Bill. Barbara Castle was by now reluctantly conceding the force of these arguments.

On Thursday, April 2 a tired and worried-looking Prime Minister arrived back from Lagos via Addis Ababa. He drove straight from the airport to the Commons to make a statement on his Nigerian visit. Imagine his annoyance at that night having to entertain President Hamani Diori of Niger at an official dinner at Downing Street! Such is the life of Prime Ministers. But there were other irritations to greet him. That same night the Whips had to abandon the planned late night sitting on the Parliament Bill and its opponents leapt up and down with joy, tearing up copies of the detested measure. The Callaghan business had also festered in his absence. Woodrow Wyatt had called in public for Callaghan to be sacked. Harry Nicholas, the party secretary, had sprung to Callaghan's defence. Tony Crosland had made a speech warning "Party squabbles and disunity have destroyed us in the past. They must not be allowed to do so again". The President of the Board of Trade called upon the Home Secretary to shut up and when Transport House had tried to suppress the speech, that too had leaked out. In addition to all this nuisance Harold Wilson was greeted by Douglas Houghton, the venerable chairman of the Parliamentary Labour Party, who in reporting to him the abysmal morale in the Parliamentary Labour Party had gone so far as to warn that there could be a backbench attempt to depose him.

The Cabinet met the next day, Thursday, April 3, the day before Good Friday. The evening newspapers that afternoon carried accounts of how Callaghan had been sternly reprimanded for his behaviour at the meeting of the party executive. There were no newspapers the next morning but on Saturday the story was still running. No Cabinet could ever have listened to such an uncompromising lecture on the subject of collective responsibility; the Prime Minister had read the Riot Act and reasserted his authority. Ministers read these accounts with astonished amusement. Their recollection of the Thursday's Cabinet meeting was entirely different. The Prime Minister had spent most of the time reporting on his visit to Africa. He had seemed tired and, according to some, was particularly boring. Towards the end he had said a few words on the subject of collective responsibility and on his favourite topic of leaks to the press. He had reminded Ministers that they were obliged to uphold Government decisions at party meetings including the national executive, and that *In Place of Strife* was a statement of Government policy not a discussion paper. He had singled out no member of his Cabinet for special reprimand and none of its members felt that Callaghan had received a stinging rebuke, least of all Callaghan himself, who beforehand had been a little nervous about the possibility that he would be sacked. The explanation of the discrepant versions lay in the fact that the Prime Minister had himself briefed political journalists after the Cabinet meeting. In their presence, and Callaghan's absence, he proceeded to talk very tough. He delivered his rebuke to Callaghan not in Cabinet but in public, through the press. The Home Secretary was able to read in the newspapers that he had been a naughty boy and could expect trouble if he was naughty again. And having thus "restored his authority" the Prime Minister left that night for an Easter vacation in the Scilly Isles.

Before doing so he had also seen various of his senior Minister. The putative "inner cabinet" had informed him of their conclusions about the strategy which should now be adopted. He was also urged to take steps to strengthen the collective leadership of his Government by establishing a proper "Inner Cabinet" or directorate of senior Ministers. And he was urged to do something about the state of the party, either by replacing Fred Peart as Leader of the House or by sacking John Silkin as Chief Whip. Listening to these entreaties the Prime Minister did his Clement Attlee act – he sucked his pipe and inquired kindly about his colleagues' holiday plans. But that Easter weekend the telephone lines were busy and the Government machine was set in motion in preparation for early legislation on industrial relations.

Harold Wilson returned to London a week later, late on Thursday, April 10. The next day he met the leaders of the TUC for the first time since the publication of *In Place of Strife*. The TUC leaders had become alarmed at reports that the Government was considering early legislation. On March 26 they had asked for a meeting with the Prime Minister but his visit to Nigeria and the Easter holidays had delayed it. Now their chief concern was to receive an assurance from the Prime Minister's own lips that there had been no change in the timetable. They also wished to inform him of the progress they were making in acting upon the Donovan Report. When the members of the TUC's finance and general purposes committee eventually saw Harold Wilson on April 11 they were already too late. Both their missions were doomed to failure: the Prime Minister's mind was made up on early legislation and the action on Donovan taken by the TUC was not within miles of the Government's requirement for "an equally effective alternative" to the policy set out in *In Place of Strife*. The TUC had understood the Government's timetable to provide for consultations lasting into June when the parliamentary draftsmen would start work on a Bill for presentation to Parliament in November. The TUC leaders considered they had received an official assurance to this effect. Now they heard the Prime Minister declare that the Cabinet was committed to no particular timetable and that he could therefore give no forecast about the timing of legislation. Frank Cousins came away from the meeting, as he told the General Council later, with the clear impression that the Prime Minister's options were open and that the trade union movement might soon face a dangerous situation. As to the action taken on Donovan, all the TUC leaders had to report was a joint statement of intention drawn up with the CBI, instigation of a study of trade union rule books, and six discussion conferences of unions grouped according to industry at which the response had been "very constructive". In Victor Feather's opinion, as he later told the General Council, these "intimate and analytical" conferences were "a unique development". The Prime Minister, however, was not impressed.

The Prime Minister took a tough, impatient line with the TUC leaders. "We can be destroyed economically and politically if we have no answer to unofficial strikes", he told them. "We cannot just fold our arms and say that because the TUC don't like it we will not do anything about it". Industrial relations were verging upon anarchy, he alleged. He pointed to that day's edition of the *Financial Times*. "Unofficial strike halts London freightliners". "Steel: new strike threat in S. Wales". "London's Upper Pool dockers may stop today". "Strike hits Welsh steel plant's output". "Electricians' strike holds up magazine production". "Walk out by 1,500 at Ipswich factory". That was one day's crop of headlines. "If we had time", said Harold Wilson, "we could see great advantage in going forward to solve the problems without legislation but it is not only a question of whether this meeting thinks it could be done in time: it is a question of whether the country as a whole thinks it could be done in time".

There was still no Cabinet decision to legislate nor on the contents of a short Bill. The Cabinet met in the Prime Minister's room at the House of Commons at 4.15 on the following Monday, April 14, the eve of the Budget. It revised the plan which had come up to it from committee in one important respect. According to this the Prime Minister's pet scheme for compulsory strike ballots was to be included in the short Bill, the reserve powers for imposing settlements in inter-union disputes were not. A number of Ministers argued that these priorities were incorrect. The strike ballot proposal would be of very limited effect and was therefore of no great urgency, yet it was one of the proposals most resented by the TUC; it would be better to postpone it, as a gesture of goodwill to the TUC, while bringing in the proposals for dealing with inter-union disputes, towards which the General Council had appeared less hostile.

Later that night Victor Feather was informed that the Government intended to legislate in the current session of Parliament. A Government car was sent down to Oxford to bring him back to Number 10 Downing Street to hear the bad news. He was told that the Chancellor would be making a statement in his Budget speech the next day. He was given no details about the contents of the proposed Bill.

Roy Jenkins rose at 3.30 the next afternoon, April 15, to make his annual Budget statement. A cry of fury went up from below the gangway on the Labour side as the Chancellor broke the bad news. Earlier there had been cheers at his announcement that the Government did not intend to seek a renewal of the powers under the 1968 Prices and Incomes Act to order delays in implementing wage agreements. These powers ran out at the end of the year. They were viable, said the Chancellor, only in exceptional circumstances and then only in the short-term. To have continued to rely on the stringent statutory powers would in the long-run have prejudicial effects on industrial relations. But the policy had been a success, Roy Jenkins claimed. Notably it had established stronger links between increases in pay and productivity, and it was doing much to improve Britain's industrial performance. However, this had to be reinforced by bringing about more orderly arrangements in industrial relations generally.

"In particular", he went on, "we need to facilitate the smooth working of collective bargaining in industry and to help prevent the occurrence of unnecessary and damaging disputes of which we have seen all too much recently, and which are totally incompatible with our economic objectives. The Government have, therefore, decided to implement without delay during the present Session, some of the more important provisions incorporated in the White Paper *In Place of Strife*."

Conservative cheers greeted this news, encouraged by the moans of pain which came from the Labour benches. Details of the Government's new plan were not given until the next afternoon when Barbara Castle intervened in the Budget debate. At 12.45 that morning Victor Feather and the chairman of the General Council, John Newton, went to Downing Street to hear an outline of the First Secretary's speech. The TUC's "inner cabinet" received a text at 4.45 and at 5.30 trooped in again for talks with Harold Wilson and Barbara Castle. The confrontation was beginning. Meanwhile, Barbara Castle had informed the Commons that the short Industrial Relations Bill would include five measures:

1. It would establish the statutory right of every worker to belong to a trade union.

2. It would give the Government power to order an employer to recognise a trade union when this had been recommended by the Commission on Industrial Relations.

3. It would give the Government power to impose settlements in inter-union disputes under pain of fines but only after, first, the TUC and, second, the CIR had failed to promote voluntary agreement.

4. It would give the Government power to impose a twenty-eight day conciliation pause in an unconstitutional dispute and to order that the *status quo* be restored and maintained. These powers would also be backed with financial penalties.

5. It would remove the disqualifications from unemployment benefit from workers laid off in consequence of a dispute in which they were playing no direct part.

An assurance was given that fines would not be permitted to lead to prison and if the trade unions did not like the Government's suggestion that this should be avoided by the automatic attachment of earnings, then alternative ways of recovering payment could be discussed.

"We believe our major proposals cannot wait", Barbara Castle declared. "They are conceived in no vindictive spirit but in a spirit of faith – faith in the future of the trade union movement in this country which has set such an example to other countries in the past, faith in its power to grow, adapt, accept responsibility, and exert its authority in its own interests and in the interests of the community of which its members form such a vital part.

"It will be the purpose of our Bill to encourage and stimulate this development. If the trade union movement will accept it in that spirit together we can build on the achievements of the past and give the country the best industrial relations system in the world."

The decisions reached in the Cabinet on the Monday evening had been intended to serve two purposes. The first was to restore the Government's authority. The second was to win over sufficient support in the Parliamentary Labour Party to ensure a Government majority on a procedural motion to send the Industrial Relations Bill to a committee upstairs. The experience with the Parliament Bill had exposed the dangers of fighting through a controversial measure on the floor of the House. In the debate on the White Paper fifty-three Government backbenchers had voted against. For the Government to be sure of a majority on a procedural motion the number of rebels had to be reduced to below thirty-five. The Cabinet believed its package would achieve this. It thought that it was making a powerful concession on the incomes policy. It had decided to admit defeat on the Parliament Bill, as was announced later that week, and it expected this to be welcome in the party. Its willingness to be flexible and reasonable on the question of recovering fines was expected to soften the opposition of the TUC and from trade union MPs. It thought that it was making a major concession on the entitlement to unemployment benefit. Of the five measures to be contained in the interim legislation, two were bound to be unpopular with the trade unions but three were designed to help them. In short, the Government was hoping to make more friends than enemies.

But once again its judgement was seriously in error. The Cabinet must have been badly out of touch with the mood in the party at Westminster and misinformed about the nature of the TUC's opposition. MPs who had at first been attracted by the idea of a trade off between the incomes policy and penalties on unofficial strikers were no longer so. The TUC leaders had never been interested in such a deal. The relaxation of the incomes policy had been too long anticipated for the Chancellor's announcement to have much impact. The abandonment of the Parliament Bill was welcome in the party but any tendency to congratulate the Government on its good sense was offset by a readiness to blame it for the getting into such a mess in the first place. Moreover, some MPs were drawing the conclusion that this backbench victory could be repeated. Their experience with the Parliament Bill encouraged hopes that the Government might be prevented from passing an Industrial Relations Bill. The Government's willingness to discuss the method of recovering fines made no impression whatsoever on the TUC: the General Council was against fines in principle and did not care how they were collected. At the very first meeting with the Prime Minister, on April 11, Victor Feather had condemned the penal clauses for trying to "introduce the taint of criminality into industrial relations". The phrase came to be many times repeated. Many MPs took their lead from the TUC on this. The concession about unemployment benefit was seen as no sort of exchange for the penal clauses. Far from restoring the Government's authority the package decided upon by the Cabinet added to alarming suspicions that the Prime Minister and his colleagues were once again embarking with undue haste upon an inadequately thought out policy and doing so for the wrong reasons.

The very fact that the decision had been announced by the Chancellor in his Budget statement added to these suspicions on the Government backbenches. This seemed to indicate that the Government was using the anti-strike measures to boost confidence in the economy and appease the International Monetary Fund. Indeed the Prime Minister was later that week to tell a party meeting that the Bill was "an essential component in ensuring the economic success of the Government". It was "essential to our economic recovery, essential to the balance of payments, essential to full employment". MPs found these assertions hard to credit. Barbara Castle herself had argued the case for her proposals on broad ideological grounds; it was her purpose, she went on insisting, to strengthen the trade unions: she had never claimed that it was the job of her reforms to increase exports or inspire confidence among international bankers. By the emphasis the Prime Minister and the Chancellor were now placing on the economic importance of the measures they seemed to many trade union leaders and trade union MPs to be blaming the unions for the country's economic difficulties. "Law courts do not make exports" said Victor Feather after the meeting in Downing Street to discuss the Government's decision. Barbara Castle's bold piece of social engineering was in danger of becoming merely a part of Roy Jenkins's "hard slog".

Roy Jenkins had himself insisted on making the announcement in his Budget speech. He was encouraged in this resolve by Richard Crossman, who saw himself as the Government's master tactician. It was not the Prime Minister's idea. Barbara Castle was quite ready to do her own dirty work. The Chancellor's reason was that he wanted to put something in the hole left by the incomes policy. The representatives of the International Monetary Fund were in London at the time and making difficulties about the terms on which Britain should receive further credits. But it was an odd political decision, nevertheless, by a Minister who was beginning to get the reputation for "keeping his head below the parapet". Did the IMF care who announced the policy? By making the announcement himself Roy Jenkins committed himself to the short Bill to a degree which he was subsequently to regret. There was no question that he did support it, indeed he had been the first to argue the case for not waiting until the 1969–70 session. But nobody was asking him to go to the lengths of mingling his blood publicly with Barbara Castle's. He was exceeding by far the terms of their demarcation agreement. This provided that she should give unqualified support to the Chancellor's economic strategy in exchange for his unqualified support for her policies on the industrial front. But now chivalry to a lady colleague was verging upon the quixotic. It was a political error for an ambitious man.

The concessions offered by the Cabinet did not impress either the party or the trade unions but they were sufficient to paper over the divisions in the Cabinet. James Callaghan had no wish to resign, Harold Wilson was not prepared to sack him. The decision to find an alternative to the attachment of workers' earnings (although the Cabinet had been unable to decide what alternative) gave Callaghan an excuse to accept the Government's decision and remain a member of it. He did not make a frontal stand against legislation at the April 14 Cabinet meeting: his criticisms were chiefly aimed at the Government's not making enough of the concessions it was offering. And the other opponents of Barbara Castle's White Paper – for examples, Anthony Crosland and Richard Marsh – had come round to the view that if the deed was to be done it had better be done quickly.

Thus in the fateful decision taken by the Government on April 14, and announced by Roy Jenkins in his Budget speech the next day, neither Harold Wilson nor Barbara Castle were prime movers. They had reacted to events and responded to pressures from colleagues, she more reluctantly than he. Later they developed an obsessive determination to force legislation through Parliament and the penal clauses became strongly identified with them personally. But the policy which was now to split the Labour Movement from top to bottom was not determined at their wilful dictates but by the collective decision of a weak government struggling to restore its authority at the end of a long run of bad judgement and bad luck. That is the manner in which politics unfold – not by conspiracies and the exercise of personal power but by error, muddle, doubt, instinct and the free play of human weakness.

That the Government was moving towards a more collective manner of decision-making was confirmed by the sequel to the decision to legislate quickly on industrial relations which came a fortnight later. On April 29 Harold Wilson announced that he was setting up a new Cabinet committee of senior Ministers and that he had sacked John Silkin, his Chief Whip. The Prime Minister had long resisted the idea of an "inner cabinet". He had no wish to share his power in any formal fashion. He did not believe in what he disparagingly called "juntas". He suspected all such schemes as plots to encircle him, usually by "Gaitskellites" who still loomed large in his demonology. The nearest he had come to an inner power grouping was in April 1968 when he established the Parliamentary Committee of the Cabinet. But this had a membership of ten, nearly half the Cabinet, and was too large to serve as a strategic directorate. Moreover, its membership was based on the order of protocol and not on the ability or political weight of its members. And it was no coincidence that it contained a built-in majority of Harold Wilson's loyalist supporters. It had no effect on his freedom of action and apparently did nothing to improve the quality of the Government's strategic decision-making. During his absence in Lagos, however, what was in effect an "inner cabinet" formed itself and it was a sign that Harold Wilson sensed the greater weakness of his position when he formalised this inner grouping of six Ministers as a committee of the Cabinet.

It was by its origins an "inner cabinet" for master-minding the trade union issue and it was for this chief purpose that the Prime Minister agreed to formalise it; the Government had staked a large slice of its fortune on being able to deal with the strike problem. But this created a problem concerning its membership. A small "inner cabinet" based on power and ability should surely include James Callaghan; a small "inner cabinet" for the purpose of putting trade union reforms on the statute book should surely not include him. The Ministers who had got together in Harold Wilson's absence were hotly opposed to admitting Callaghan to their club. They were convinced that he would sneak to his trade union friends. However, to their annoyance and surprise, Wilson at the last moment invited the Home Secretary to be a member. The six became the seven. It just showed what a "softie" he was, said one Cabinet Minister, quoting the *Daily Mirror's* verdict on the Prime Minister.

Wilson had also been under strong pressure to end the Silkin regime. Apart from the complaints about his style of operation, poor John Silkin's competence was now in doubt. On April 21 the Government's majority slumped to twenty-eight on a vital Budget resolution giving effect to the increases in Selective Employment Tax. It was a vote of confidence but thirty-nine Labour MPs abstained. The extent of the rebellion came as a shock. Roy Jenkins went to the Prime Minister and complained angrily about the performance of the Whip's Office. Other Ministers had urged that Silkin must go on the day after the Prime Minister's return from Africa. That was after the committee stage of the Parliament Bill had reached its final fiasco. Wilson then said, "Yes, I have been worried about John for some time". Indeed, in the previous summer he had intended to make Silkin the Minister for Housing and Local Government in place of Anthony Greenwood. But his endeavours to make Greenwood the general secretary of the Labour Party had been foiled. Now Silkin had to be content with the Ministry of Works and no seat in the Cabinet.

Harold Wilson's choice for his new Chief Whip – and it was entirely his own idea – was Robert Mellish. Wilson was after a tough right-winger, not to sweep away the liberal regime but to stop the nonsense in the party, notably on the left-wing. Mellish seemed just the ticket. A real toughie from Bermondsey, of working class origin and trade union background, an engaging Cockney and experienced in the Commons. He was a popular figure, save on the left who recalled some attack he had made on Nye Bevan, and was famed for his iron ward-heeler's control of the London Labour Party. Mellish – though by no stretch of the imagination a Wilson man – seemed the very man the Prime Minister needed at that moment. His assignment was to get the industrial relations bill through the Commons. John Silkin departed in tears; his liberal regime had ended in tears. In order to restore his own authority the Prime Minister was obliged to sack a man who had served him with unquestioning loyalty – but served him less well, perhaps, for that very reason.

But none of these moves – the decision to bring forward a short Bill on industrial relations, the abandonment of the Parliament Bill, the appointment of an "inner cabinet" and the reluctant sacking of a personal favourite who had become an unpopular Chief Whip – had yet succeeded in restoring Harold Wilson's lost authority as Prime Minister. Since his return from Lagos he had not been his resilient bouncy self. Devaluation had been a great trauma but this was perhaps the unhappiest and most unnerving period of his Prime Ministership to date. For once he seemed to his colleagues to be rattled. He paced uneasily in his lair and at night slept not as soundly as he was accustomed, over the shop at Number 10.

6 *Douglas Houghton asks 'Can I help you?'*

BETWEEN Easter and Whitsun Harold Wilson for the first time became precariously balanced on his throne. How great a danger he was in – or how little – we shall see, but he was the nearest he had ever come to downfall. The reason for his vulnerability was the classical one: he was in danger of losing the support of his party.

It was amazing to behold Harold Wilson in this position. Three years previously it would have been thought hardly possible. His situation now offended against every previous stereotype of him. From the moment he became Leader of the Opposition on February 14, 1963, until the moment he transformed a majority of four into a majority of ninety-seven on March 31, 1966, he had shown consummate skill as a party manager. Whatever failings were attributed to him during that period, lack of tactical aplomb was not among them. Indeed one of the most common allegations was that here was someone who would ruthlessly and cunningly put party before country. He had become famous – or to some notorious – as the man with the open options, the pragmatist of pragmatists and the politician for whom ten days was a long while. How had he come by 1969 so to neglect or ignore his own party?

In the past he had shown an almost pathological aversion to party rows. His biographer Leslie Smith records his saying in 1955 to Hugh Gaitskell, "I'll back you for the leadership wholeheartedly so long as you stop trying to force every issue by always trying to get a majority decision on everything that crops up. If you'll really try to work with the whole party and take a unifying not a divisive view of your responsibilities you can count on my complete support when Attlee goes and on my continuing loyalty". When he challenged Gaitskell's leadership in 1960 it was not because he differed with him on principle, either about public ownership or defence, but because he thought it wrong to split the party when its differences could be patched up. In conversation he never showed the slightest interest in the constitutional or ideological speculations which so divert many Labour politicians. It was no good asking him to try to define Social Democracy or describe the nature of the Labour Movement; the clashes of belief and conflicts of interest within it were best left to lie like Walpole's sleeping dogs and if they growled to be quickly put to sleep again. He accepted the Labour Party as it was and in order to lead it was prepared to say one thing, do another and then explain how he had done something else. He knew how to play the centre against both ends. James Maxton, the famous left-wing leader of the twenties, once said, "the man who cannot ride two bloody horses at once doesn't deserve a job in the bloody circus". Harold Wilson could ride three horses if necessary. He was the Circus Master.

Yet as Prime Minister he gradually evolved a completely different concept of himself as leader. In the course of trying to establish his party as the National Party, a very proper ambition, he adopted a doctrine of almost Old Testament severity. He expounded it with remarkable frankness in an interview he gave to the Political Correspondent of the *Evening News* in November, 1968, on the anniversary of devaluation. "There is one question you didn't ask so I'll ask myself for you," he said; "What was the hardest thing I had to do in a hard year? Without doubt it was to tell my own supporters they had got to do things totally opposed to them and everything they had been brought up to believe. But if you cannot do that when it is necessary you will not only never come through. You won't deserve to". The test of fitness to govern was self-immolation? So it almost seemed, for time and again Harold Wilson relished the unpopularity of his Government in the exercise of its duty, and, as time went on, seemed even to relish his own unpopularity as if it were the proof of his statesmanship.

His talents, it has been said often, were ideally suited to leading the Labour Party in opposition. But they were even more appropriate in the unusual circumstances between October 1964 and March 1966. The wafer majority of his Government placed a high premium on tactical ability and permitted small scope for strategic choice. Rhetoric had to serve for action in such a situation and leadership necessarily involved a large element of showmanship. What was not appreciated at the time, and what had hardly sunk in three years later, was the overnight transformation which took place on March 31, 1966. As he travelled back to Downing Street from his campaign headquarters in Liverpool he told a colleague: "Now you must forget everything you knew about me. It's all different now. We are a real Government from now on. I don't have to sell myself any more."

The short view of politics – "ten days is a long while" – gave way to an excessively long view. His tactical sense got lost in grand dreams of building the "New Britain" and establishing his party as the natural party of power. After Labour's victory at the polls in 1966, unprecedented in normal peacetime conditions, he could have done anything he wished. That was the time for the "hundred days". But instead he seemed to sink back into a satisfied inaction. Perhaps the struggles of the past three years had exhausted him momentarily. The economy was allowed to drift into the crisis of July 1966 and that was the start of all Harold Wilson's troubles. The time scale of his purposive dreams never again related to the timetable of reality and devaluation of the pound sixteen months later smashed his reputation for strategic judgement. He had spoken in the language of priorities but did not appear to possess a clear set. From July 1966 there had been only one priority – the maintenance of $2.80 parity. Most of the major changes in Government policy which took place were forced upon him by events – deflation and a statutory wages freeze, withdrawal from East of Suez, devaluation, cuts in the growth of social expenditure (including the symbolic reintroduction of prescription charges). But to show itself a ready victim of events was taken by Harold Wilson – so it seemed – to prove the credentials of a party of government. He combined an ability to change course with an inability to admit error. The tone he adopted in his devaluation broadcast in November 1967 suggested that it marked not a defeat but a new stage in some cunningly planned campaign to beat the economic problem. It was as if being wrong was for him a necessary stage in the process of being right.

His party took a lot from him. He led his supporters up the Himalayas and down again; they stood with him in the last ditch to defend the pound sterling; they sat on the see-saw of rising unemployment and wage restraint; they watched him herd sacred cows to the sacrificial altar. True there were plenty of rebellions, mostly on the Left of the party; but none seriously threatened the Government or his leadership, and it was the Left who persisted longest in the belief that, in spite of everything, he was the best Prime Minister they were likely to get. Perhaps it was this success in keeping his party together which went to his head, for by 1969, after three years of battering disappointment, the cohesion of the Parliamentary Labour Party remained more remarkable than its divisions. The Left, of course, was opposed to the direction his policies were leading, but the remainder of his party had no fundamental quarrel with his objective which was the same as Gaitskell's – to complete the transformation of a party of protest into a broadly-based party of Government. It was his judgement and timing which increasingly caused alarm. The man who Aneurin Bevan had quite wrongly described as "all bloody facts and no imagination" turned out to have a strong romantic and reckless streak in his character. Typical was the manner in which he decided Britain should join the Common Market. It was a conversion as sudden and blinding as St. Paul's. During a train journey to Wigan in the autumn of 1966 he looked up from *The Economist* in which he had been reading an article by François Duschene – a former aide of Jean Monnet, the grandfather of the European Movement – and announced "Right, we're going in". The premature Grand Tour of the European Capitals was decided over lunch that day. "Ring George Brown's private secretary and tell him I'm a European now" he instructed. This style of operation – the self-dramatic interventions, initiatives and mercy dashes – was as characteristic as the former President of the Board of Trade's meticulous interest in some Scottish gas works; both lacked a sense of proportion.

One of Herbert Morrisons' maxims was "Socialism is what the Labour Government does". For Harold Wilson government became what Harold Wilson did next. With each reckless play he would test the nerve of his party as a party of government. He saw the trade unions as a problem he would have to do something about if he was to hold the centre of British politics, the secret of his success in 1964 and 1966. But there is no evidence that he set out fundamentally to challenge the balance of power within the Labour Movement or to fight a symbolic battle as Gaitskell had done over Clause Four of the Labour Party's constitution, the clause which committed it to the "common ownership of the means of production, distribution and exchange". No, what happened was that he developed one of his enthusiasms. He gradually increased his stake on the one hand of cards. Each time the game went badly he doubled up. What had begun as a longish-term institutional reform became a matter of urgent economic necessity. What had started as a White Paper was allowed to become an absolute commitment on which depended the whole future of the Government. By April 1969 it was not his motives which worried the bulk of his party but the soundness of his judgement. His appearance at the party meeting in Budget week did nothing to restore confidence in his leadership. Rather the reverse, for he said: "The Bill we are discussing tonight is an essential Bill – essential to our economic recovery, essential to our balance of payments, essential to full employment. It is an essential component in ensuring the economic success of the Government. It is on that economic success that the recovery of this nation, led by this Labour Government, depends. That is why I have to tell you that the passage of this Bill is essential to the Government's continuance in office. There can be no going back on that".

The first reactions in the Parliamentary Labour Party to *In Place of Strife* had been deceptive. The Left was up in arms at once but there was nothing remarkable in that. The trade union group was suspicious and worried, as was to be expected. But there was also a good deal of support in the party for Barbara Castle's approach. Some were ready to regard the White Paper as a fair swop for ending the incomes policy in the compulsory form. Compulsory wage restraint was seen as a greater evil than a degree of limitation, probably not very effective, on the right to strike unconstitutionally and damn the consequences on other workers. And there was a great deal in the White Paper which in all reason should be welcome to the trade unions, for example legal recognition.

The first storm signal was the division list after the debate on the White Paper in the Commons on March 3. The number of votes against, and the abstentions, were larger than the party managers had expected. Fifty-seven Labour members voted against the Government and an estimated thirty more abstained. A number of usually loyal centrists went into the "Noe" lobby, among them the chairman of the trade union group, James Hamilton, MP for Bothwell. But the most significant hint for the future lay in the behaviour of the Liaison Committee. The Liaison Committee consists of the Leader of the House of Commons and the Chief Whip representing the Government, a representative of the Labour peers, and four representatives of the PLP. These four were Douglas Houghton, the elected chairman of the party and the three elected vice-chairmen – Willie Hamilton, a well respected if somewhat soured backbencher; Will Howie, a former Government Whip; and Joyce Butler, a Co-operative Party sponsored MP of Leftist leanings. Of the four only one – Will Howie – voted with the Government.

By the end of the month Howie had changed sides. On March 29 he issued a statement from his constituency which said in part:

"It is beyond question that the Government's prices and incomes policy and its proposals for the reform of industrial relations are right both in socialist theory and socialist practice.

"Unfortunately, the first has alienated the main body of Labour support and the strike provisions of the latter are making sure that they stay alienated.

"A party without support is like a head without a body. The body must be brought back – and soon.

"It is now time to end the statutory prices and incomes policy and to abandon the strike proposals, however desirable they may be. They can only continue at the expense of the Labour Party.

"As the saying is, enough is enough. It is time for a change of direction."

This was no more than the view of one modestly influential back-bencher, but it was indicative of the rend in the party. The grounds of the argument were shifting. Hitherto the White Paper had been opposed chiefly on grounds of principle and inpracticability; now middle-of-the-road MPs who had not quarrelled with it in principle were beginning to oppose it because it was too politically damaging. Howie's turn around also meant that all four elected officials of the party were now against the Government's trade union policy. Between them they represented all important sections of the party, save the hard core left. They represented young and old, new and senior, trade union and non-trade union. The disaffection of the Liaison Committee showed the extent of the gap which had opened up between Government and party.

At the end of March the Liaison Committee got wind of the discussion going on inside the Government about interim legislation on industrial relations. Douglas Houghton asked to see the Prime Minister in order to be reassured that there was no truth in this alarming rumour. The Prime Minister was leaving for Africa but on April 2 there was a meeting of the Liaison Committee at which the Chief Whip was present. The party representatives received the impression that early legislation was not very likely. As we have seen, there was no Cabinet decision at that time and Silkin may not have been fully informed of what had been going on among senior Ministers. Nevertheless, the party representatives warned him that an interim Industrial Relations Bill containing penal clauses would very likely suffer the fate of the Parliament Bill, a view which Silkin did not accept. Thus a significant revolt, involving influential MPs normally loyal to the Government, was brewing up even before the Easter recess. However, it was the announcement by

Roy Jenkins on April 15 in his Budget speech that the Government proposed to legislate urgently on industrial relations which set in motion not only a determined, organised opposition to the Government's policy but also a backbench challenge to Harold Wilson's leadership.

It became apparent very soon after the Budget that the Cabinet had gravely misjudged the temper of the party. It was by now in a highly emotional state. Although there was as yet no Industrial Relations Bill, not even in draft, it had taken on for many MPs a physical presence – they talked about it as if it were already a nasty fact, not merely an unpleasant intention. The Labour Party at Westminster became almost wholly obsessed by it. The opponents of the penal clauses were very little interested in the details – how the fines were going to be collected, etc.; however the pill was sugared they did not want to swallow it. The threatened Bill also took on a symbolic significance; rational argument about its merits or demerits gave way to apocalyptic concern about the unity of the Labour Movement. MPs who had previously had some sympathy for the Government's approach to the union question now came to oppose it on tactical considerations. The historical relationship between the Labour Party and the trade union movement was seen to be at stake, the foundation of British Social Democracy – the partnership between Socialist reformers and the representatives of work-people – seemed to be threatened. It was no good Harold Wilson claiming in his May Day speech that the Government had been misunderstood. He complained: "From the very moment we decided to act, when we announced our proposals, the whole problem we are seeking to deal with became obscured in controversy, a controversy where apparently the main qualification for pronouncing on the Government's proposals is failure to read the White Paper. Recognition of the problem and responsibility for dealing with it are in danger of being sacrificed to slogans. You would have thought we were going to re-enact Tolpuddle". That indeed was the atmosphere of the moment, a great many people did believe that here was an ugly landmark in the history of the Labour Movement. The Cabinet in April acted as if the party were susceptible to rational argument on the question of industrial relations, but for the time being the party was not.

At the end of Budget week Michael Foot, whose sword is his pen, for the first time lunged personally at Wilson. In a signed *Tribune* article Foot wrote:

"Harold Wilson and the Labour Cabinet are heading for the

rocks. . . . It is the maddest scene in the modern history of Britain and if the Labour Movement as a whole can succeed in rescuing the Labour leaders from their folly, historians will look back on it with amazement and incredulity". He went on to accuse the Government of declaring war on the trade unions, nothing less. The advice of experts in industrial relations, of the Donovan Commission and middle-of-the-road Labour MPs who knew how industry really worked, had all been rejected. The Cabinet, headed by the Prime Minister (Foot singled him out for special blame) had embarked upon a course which threatened "to break the Government and tear the movement to shreds". It was a "situation of matchless absurdity"; "An hysterical press campaign, whipped up by Ministerial and Prime Ministerial leakages, clamours for a Labour Government to drink the poison that could kill it". The only way to save the Labour Movement, wrote Foot, was for everyone in it to make it as clear as possible that the anti-trade union legislation would not be tolerated. Evidently he considered the Labour Government beyond redemption for the article concluded – and the sting was in the tail – "Only after that shall we be able to pick up the pieces. The choice about the time when we can start upon that fruitful work of construction rests with the Cabinet and the party's leaders, *whoever they may turn out to be*". (Author's italics.)

Foot was not the only former friend now to cast public doubt on the continuance of Harold Wilson's leadership. Budget week began with side swipes from the two newspapers which had given him the most consistent support. *The Guardian*, formerly Liberal but since 1964 sympathetic to Labour and to Harold Wilson, said "Either Mr. Wilson must be supported – and with him the main proposals on union reform – or someone else must quickly take his place". The *Daily Mirror*, which at each election since the war had powerfully enjoined its fifteen million readers to vote Labour, now urged the Prime Minister to put country before party; the overwhelming majority of the nation would be behind him if he pushed ahead with the Bill but, commented the *Daily Mirror*, "he's a softie at heart". Ray Gunter, the disgrunted former Minister of Labour, had earlier expressed broad approval of the policy adopted by his successor Barbara Castle but now he stated publicly, "I see no hope of the Labour Party winning the next election, certainly not under its present leadership".

The Tribune Group at Westminster called for a joint meeting of the Parliamentary Labour Party and the Labour Party National Executive Committee. The very thought set the skeletons rattling, for the last such meeting had taken place in 1931 after Ramsay Macdonald's abdication. *The Times* found the moment appropriate to editorialise on the constitional position concerning the dissolution of Parliament. Ought the Queen to grant a dissolution to a Prime Minister for the purpose of involving his party in his own downfall? No, concluded *The Times*; the Queen in these circumstances should follow the nineteenth century practice and grant the dissolution to the Cabinet rather than to an individual.

It was in this atmosphere that active Labour backbenchers embarked upon two overlapping, sometimes complementary and sometimes conflicting, enterprises. One was to prevent the passing of an Industrial Relations Bill containing penal clauses. The other was to overthrow the Prime Minister. Some MPs were interested only in stopping the Bill. Some approved of the Bill or had no great objection to it but wanted to use it as a device for getting rid of Harold Wilson. Some wanted to kill the two birds with one stone, others wanted to throw all their stones at one or other of the birds. The organised campaign against the Bill by people who were not directly interested in the leadership question assisted the anti-Wilson plotters, for it was his deepening commitment to the Bill, and only that, which made a backbench coup at all plausible. Conversely, the activities of the plotters provided extra ammunition for the enemies of the Bill, for they were able to warn the Prime Minister that his own position would be in doubt if he persisted with the policy.

The opponents of the penal clauses began to organise themselves as soon as the short Bill was announced in the Budget speech. An "action group" was set up. It was organised by Eric Moonman, one of the 1966 intake and a member of one of the printing trade unions, a centrist – no professional rebel. It set itself the limited aims usually necessary to the success of a pressure group. It was purely a canvassing organisation, it had no candidate for the leadership. It took for its quota sample the one hundred MPs who had either voted against the Government or abstained in the debate on *In Place of Strife* and it kept a running count of how many of them were prepared to defy the whips when the Bill was presented. At the first reckoning there were fifty pledges to vote against and thirteen more to abstain. Thus no sooner was the Government's intention to push through a short Bill announced than it became extremely doubtful whether it could command a majority for sending it upstairs to committee or for a "guillotine" motion if necessary. The Opposition had quickly made clear that, although not opposed to the steps the Government was proposing to take against unofficial strikes, it would not support the Government on these procedural motions. With the Tories voting the Government could afford no more than thirty-five rebels. So already there was the danger that the Industrial Relations Bill would suffer the same fate as the Parliament Bill on the floor of the House.

At about the same time, encouraged by the results of Moonman's researches, groups of MPs who had lost their faith in Harold Wilson's leadership began to explore ways of getting rid of him. There were only two ways of going about it. A Prime Minister of sound body and mind could be deposed either by a Cabinet coup or a backbench coup. The scenario for a Cabinet coup was simple. A body of senior Cabinet Ministers would go to the Prime Minister and say "Harold, either you resign or we all resign". The scenario for a backbench coup was more complicated. The Prime Minister would have to be deposed from his party office as leader by an adverse vote at a party meeting. He would then presumably be obliged to resign as Prime Minister. However, arranging for a vote to be held at a party meeting was easier contemplated than done. The PLP's rules provided adequately for selecting a new leader to fill a vacancy but not for creating the vacancy. It had been assumed that a vacancy would only occur through natural causes. While in Opposition the Labour Party elects its leader annually. In the event of a contest the procedure is for a first ballot to eliminate all candidates but two and for a second ballot to decide between them. Voting is secret. After Hugh Gaitskell's death in 1963 Wilson, Bown and Callaghan contested the first ballot and Wilson and Brown fought it out in the second. The second ballot took place a week after the result of the first was known. Clearly this procedure could not be followed when Labour was in office and therefore a modified, truncated version of it had been invented. The incentive to do this was provided by the behaviour of the Conservatives after Suez. Labour was alarmed at the process by which Harold Macmillan had succeeded Anthony Eden at the expense of R. A. Butler. Arrangements were made to ensure that if a similar situation ever arose with a Labour Government the choice of leader would be the party's not the Queen's. A procedure was established similar to that used to elect a Pope. The PLP would be locked up in a room and the smoke would not appear from the chimney until a new leader had been elected by multiple ballot. This arrangement had the additional advantage of protecting a Prime Minister from a Cabinet coup. For if a group in the Cabinet formed around an agreed successor they could never be certain that the man they had chosen would be elected by the party or that members of the cabal would not defect and run themselves.

However, these arrangements applied only to filling a vacancy which had for some reason occurred; there was no special procedure for dismissing a Prime Minister and no provision for a secret ballot. A motion of "no confidence" in the leader (or it could be disguised as a motion of confidence) would have to go forward like any other motion. That is to say it would have to be submitted to the chairman of the PLP a week before the party meeting. If the chairman accepted the motion he would be obliged to post it on the notice board in the Whips' room. Thus a move to vote down the Leader at a party meeting would be a matter of public knowledge. The Prime Minister would be given a week in which to mount his defences. During that time there would probably be panic on the foreign exchange markets and politics would be in turmoil. It was no wonder that even those who were now trying to depose Harold Wilson had doubts about the feasibility of their enterprise.

Ironically, among the would be assassins was the author of the theory that it was well-night impossible to depose a modern Prime Minister. This was John Mackintosh. A professor of politics before entering the Commons in 1966, Mackintosh was author of the standard work *The British Cabinet*, a revised edition of which had appeared shortly before he now set out to disprove his own thesis. In it he said that there were "only two ways a Prime Minister can be removed providing he has a majority and retains his health. One is a Cabinet coup, the other is overthrow at a backbench meeting of his party. Both are so unlikely as to be almost impossible". Although a Prime Minister might lose his authority when he was under fire and things were going badly for him, the powers at his disposal nevertheless protected him from removal. "The lesson for students of British Government", wrote the student now turned practical experimenter, "is that even at times when the record and capacities of a Prime Minister are under the maximum criticism and therefore the office is at its weakest, overall direction can come from no other source, no junta can take command, powers that are circumscribed are not taken up by others but merely fall into abeyance and the only way out of the impasse is the recovery of the authority of the Prime Minister".

John Mackintosh and his friends quickly satisfied themselves that there was no possibility of a Cabinet coup. So they were left with the second method – the overthrow of the Prime Minister at a party meeting.

There would not be a Cabinet coup for a simple reason: there was no agreement in the Cabinet as to who should succeed Harold Wilson. The senior Ministers who would have to threaten their collective resignation in order to oust Wilson still preferred him to either of the alternatives who were James Callaghan or Roy Jenkins. This situation illustrated the complete success of the Prime Minister in preventing the emergence of a Crown Prince. It had been his first rule at each reconstruction of the Government. In 1966, after the July crisis, he sent George Brown to the Foreign Office, because he knew that Brown was no longer a threat, but he held Roy Jenkins down at the Home Office and kept him away from the centre of economic power. When eventually obliged to appoint Jenkins to the Treasury in place of Callaghan it looked for a while as if he had at last been forced to anoint a Crown Prince. But Harold Wilson took effective precautions. Denis Healey was the obviously qualified candidate to succeed Brown when he later resigned from the Foreign Office, but Wilson instead re-appointed Michael Stewart and kept Healey locked up at the Ministry of Defence, where he had been since the formation of the Government. Wilson could risk Jenkins at the Treasury or Healey at the Foreign Office but not both. Then by sending Barbara Castle to the Department of Employment and Productivity with responsibility for prices and incomes policy he created a rival pole of economic power to offset the Chancellor's. And the Parliamentary Committee, which he set up at the same time, ensured that there was a majority of loyal Wilson men at the centre of the Government to prevent him from being crowded by too powerful colleagues. These precautions now stood Harold Wilson in good stead. Roy Jenkins was manacled on the one side to Barbara Castle and on the other to Wilson himself. Callaghan was out on his own and had been removed from the centre of affairs. Denis Healey was still soldiering on at Defence.

The one advantage of a backbench coup over a Cabinet coup was that it was not necessary to have prior agreement on a successor. The party would elect a successor when the time came; in the meanwhile the task was to bring about a negative vote against the Prime Minister at a party meeting. A group of MPs who had met in John Mackintosh's room at the House of Commons thus set out to collect signatures for a letter to Douglas Houghton requesting him to call a meeting of the party at which the leadership question would be discussed. At the same time they conducted more discreet soundings among MPs about who, if anyone, they would prefer to Harold Wilson.

The leaders of this group are difficult to place in the spectrum of Labour Party politics. They were not a part of the organised Left, nor were they for the most part members of the "radical Right". The young Right-wing intellectuals associated with the Gaitskellite "Campaign for Democratic Socialism" which remained in existence, although only about twenty now attended its meetings, had burnt their fingers a year previously when they had canvassed the cause of Jenkins for leader. This time they played a lesser role. The men who met in Mackintosh's room belonged on the Left- and Right-wing fringes of the centre. They were not a party group in the same sense as the Left or the "radical Right". A good proportion of them had entered the Commons in 1966. They were the generation of Wilson's "technology speech" (at the Scarborough conference of 1963) which had led many of them to believe they could expect from him a radicalism which was neither conventionally Left nor Right in Labour Party terms. They tended to agree among themselves on such questions as Rhodesia and aid to under-developed countries and, indeed, it was fear of a sell-out to the Smith regime which had first brought them together for occasional meetings. Now they had another clear common interest and that was in the possibility of changing the leadership of the party. The only possible explanation of why the Government was functioning so badly, they had concluded, was the way in which it was led. They were all the more disillusioned with Harold Wilson for at first having admired him. Their chief complaint was that the Government under his leadership blundered along according to no apparent system of priorities. They felt that they had been marched half-way up the hill and down again too often, for example on the incomes policy which they had first been led to believe was based on priorities of social justice but had recently been told at Question Time that this was not one of its purposes. They could no longer even credit Wilson with being a good party tactician. They had severe misgivings about his judgement of people. Some of them may have been disappointed themselves in hopes of office but their chief complaint, so they insisted, was that he had appointed to junior posts men who commanded no respect even in the sections of the party they were intended to appease, for example some of the second-rate trade unionists brought into the Government in 1967. They were not opposed to a strong policy towards the unions but they feared that the history of the prices and incomes policy was about to repeat itself.

From sources within the Government they had gathered that Barbara Castle's proposals were in all probability unworkable. But their chief purpose now was not to destroy the Bill but to depose the Prime Minister, and the man most of them wanted to succeed was Roy Jenkins. This made for additional difficulties, for Jenkins was heavily committed to the Bill and the Bill was the essential lever for prying Harold Wilson out of Number 10 Downing Street. Jenkins's attitude was as follows. He was completely committed to the Bill. Moreover, he had entered a pact with Barbara Castle and could not go through with his "hard slog" policy without her support. Therefore he would greatly prefer it if his supporters made no move until the Bill was out of the way, one way or the other. "It's too early to strike", he was heard to say. But if Wilson was by some means or another to be removed there was no doubt that Roy Jenkins would be a candidate for the succession.

It was therefore essential to the Jenkinsites that the Callaghanites should move first. They could not promote their man directly because of his commitment to the Bill and because of his lack of sex appeal in the tea room where the trade union MPs gathered to wonder what the world and the Labour Party were coming to. In order to achieve a negative vote against Wilson it was necessary to hold together all the opponents of the Bill who might be prepared to change the leadership. A move by Roy Jenkins was liable to misinterpretation as a naked bid for power; Callaghan on the other hand was identified with the trade union issue and could purport to be challenging Wilson on a question of principle. Therefore the Jenkins men hoped that the Callaghan men would dig the hole but that Roy might be able to jump into it before Jim.

Callaghan's position was indeed the very opposite of Jenkins's. His only hope of succeeding was while the Bill remained a controversial question dividing the party. Once the question was settled one way or the other his claim to be able to provide a different "style of leadership" would quickly evaporate. Consequently he let it be known to a caller that he was a man "not without ambition, in which there is nothing dishonourable". The Callaghanites, the chief of whom was the Scottish MP George Lawson who had organised Callaghan's bid for the leadership in 1963, were predominantly the solid men of the centre and old Right. In 1963 Callaghan had received forty-one votes in the first round, two-thirds of which went to Wilson on the second ballot. Since then he had failed as Chancellor and alienated the left and liberal wings of the party by some of his activities as Home Secretary. The hard core of the trade union group, the manual workers, did not regard him instinctively as a sound trade union man. But he was the only powerful figure in the Government identified with an alternative policy on industrial relations and he was closest in style to the sort of leadership the centre expected from a Labour Prime Minister. He stood a good chance of being more acceptable to the party as a whole than either Roy Jenkins from the "radical Right" or any candidate the Left put up – but once again it all depended on opening up the leadership by challenging Wilson.

According to the canvass carried out by the Jenkinsites sixty MPs were prepared to join in requesting a meeting of the party to decide the leadership. An additional forty were believed to be prepared to vote against Harold Wilson in a secret ballot if a party meeting could be arranged but were not prepared to be active in promoting a leadership crisis. The one hundred dissident MPs included twenty members of the Government (about a quarter of the "pay roll vote", which would have to split if Wilson was to be defeated) and, significantly, half of the seventy-one MPs elected for the first time in 1966. The opposition to Harold Wilson's leadership was far larger than ever before but it still fell well short of Douglas Houghton's requirement for calling a meeting of the party to vote on the question. For the party chairman had let it be known that he would want not less than one hundred and twenty signatures before he would be prepared to put the leadership on the agenda. He was saying in effect that he would need to be convinced that the Prime Minister would almost certainly lose the vote before he would risk calling it. For Houghton, as we shall later see, was not prepared to allow a halfcock attempt to remove Wilson to interfere with the campaign to kill the Industrial Relations Bill which he passionately believed was in danger of destroying the Labour Movement.

But meanwhile another group of MPs were trying a different tack. Instead of trying to collect lots of signatures they were attempting to gather a few very influential ones. This enterprise was organised by Willie Hamilton, one of the elected vice-chairmen of the PLP. Hamilton, although a somewhat embittered man, office having eluded him, was one of the most able backbenchers on the Labour side of the House, one of the stars of question time. He sat for a mining constituency, one of the very few ever to have returned a Communist to the House of Commons, but he was not a man of the Left save when it came to issues involving the Monarchy and the Scottish aristocracy on which he took an extreme republican position. He was a schoolmaster by profession, had been in the House since 1950 and during the Labour Government had been chairman of the Select Committee on Estimates. It was under the cover of this capacity that Hamilton held two meetings in his room for the purpose of trying to gather twenty signatures of an unimpeachably respectable character. Houghton, it was thought, would be more impressed by an appeal of this kind for a party meeting on the leadership than by sheer numbers. The signatures would include no sacked Ministers, no hard core leftists, no left-over extreme Gaitskellites but all belong to good solid party men with no previous record of anti-Wilson activities. The sort of men he had in mind for this purpose were Eric Heffer, a Left-winger verging on the centre, well-liked for his straightforward honest qualities and who had been offered a job by Wilson which he had refused; Arthur Palmer, a long standing centrist; Carol Johnson, the secretary of the PLP until he had entered Parliament in 1959; Cyril Bence, a good solid trade union MP sponsored by the Amalgamated Engineering and Foundry Workers' Union; Ernest Thornton, another sound trade union man who had for a while been a junior Minister at the Ministry of Labour but had returned happily enough to the backbenches.

Where did the Left stand in all this? Its attitude was one of the reasons why the men who were trying to get rid of Harold Wilson believed that on this occasion they might conceivably succeed. For the Prime Minister's praetorian guard had begun to desert him. The Left had always taken the line that its object was to change the party's policy not its leadership. The MPs of the Left continued to entertain romantic delusions about Harold Wilson being one of them at heart. They remembered that he had resigned from the Attlee Government with Aneurin Bevan over health service charges and defence expenditure and they remembered how he had stood against Gaitskell for the leadership in 1960; they conveniently forgot that he had voted for Gaitskell in 1956 and had supported him in steering the party away from a policy of wholesale nationalisation. Long after he had adopted many policies hateful to the Left they continued to believe that they would get more from him than from any likely successor. Jenkins was even less of a Socialist – he hardly pretended to be one and deliberately avoided using the word. Callaghan had pursued what they regarded as bankers' policies at the Treasury and was pursuing what they regarded as policeman's policies at the Home Office, for example, closing the frontiers to the Kenyan Asians in spite of their British passports. "Policeman Jim" they called him. The Left therefore had always attacked Wilson's policies but rallied around him when his leadership was called into question. A year previously when young MPs on the "radical Right" were canvassing in favour of Roy Jenkins for Prime Minister it had been Michael Foot who sprung first to the Prime Minister's defence. It was he who exposed the "plot". Who were these people?, he demanded to know at a party meeting; why didn't they stand up and reveal themselves? "I'm not letting people go for Harold", he said afterwards. But now Foot was to be heard wishing he could suppress the short biography, published before the election in 1964, in which he had offered a fulsome if not downright sycophantic assessment of Harold Wilson's character and abilities. In the *Tribune* article in Budget week he had for the first time attacked Wilson personally. Other Left-wingers were also turning against him personally for the first time. One man reported that in his constituency the bingo callers could no longer announce "Number Ten, Harold's Den" because of the cat calls and boos. Some members of the Tribune Group began to look round for a candidate, for they began to realise that they were not going to change the policy of the party unless they could change its leader. But who? A few still said Barbara Castle, in spite of the fact that she was the author of the policy which was causing all the trouble. Some said Richard Crossman but even Crossman himself confessed that this project lacked plausibility – although he firmly believed he would make an absolutely splendid Prime Minister. Unable to discover a candidate who was both credible and acceptable, the Left back-tracked somewhat between April and mid-May when the backbench movement against Wilson reached its climax – or, rather, its anti-climax. Only a handful of the Tribune Group were prepared to pledge themselves to the Jenkinsites. Nevertheless, Harold Wilson could no longer rely upon the Left to act as his personal bodyguard.

The elected party representatives on the Liaison Committee had reason to believe that at its meeting on May 14 it would receive a formal request to place the leadership question on the agenda of the next party meeting. Douglas Houghton was still against doing this, although he would have carefully assessed the support for the request both in the terms of the number of MPs and, more particularly, who they were. Willie Hamilton, Will Howie and Joyce Butler were expected to be favourable. Fred Peart and Robert Mellish obviously would be against. The representative of the Labour peers, Lord Campion, it was hoped would stay out of it. So there would be three against two, with Douglas Houghton holding the balance. But all these considerations turned out to be purely academic for the request was never received – the backbench revolt against Harold Wilson's leadership fell apart.

The request for the party meeting was to have come from the Callaghanites. The Jenkinsites had informed Houghton of the strength of support they had discovered for a vote to be held on the leadership but, in accordance with their strategy, they were still not prepared to strike the first blow. In any case they too expected the Callaghan army to move. But at the last minute the Callaghan camp split.

On May 9 Jim Callaghan made a mistake, in fact his error was twofold: he repeated himself and he went too far. On that day a long previously arranged meeting between the Cabinet and the National Executive Committee of the Labour Party took place. This get-together was becoming an annual event; its purpose was to promote a greater understanding between Government and party. It took place on this occasion at an awkward moment, although it would have been hard at that time to find a moment which would not have been awkward. A financial crisis was raging in Bonn and upsetting the exchange markets. Labour had just suffered further body blows in the local government elections, although some mathematical consolation could be found in the size of the swing. Richard Crossman had chosen the eve of the local government elections to announce increases in the charges for National Health Service dentures and spectacles. "Teeth and specs" were unfortunate items to crop up at that moment for increased Health Service charges were the occasion of Harold Wilson's resignation from the Attlee Government. So it was at the end of another bad week that the meeting between the Cabinet and the NEC took place.

The Cabinet had met the previous day and James Callaghan's colleagues had understood him to give an assurance that he would not renew the opposition to the industrial relations policy which he had expressed openly at the meeting of the NEC on March 26. But he did. At the joint meeting he entered a powerful plea on behalf of the unions and against the Government. He argued that it was the job of a Labour Government to help its friends; it should not be encouraging the public to hold a hostile opinion of the unions but rather explaining trade unionism to the public so that the unions came to be seen in a more favourable light. Once again Barbara Castle was furious. She shouted back at Callaghan that it was the job of a Labour Government to give the unions the chance to make themselves more popular and that was just what she was trying to do.

Labour politicians and trade union leaders will fight with knives with the best, but they have certain standards or, perhaps we should say, inhibitions. The people in the PLP who were well disposed towards the idea of Callaghan in place of Wilson were the very people who clung instinctively to such old fashioned virtues as loyalty to the leader, strict party discipline and getting on with the job. Even the trade unionists who appreciated the sentiments expressed by Callaghan were told by their nostrils that there was something wrong about his style of behaviour. He had declared himself once at the NEC meeting in March. Since then the Government had decided to legislate but he had not resigned from the Cabinet. His conduct again seemed to be ambivalent to those who thought that his proper course was either to come out openly and fight with the gloves on or stay quietly in his corner. The result was that the Callaghanites split. Some were so offended by their man's behaviour that they refused to go ahead with the move to request the party meeting. "I'm sorry," said George Lawson to the waiting Jenkins men, "but our thing broke down".

Willie Hamilton's "thing" also broke down. By this time it was known that the TUC had prepared an alternative plan for dealing with unconstitutional strikes. Discussions between the General Council and the Government had begun. A special Trades Union Congress had been called for June 5 to endorse the TUC's plan. Hopes began to rise that, after all, there would be an agreement between the Government and the TUC and that the Government in consequence would drop the penal clauses. So the senior party worthies convened by Willie Hamilton also decided to hold their hand for the time being.

What would have happened if the leadership question had been opened at a party meeting? Almost certainly Wilson would have survived, if not Callaghan might have won. The Jenkinsites believed that their man could have squeaked home on a second ballot, but they were not very confident and that was one reason why they were so cautious about triggering off a contest themselves. Their researches showed about sixty to seventy votes for Callaghan on the first ballot out of a sample of a hundred. Senior members of the Cabinet, who were kept in touch with what was going on by their parliamentary private secretaries, were of the opinion that if it came to it Callaghan would be the man they would have to stop. There might have been a move from the Cabinet to draft Healey as a dark horse. Roy Jenkins, as he himself had realised when approached by his fans, was the prisoner of the Prime Minister and Barbara Castle for as long as the Bill was on the agenda. In any case, in so far as the mood in favour of a leadership change represented the desire for a true party man to come to the aid of the party, Roy Jenkins was not the man for that moment. Not enough of the solid men of the party, for instance, the Welsh miners – the folk from whence Roy Jenkins came – could see him as a Labour leader. The word had got down from Cabinet that he was too dilettante, not a serious enough politician – a man with good strong views on subjects which interested him but no clearly known views on some of the gut issues which concerned the mass of the party. For example, what did he really believe on the union question? Had he thought deeply about it, or was he just following Barbara Castle for motives of political convenience? As for James Callaghan, he was offering the party a different style of leadership but a good many in the party did not think much of James Callaghan's style of behaviour. They might have chosen him if forced to choose but they did not want him enough to push him forward; and without that the Jenkins men were stuck too.

So the text books were proved right. And so was Harold Wilson who said in a public speech, "May I say for the benefit of those who have been carried away by the gossip of the last few days, that I know what's going on – I am going on". The reasons Harold Wilson remained Prime Minister were that – as Mackintosh had written – when a Prime Minister is in good health and has a majority it is "almost impossible" to overthrown him; that there was no Crown Prince, as he had carefully ensured; that Callaghan had over-played his hand and Roy Jenkins under-played his; and that a majority in the party was still chiefly concerned with avoiding a disastrous split on the question of trade union reform and still hopeful that Harold Wilson would reach an accommodation with the TUC. But there was one other extremely important factor in the situation, and that was the chairman of the Parliamentary Labour Party, Douglas Houghton.

Houghton occupied a position of considerable independent power, a position without parallel in the Conservative Party. The Prime Minister might sack him from the Cabinet, which he had done on grounds of his age, but he could do nothing to remove him from his party office to which he had been elected, and elected more recently than Harold Wilson to his as Leader. He had won great respect for his fairness and sense of responsibility from all sections of the party. As party chairman he controlled the agenda of party meetings almost as effectively as a Prime Minister controlled the agenda of the Cabinet. Houghton's consent was required for the leadership, or any other question, to be discussed. He had no reason to love Harold Wilson. He had no special interest in preserving him from a backbench coup. But he was prepared to allow nothing to come into the way of his first objective at this time which was to prevent the passing of an Industrial Relations Bill of the kind which he feared might destroy the Labour Movement. He had been against the penal clauses from the very start. His attitude was identical with that of the moderate progressive members of the TUC General Council, of which he had himself for eight years been a member. That is, he knew the need for trade union reform but believed that the Donovan Commission's approach was the correct one and Barbara Castle's the misguided one. For thirty-eight years he had been the general secretary of the Inland Revenue Staff Federation. In that capacity he had appointed James Callaghan to his first trade union job and he saw no reason now for making him Prime Minister. He was afraid that a back-bench attempt to vote down the Prime Minister would fail and that the party would be left with both Harold Wilson and the Bill. He was prepared to work with Callaghan, indeed with anybody, providing the objective was not to divide the party but to reunite it by disposing of the penal clauses. The plotting against the leadership, of which he kept very careful track, was for him another lever for changing the Government's policy. Before this present crisis had cropped up he had been concerned about the state of communications between the Government and the party and it was at his suggestion that regular Tuesday evening meetings were arranged between himself and the Prime Minister. He now used these to give the Prime Minister repeated warnings about forcing through legislation against the will of the party. On the Prime Minister's return from Nigeria in April, when the controversy over Lords reform was still raging, Houghton warned him of the danger to his leadership. Wilson replied grandly, "I hold my office from the Queen not from the Parliamentary Labour Party" and claimed he did not care how many backbenchers voted against him, he would still go on. It was this sort of intransigence which convinced Douglas Houghton that he must do something more to stop the Industrial Relations Bill.

He was a man who carefully considered his words and actions. He was remembered by the public as the trusted adviser on family finances of the BBC's "Can I help you?" programme, a popular long-running radio feature during the wartime and early post-war period. Douglas Houghton now decided it was time to be unhelpful to Harold Wilson. At the meeting of the PLP on May 7 he delivered a very carefully pre-pared statement. The text of it was released in full to the press and copies were made available to Ministers not present. He began by appealing to all sides to avoid taking entrenched positions. "Much is going on," he said; "consultations are taking place. In my own way I have been active myself. The divisions in the party and the trade union movement are deep and serious, but we must work to narrow and not to widen them.

"We want something in place of strife in our own party. No good can possibly come of any clash or split within our movement. No good that any contentious Bill of this kind can do to industrial relations or the economy will redeem the harm we can do to our Government by the disintegration or defeat of the Labour Party.

"Our unity and our political purpose matters more to the country than the marginal damage done by unconstitutional strikes. I know that as we continue to debate, the Government is searching for a solution. They are going to see the TUC on Monday. I hope that contributions to our debate here can now suggest possible courses of action. There has been enough deunciation of the Government's proposals. Can we now hear more of the way forward? It is not simply enough to go on hammering the Government's proposals."

Houghton then made his own position on the industrial relations question clear. He fully endorsed the position taken by the Donovan Commission. The responsibility for ridding industry of unconstitutional strikes, he said, lay first and foremost with management and the unions themselves. It would be a mistake for the State to shoulder that responsibility. He would put the unions and management on the spot rather than the Government and the Minister.

He then went on: "Despite the events of recent days (he was referring to the speculations about the leadership), we must not despair. We have been through bad times before. But we are still the Government. We still have the power to influence events our way. But the best hope of all is in a united party, here and outside. The Government and the party are one, and the sooner we become indivisible the better. Ministers must not fall into the error that their determination and their resolve to force things through the party and through Parliament is either desirable or possible. It can only be done with us, it cannot be done without us. We must all strive to prevent government by disintegration of the Labour Party – there is no future in that for anybody, least of all for industrial relations."

This was a remarkable statement and an important one. Houghton had given many warnings in private but this was the first time he had spoken out in public. It was also the first time he had made publicly known his views on the trade union question. In trade union parlance he was, so to speak, declaring the backbenchers' dispute with the Government official. But like an experienced trade union official he was not looking for a showdown but for a negotiated settlement. A few days previously he had made his first contact with Victor Feather; they had spoken on the telephone between London and Newcastle where Feather was on TUC business. Feather briefed him on the steps being taken by the TUC to do something itself about unconstitutional strikes. The TUC's plan was not yet published, indeed Ministers had not yet seen it, but Houghton in his statement of May 7 was advising them in advance, and in public, that they would do well to use it as the basis for a compromise.

However, his speech was made in the atmosphere of the leadership crisis and was therefore taken to be a sharp personal warning to the Prime Minister. Harold Wilson was furious at what he took to be an ultimatum to the Government from the party. Newspaper headlines had portrayed Houghton as throwing down a gauntlet to the Prime Minister and demanding the Government's surrender. At question time the next day the Prime Minister found the opportunity to point out that the chairman of the Parliamentary Labour Party did not exercise influence over the Treasury Bench in the way that Enoch Powell, so he claimed, exercised influence over the Opposition Front Bench. The Prime Minister angrily summoned Houghton and complained that he had understood from their last conversation that he would not be making such a statement to the party. Houghton replied that what he said or did not say to the party depended on what the Prime Minister said to him and could not be decided in advance. That was the nature of their relationship at the time – Wilson expecting Houghton to act as a channel of communication with the party and Houghton reserving his independence of action as the party's elected officer. However, he did climb down a little, in tone if not in substance, and the next evening made a second statement to the party in clarification of his first. He said:

"There has been a lot of publicity given to my statement yesterday – rather more than I expected or desired. What I did was within my function as chairman of the PLP – namely to sum up what I believe to be the feelings and deepest hopes of the party for the reconciliation of the present differences between the Government and the trade union movement on the more controversial proposals in the White Paper on industrial relations.

"The party chairman does not dictate to the Government, or call for any surrender, or throw down gauntlets to the Prime Minister. He advises the Government, in good faith, of the state of mind of the party, mostly in private and only rarely in public. This time – and for the first time – I did it openly at the party meeting because I believe the present situation justified doing so.

"Once over this hump of the interim Industrial Relations Bill, I believe we shall be set for a forceful and successful run-up to the General Election, with many impressive achievements by our Government which otherwise may be lost sight of in the dust of internal strife. But we must be united to do it. By unity, I mean full accord in the wider movement as well as in the PLP. The trade union movement is an integral part of the Labour Party. We must not be torn apart. This is the rift our opponents are hoping for.

"It requires *mutual* effort," he went on – emphasising the word – "to avert it. The attempts to solve the complex problems of industrial relations do not rest with the Government alone. I am sure we all hope for a response from the TUC just as strongly as we hope for a response from the Government to our deep anxiety for a speedy removal of present difficulties over this Bill.

"There is no ultimatum in this," he asserted, "no challenge to the Prime Minister or the Government. I said yesterday what I believe a very large section of the PLP is thinking. We want to reunite our party: we search for an honourable basis upon which we can pledge our firm loyalty to the Government through the testing days ahead."

Houghton's public warnings reflected not only the degree of opposition which had built up in the party against the penal clauses, but also the hopes of an amicable compromise between the Government and the TUC which MPs were beginning to entertain.

The effect that the proposed penal clauses were having on the loyalists in the party was illustrated in the case of Tom Bradley who was at the same time the president of the railway "white collar" union (The Transport and Salaried Staffs' Association) and Roy Jenkins's devoted Parliamentary Private Secretary. Bradley faced an agonising choice but had no doubt that on this occasion, on an issue as fundamental as this – as he saw it – he must choose the trade union movement. At his union conference in May he launched into a swingeing attack on the Government's policy, even querying – quite unwarrantably – whether either Harold Wilson or Barbara Castle had ever read the Donovan Report. And as MPs attended the series of party meetings on the subject of trade union legislation their doubts also increased as to whether the Government knew what it was doing in this field. At one of these meetings the Lord Chancellor, Gerald Gardiner, came down to lecture backbenchers on the law of garnishment – the recovery of debts from third persons. Gardiner, eminent leader of his learned profession, splendidly liberal man and zealous and humane reformer of the law, was trying to reassure backbenchers about fines leading to the imprisonment of trade unionists. It was very rare for debtors to finish up in jail, he assured them, and he gave figures. There were something like 170,000 committal orders a year but more than 90 per cent paid up when the bailiffs arrived. What if they didn't? Then it was a matter for the courts, the Lord Chancellor explained, but even then only about 3,000 cases finished in prison. A whistle of amazement went up – only 3,000 trade unionists a year locked up for going on strike! In what strange world was the Government living, wondered the MPs – many of them trade unionists and representatives of industrial constituencies? Was this a Labour Government, a Labour Lord Chancellor? And well might they wonder, for the plan to attach workers' earnings had gone through the Cabinet originally without a murmur. Nobody had seen the significance of it or sensed the emotions it would arouse in the trade union movement. Admittedly, the TUC had given evidence to a committee of inquiry in favour of attachment in maintenance cases. But experienced trade union MPs like Charlie Pannell were quick to see the furore which this would cause when extended to the recovery of fines. Only then did the Cabinet give the matter serious thought. There was no one in the Labour Cabinet, save a junior member of it – Roy Mason, a coal miner – who really knew the working class world at first hand.

The strength of the opposition in the party to penal legislation was one of the reasons why many MPs began to expect a compromise. The Moonman action group's count was by mid-May up to sixty-one MPs pledged to vote against the Government with another thirteen pledged to abstain, and this was after Bob Mellish had made it clear that even a procedural vote would be treated as a vote of confidence in the Government. The Chief Whip was kept closely informed of this and other developments in the party. For example, on May 19 Barbara Castle addressed the party's prices and incomes group, a body predominantly of loyalist centre MPs. She gave the impression, in the words of one member, "of a martyr looking for a cross to nail herself on". After this encounter Ron Brown, George's brother, and James Hamilton, the chairman of the 130-strong trade union group, went to Mellish to make it absolutely plain to him that they were not going to vote for Barbara Castle's Bill. Without votes like Ron Brown's the Government's supply of lobby fodder would fall below subsistence level.

Because MPs could no longer see how the Government could possibly get the Bill through they began to conclude that Harold Wilson – surely his genius for getting out of awkward corners had not wholly deserted him? – would in the end fudge up some sort of formula with the TUC. Some encouragement for this view was derived from the Prime Minister's May Day speech in which he drew the loudest applause from a faithful audience at the Festival Hall for a renewed, and somewhat extended, pledge to listen to any proposals from the TUC for action which would be "as effective" as the legislation proposed by the Government. There even grew up the idea that Harold Wilson had been cunningly working for a compromise all the while. MPs could not get it out of their heads that he would find a party political answer. They could not grasp the possibility that the Prime Minister, unscathed by the plots against him, might be acting according to conviction and principle.

Thus by the end of May all eyes were turned hopefully upon the extraordinary Trades Union Congress – only the second in the TUC's one hundred year history – which was to be held at Croydon on June 5.

7 *The cart horse snorts and is seen to move*

It was an all Yorkshire affair the protracted negotiations between the Government and the Trades Union Congress, a civil war of the White Roses. Victor Grayson Hardie Feather was Yorkshire through and through, Bradford born and bred. Four years before his birth Harold Wilson's parents had taken the precaution of emigrating from Lancashire to Milnsbridge, a mile outside Huddersfield. Barbara Castle's parents were more careless and she was born three months before they crossed the frontier from Chesterfield, Derbyshire, to Pontefract where she soon developed a life long passion for liquorice allsorts. Harold Wilson and Barbara Castle were both educated at Oxford University and both now sat for Lancashire constituencies but their Yorkshire accents could still thicken on demand and did so in the presence of Vic Feather. All three by blood and upbringing had it in them to be tricky, pig-headed and bloody-minded, although Feather regarded himself as the only *bona fide* professional at the Yorkshire game.

In Victor Grayson Hardie Feather (his names were a recital of the Socialist pioneers) the Government had mistaken its man. He had spent many years at the TUC but he had never become a trade union bureaucrat. He did not share George Woodcock's view that party politics were best left alone by the TUC or that the institutional link between the union movement and the Labour Party was of diminishing importance now that the TUC dealt with governments in its own right. Feather remained a Labour politician. He appeared on Labour Party platforms. He had been treasurer of the London Labour Party. He had been involved in most of the great controversies within the party in which his vast range of contacts and his talent for fixing had been greatly valued by the party leaders. For example, he had played an important if unseen role in recultivating the grass roots on behalf of Hugh Gaitskell at the time of his conference defeat on the bomb issue. He was firmly on the Right of the party and did not have much time for ideological Leftwing Socialists of the Barbara Castle variety, although he had been much influenced and helped in his early career by her father, Frank Betts, the editor of a socialist paper in Bradford. Feather's experience in Labour politics stretched back into the days when the big shots on the General Council – Arthur Deakin, Tom Williamson and Will Lawther – took it to be their function to hold the party steady in the face of ideological assaults.

Thus it was not unreasonable for Harold Wilson to have hoped that Feather would be more disposed to help a Labour Govermennt than George Woodcock. This had been one of the reasons for appointing Woodcock to the Commission on Industrial Relations. But the hopes of Victor Feather were based on a mistaken view both of the man and the office. In the first place Feather could not succeed Woodcock until he had been elected general secretary by the annual Congress. Until that time he was only the acting general secretary. There was not much doubt that he would succeed. He was sixty-one which gave him less than four years to serve before retirement, but the trade unions always like to give Buggins his turn. Moreover, the members of the General Council were well aware of Feather's loyal service to a difficult master and of just how much of the donkey work he had done during Woodcock's nine years. He deserved his reward. And he was exactly the man for the moment. An antidote was needed to the Philosopher King, and Feather, although far from being an uncultivated or uneducated man, was in manner and approach the very opposite of his predecessor. Woodcock was inclined to be gloomy, introspective, lethargic, introverted, grumpy and aloof; Feather was cheerful, extrovert, energetically practical and amenable. Vic was one of the boys. But he was not a man to count his chickens and now that his patience and dedication were on the point of reward, he was taking no risks. He knew what sticklers for form and protocol were the men who would solemnly confer upon him the highest honour of the trade union movement. He knew all that there was to know about their vanities, their jealousies and their pettiness when it came to questions of seniority or precedence. You would no more upstage the general secretary of a powerful British trade union than Callas at the Scala. Therefore he proceeded with the utmost caution. He very carefully did not set up shop in Woodcock's spacious office at Congress House; he took possession of it subject to survey and contract, used it only for receiving visitors and did not hang his picture collection on the walls.

Nothing could be more calculated to upset this racing certainty than for him to let it be thought that he was the Government's man for the job. It would be fatal for him to give the impression that his loyalties were divided between the Labour Party and the TUC. It was vital for him to show that he was the loyal and trusty servant of the General Council of the TUC and none other. Furthermore, he was obliged to take account of the changed political balance of the General Council. It had tipped quite sharply to the left. Hugh Scanlon had replaced Lord Carron at the head of the second largest trade union, the engineers'. Jack Jones was poised to take over the leadership of the giant transport workers' union from Frank Cousins, a much mellowed giant and something of a spent force since returning from his miserable and ineffectual spell as a member of Wilson's Cabinet. Jones was already the real power in the TGWU. Scanlon and Jones represented a new form of militancy. It was a difference more of kind than of degree from the older left-wing militancy of the trade union movement. They were left-wing socialists (indeed, both were former Communists) but they had broken from the tradition of centralism. They knew where the industrial power of the workers now resided – on the shop floor – and it was there they expected it to find its political expression. They were interested in workers' control, a subject for which the TUC over the years had shown a disinterest enlivened only by distaste. Their formative backgrounds were very similar. Scanlon had come recently to the national scene from a long experience as shop steward and district officer in the North-western engineering industry. Jones had been the regional officer of his union in the Midlands, the heart of the British engineering industry and, in particular, the motor industry. Both men were hard trained in the jungle warfare of piecework – the purest example of man-to-man combat in the power struggle between management and men. They were much closer to the anger of the shop floor than were the trade union leaders of the old Establishment; they were more sympathetic towards it and more ready to release it. Socialism, if it came, would result from this struggle, Scanlon and Jones believed, not from cosy chats in London between the trade union movement and what called itself a Labour Government.

In whatever Feather did he had to carry Jones and Scanlon with him. He not only needed their support to cement his own position at the head of the TUC but also in order to conduct a credible diplomacy with the Government. For without their concurrence he could not enter into a bargain worth the paper it was written on. For that reason alone he was going to have to drive a hard bargain in Downing Street. Yet even without these pressures upon him it is unlikely that Feather would have proved very much more amenable. It is a common mistake to assume that because the leaders of the unions owe a double loyalty to the trade union movement and the Labour Party their loyalty is divided and can be played upon. Their first loyalty to their own unions is almost total. Trade unions, no less than public schools, colleges, regiments or even football teams, command a fierce allegiance from the men who devote their lives to them. The pay is usually poor, the conditions of work onerous and the responsibility great; yet over and over again professional trade union leaders have chosen advancement within their own organisation in preference to seats in Parliament, jobs on public boards or full-time Party positions. For example, there were no takers among established general secretaries of appropriate calibre for the general-secretaryship of the Labour Party in 1968. Feather was approached then and had been offered it previously. Yet the uncertain prospect of the general secretaryship of the TUC was more enticing to him than the certainty of the party job. This scale of priorities is reflected in the system whereby the first rank of union leaders attend the General Council and the second rank sit on the National Executive Committee of the Party. The Labour Party, as Bevin said, was created in the bowels of the trade union movement. The trade unions came first – they still came first, the horse before the cart. Political activity was the complement of industrial activity, for governments come and go but trade unionism goes on.

Labour Party card holders, contributors to Party funds, an integral part of its decision-making machinery, the union leaders are for the most part curiously unpolitical animals once ventured beyond their own domain. Respectful of the mysteries of craft – what does a caulker know of a rivet? – they recognise a system of demarcation between themselves and the politicians. As far as Victor Feather was concerned Harold Wilson knew next to nothing about trade unionism and Barbara Castle "couldn't even spell it". But it was not for him to tell them how to suck their political eggs. The politicians must master their own craft; the TUC could only explain to them how the trade unions went about their work – imperfectly, perhaps, but better than any unskilled man or jumped up dilutee of a politician was going to do it for them. "We don't tell each other how to do each other's jobs", said Frank Cousins in 1956. And now, even when it had been recognised that Government, charged with maintaining full employment and promoting economic expansion, had a legitimate interest in the wages question (although it was still not accepted that Government should have any powers in the matter), the unions were still not ready to allow the Government a direct role in the bargaining process itself. This was one demarcation they were not going to relax. Unconstitutional strikes were a problem, that was no longer denied; but it was *their* problem. The political context in which Governments had to operate was only dimly perceived through the blinkers. The union leaders painfully realised the unpopularity of the unions, but they blamed it chiefly on the press and on ignorance. They recognised the need for change, but it could only be brought about in their way, at their pace and in accordance with their own overriding objectives. They found it hard to see that in a modern pluralistic society they had become accountable. The Chinese had for long believed that China occupied the centre of the world, whatever the geographers' maps might say. The British trade unions saw politics as something which went on round them, not as something of which they were a part but not – even under a Labour Government – the point of reference.

The leaders of the TUC approached their dispute with the Government rather as if it were a dispute in a factory between management and workpeoples' representatives. It should be settled between professionals by the time-honoured means of negotiation. Trade union leaders, unlike politicians or diplomats, do not usually act according to general appraisals based on political intelligence and analysis: they act very much according to what they see and hear and know for themselves. The General Council in 1969 seemed to have no very clear assessment either of the political forces which were pushing the Government into trade union legislation or of the political forces which might turn it back. The confrontation was across a table, Ministers (management) on one side, workers (the TUC) on the other – two sides trying to solve a practical problem of industrial relations. The nuts and bolts of it were what concerned the TUC not such extraneous matters as the authority of the Prime Minister, the state of public opinion or foreign confidence in the pound sterling. "What about funeral benefits?" It was in the spirit of this tradition that the TUC now donned its blinkers and lumbered off in the direction of the enemy, a Labour Cabinet rich in Oxford and Cambridge "Firsts" but containing not a single trade unionist of stature.

On learning that the Government was going to legislate in haste Victor Feather's first reaction was to determine to produce an alternative plan as quickly as possible. The Government was demanding action by the TUC against unconstitutional strikes which would be "equally effective and urgent" as the action the Government was going to take by legislation. This was an impossible task for the TUC. At the very first meetings at Number 10, on April 11 and 14, Victor Feather and Sydney Greene, the railwaymen's leader, had made the point that the TUC could not undertake to be equally effective in doing something which it believed would be ineffective. Punishing strikers, it believed would do more harm than good to industrial relations. Nevertheless, the TUC had to have a plan. General secretaries of the TUC are ever looking for ways to enhance the authority of the central trade union body and Feather saw here an opportunity to extend the TUC's influence in ways which were necessary and desirable quite regardless of the Government's requirements. Furthermore he knew the rules of the trade union game and one of the first rules was "Never have a meeting without an agenda". A special meeting of the Congress had to be called now that the Government was proposing to legislate before the annual Congress would be held in September. But it would be worse than useless if it met solely for the purpose of abusing the Government and declaring against the penal clauses; it had to adopt an alternative programme. In any case the TUC had intended to do something about Donovan; what needed to be done now could be presented as an acceleration of what would have been done any way.

One of the reasons Barbara Castle had come round eventually to the idea of an urgent short Bill on industrial relations was her growing belief that the only language the General Council understood was a pistol pointed to its head. She may have been right; since the publication of the Donovan Report in June 1968 the TUC had done next to nothing: now in April 1969, under the threat of legislation, it moved with remarkable alacrity. On the morning of May 12 a document called *Industrial Relations: Programme for Action* was rushed down to Number 10 Downing Street an hour and a half before the General Council trooped in for the first of what were to be six long gruelling encounters with the Prime Minister and the Employment Secretary. "I'll need my large pipe", said the Prime Minister before the meeting began and he was never seen without it at the subsequent encounters.

The TUC's document covered much more ground than was under dispute with the Government. It was a fairly comprehensive follow-through to the Donovan Report. But the two questions in which the Government was interested were (*a*) what action would the TUC take in unconstitutional strikes, and (*b*) what action would it take in inter-union disputes? The answer to the first question was that the TUC was now prepared to intervene in unconstitutional or unofficial disputes on the same basis as it could already intervene in official disputes. That is to say, unions would in future be obliged to inform the General Council of such disputes and the General Council would be entitled to give its "considered opinion and advice" to the organisations concerned. The answer to the second question was that the existing rule of Congress which gave the General Council the power to adjudicate in inter-union disputes, under the ultimate sanction of expulsion from Congress, would be amended so as to make it clear that unions were not entitled to authorise stoppages of work until the General Council had been consulted and were under "an obligation" in the case of an unofficial strike "to take immediate and energetic steps to obtain a resumption of work."

On a hurried first reading of the *Programme for Action* Harold Wilson and Barbara Castle were impressed by the action proposed in the case of inter-union disputes but not at all impressed by the action proposed for dealing with unconstitutional strikes. Castle wanted to know, "What are the unions prepared to do to ensure that their members return to and remain at work during negotiations?" The General Council in its document talked about using its influence, she said, but without a clear definition of this "influence" the proposal was "little more than a vague and pious hope." Feather replied that unions which did not accept the General Council's advice could be reported to Congress, which was a serious matter, and one which unions took seriously. Harold Wilson asked about a situation whereas small group of workers refused to obey their union's instructions to go back to work. To what extent would the TUC insist that unions imposed sanctions against their members in these situations? To what extent would they hold unions accountable for disciplining their members? Feather replied, "The General Council is not trading sanctions with the Government. Unions and their members generally accept the judgement of their peers and immediate threats of sanctions, whether by the Government, by unions or by the TUC, would be self-defeating".

There was a heated intervention from Frank Cousins. The Prime Minister was mistaken, he said, in thinking that legislation or equally effective action by the TUC was essential for the survival of a Labour Government. Another alternative should not be ruled out, namely that another Labour Government could continue in office. This remark was understandably not recorded in the official minutes.

These initial exchanges measured the gap between the Government and the TUC. The Government was demanding, as an alternative to its own penal clauses, some form of automatic penalty – fines or expulsion – against unions or their members who defied the TUC. The General Council was proposing, in the words George Woodcock would have used had he been there, "to do the best we can", in a flexible fashion working by persuasion. That remained essentially the difference throughout the long argument.

However, at its next meeting (on May 15) the General Council tried to do a little better. On the previous day it had received from the Government an uncompromising memorandum which expressed "serious doubts" about the effectiveness of the TUC's proposals and which contained a long list of awkward questions to which the Government would require convincing answers. In response the General Council worked on what Harold Wilson had called "the fuzzy edges" of its document. It moved towards meeting his complaint that the rule concerning unconstitutional strikes was less specific than the rule governing inter-union disputes. Six new explanatory paragraphs were added to the document and Rule 11 of Congress, the rule which concerned industrial disputes, was amended to underline the fact that a union which refused the "assistance or advice" of the General Council could in the last resort be expelled. The additional paragraphs made it clear that a "recommendation" by the General Council was something which unions were expected to obey and which over the years they invariably had obeyed. In seeking to comply with a General Council "recommendation" unions would be expected "to take action within their own rules if necessary."

There was nothing really new here, as Feather himself emphasised in the privacy of the General Council; "no new policy is involved", he said. However, the General Council did make one important tactical decision at this meeting: it decided to make the entire *Programme for Action* conditional on the Government dropping the penal clauses. Feather himself never took this ultimatum very seriously. He believed that the TUC should be taking the steps it was now proposing regardless of what the Government did and purely on their own merits. He was well aware of the danger that unless the trade unions acted to put their own house in order other Governments would come along to administer larger and larger doses of State intervention. But he had to pay a price for the support of Scanlon and Jones and this was the price. It was also because he knew that he must carry them with him in everything he did that he was now taking the entire General Council, an unwieldly body of thirty-nine, along with him to Number Ten. More usually the finance and general purposes committee, the so called "inner cabinet", acts as the General Council's negotiating team. But its membership was according to seniority, not power or ability, and therefore neither Scanlon nor Jones were members.

On May 21 the TUC presented the second edition of its programme and delivered its ultimatum to Harold Wilson and Barbara Castle. The Government had meanwhile undertaken not to produce a Bill before the special Congress at Croydon on June 5 (the Bill was not ready in any case) and it now also undertook not to reach a decision about legislation until the question had been further discussed with the General Council in the light of Croydon. But although there was now more time, the two sides were still no nearer to what Harold Wilson at the previous meeting had called a "copper-bottomed" compromise. "Copper-bottomed" was a nautical expression he had picked up during the merchant navy strike of 1966.

The ground covered at this second meeting between the General Council and the Prime Minister was the same ground covered at the first. One of the most effective weapons in the TUC's armoury is boredom. It has the capacity to deliver boredom by the megaton, the desolation it can inflict on the other side of a negotiation table can be terrible to behold. Many a rapacious capitalist had laid down his arms and put up his money at the rumbling of trade union leaders going nuclear. What a prospect for a Prime Minister to awake to on a summer's morning with the birds singing in St. James's Park – four hours with the General Council! The sight of them shuffling in, settling round the table in strict order of senility – so many of them! Harold Wilson would struggle with matches and pipe trying to remember some of the dreary fellows' names – who was that one, Alf, Bert or yet another Bill? Listening to them – "speaking from long experience" (tendentious reminiscence); "plain words" (cliché); "making it quite clear" (unnecessary repetition); "brief intervention" (long-winded monologue); "point of information" (fatuous question); "expediting the proceedings" (wasting more time); "useful suggestion" (red herring); "summing up" (going over it all again); "valuable progress" (hours wasted); "another meeting?" (Oh God!). "The TUC doesn't like rush", Feather had said. It was a war of attrition; the TUC's tactics: grind the enemy down, wear him to a standstill, bore him into submission.

Harold Wilson on seeing the amended document congratulated the TUC on a very great step forward. In his view they had moved further and faster and more comprehensively than at any time in forty years. (He was later to say this several times in public; it was a mixed compliment.) But the Government was still not convinced that the TUC's proposals for dealing with unconstitutional strikes were adequate, he said. There was still a "missing link", he said, and this was a "guarantee that sanctions, either in the form of fines or, in the last resort, expulsions, would be imposed on union members who refused to return to work or go through procedure." Victor Feather replied that the TUC's proposals had been "pushed to the limits of feasibility." He had a heated exchange with Barbara Castle, which underlined the difference of approach between the TUC and the Government, a difference which went far deeper than the semantic arguments about rules. Feather accused Castle of not being interested in the TUC's alternative. She replied that the Government was not interested in judging the merits of disputes, as the TUC would be doing in its attempts to enforce settlements, but in enforcing a resumption of work and ensuring the continuation of discussion through procedure. Feather replied that this emphasis on getting people back to work, rather than on securing an agreed settlement of a dispute, underlined the fallacies in the Government's whole approach. The aim should be to prevent disputes and, if they arose, to settle them.

The meeting ended as it had begun – in fundamental disagreement. But not before Harold Wilson delivered a stern political warning to the trade union leaders. He had been rattled by this time by the attacks within the party on his leadership. The party managers were warning him of the by now formidable difficulties of carrying through a Bill. He had just been obliged to sack Callaghan from his "inner cabinet." Alarming trade figures had been published that week. The International Monetary Fund was insisting upon stringent conditions for a new stand-by credit. Things were going badly all round. He now said:

"I have to give you my political judgement. You have given your judgment about the industrial implications. But the question at issue really is whether this Labour Government can continue. When I addressed the Parliamentary Labour Party on April 17 and when I informed them of our intention to meet the General Council I said, 'I have to tell you that the passage of this Bill is essential to the Government's continuance in office'."

"In our joint consultation what we are talking about is a deep fundamental split between the two wings of the Movement. This is serious – extremely serious in any circumstances. We all recognise and approach it with that degree of gravity. I believe it means something more – whether this Labour Government or any Labour Government can continue."

The leaders of the General Council were unmoved. The continuance of a Labour Government did not depend on fining strikers. Nonsense. If that was the Government's attitude the dispute could be resolved in one way only – by one side or the other backing down. And with that the TUC leaders returned to Bloomsbury and there decided unanimously to budge no more.

Allowing for an element of psychological warfare at this point – the Croydon Congress was a fortnight away – we should assume that Harold Wilson believed what he said. Not only was his Government at stake but British Social Democracy. For him, no less than for Barbara Castle, the Bill had now become an end in itself, the test of a Labour Government's competence to govern and its ability to "do something" about the trade unions and strikes. The point at issue between the Government and the TUC was whether Parliament legislated penalties against unconstitutional strikers or whether the trade unions legislated penalties against them through their own rules. The insistence which the Prime Minister and Barbara Castle placed on the rewriting of the TUC's rules was the result of their knowing perfectly well that Jack Jones and Hugh Scanlon were interested in the TUC's proposals solely as a device for persuading the Government to abandon the penal clauses. Scanlon's attitude had been made clear at the meeting on May 12 when he had intervened to say, "Let it be clearly understood – we will decide whether action will be taken under our rules or not." The context of that remark made it plain that the "we" was the unions, not the TUC, and Scanlon appeared to be addressing Victor Feather no less than Harold Wilson. The TUC leaders frequently suggested that the Government should take credit for having prodded the TUC into action as a means for gracefully dropping the penal clauses. But the attitudes of Jones and Scanlon convinced the Prime Minister and First Secretary that no undertakings by the TUC would have credibility unless they were embodied concretely in the rules of Congress.

That evening Harold Wilson spent more than a hour with the officers of the trade union group of MPs. He went out of his way to disabuse them of any notion that Barbara was the "hawk" and he the "dove". Whether he believed that a rule of Congress would make much practical difference to the behaviour of the powerful unions led by Jones and Scanlon we may only guess. To some extent it was now a matter of appearances. At the meeting with the General Council the Prime Minister had said he was looking for "a demonstration of will by the unions" – a demonstration. Negotiations can develop a momentum of their own. Words in drafts, and communiqués become fetishes; the negotiators may forget what it was they were originally negotiating about; they become afflicted by a lack of proportion; a comma on a piece of paper becomes like a yard gained in infantry battle fought on thick mud. They can become shell shocked with words, words, words – reduced to gibbering formulae and jargon. It may have been that Harold Wilson's and Barbara Castle's brains got washed in the repetitive flow of their own spoutings until they genuinely mistook the form for the reality. But it is not very likely. For about their political position they were quite realistic: in view of the positions of Jones and Scanlon, they had to have the Bill.

From the very start Victor Feather had been convinced that the Government's motives were political. Too clever by half, that was Harold's and Barbara's trouble. "Ho Ho", he could hear them chortling gleefully, "We've stolen Ted Heath's trousers". Over and over again, in public speeches and in the arguments with Ministers, Feather demanded to know what were the economic reasons and what were the industrial reasons for what the Government was doing and doing in such an indecent hurry? He believed it was doing the wrong thing for the wrong (political) reasons – to appease the middle classes, impress the foreign bankers, put the blame on the workers for the country's difficulties. The TUC was advocating the correct course based on a proper understanding of the facts of industrial life in factory, pit and port. But although he was convinced that the Government's reasons were political he was meticulous in his care not to be drawn into a political campaign against the Government, not at this stage. He kept well clear of Westminster. When the trade union group of the Parliamentary Labour Party asked him to attend one of their meetings, he declined; its officers could visit him in his own office at Congress House, at their request, to hear what the

TUC was thinking and doing. His dealings with Douglas Houghton had been so far at Houghton's initiative. When Feather shared a platform with Wilson at the 50th conference of the Union of Post Office Workers on Sunday, May 11 he said, "The TUC has no hand or part in any political shennanigans at Westminster or anywhere else". He was referring to the attempts to depose Wilson. And it was true. Feather was staying completely out of party politics, not for reasons of high principle but for good practical ones; he was saving his fire. If the Government finally decided to legislate he would then be prepared to launch an all-out political campaign, making use of the trade unions' MPs, taking to political platforms, cracking the trade union purse strings around the Government's ears. But for the time being he was going to play it straight and deal with a Labour Government just as, as TUC general secretary, he would deal with any other government.

Nor did Hugh Scanlon or Jack Jones, the most militant and powerful of the union leaders, become involved in party shennanigans. Their objective was to change the Government's policy not its leader. However, both were prepared to press their opposition to the Government's policy to the limit, and by that they meant the survival of the Government itself. They did not support the call from a few small left-wing unions for a token general strike on May 1. Some 80-90,000 workers did stay away from work on May Day but the only effective strike was the one which stopped the national newspapers. But Jones and Scanlon were prepared, if it became necessary, to declare a cold war against the Government. They had in mind the TUC breaking off diplomatic relations with the Wilson Government, withdrawing its representatives from the scores of joint committees on which they sat from the National Economic Development Council downwards. Scanlon did nothing to interfere with his union's MPs. Jones did remind the TGWU's MPs that the union's sponsoring arrangements would be reviewed, as usual, after the next General Election. He saw no point in sponsoring MPs at Westminster unless they gave support to the union. In April he attended a meeting of the TGWU group in the House of Commons – only one Minister turned up – at which those present unanimously backed the union's line against the Government's. But in general both Scanlon and Jones took the traditional position that politics was politics and trade unionism trade unionism. They were concerned for the future of the Labour Party and the Labour Movement and were more interested in that than in the fate of the

Wilson Government. But for the purpose of changing the Government's policy they looked first to the TUC, not to the politicians at Westminster. There was no suggestion at this stage that they would seek to use their immense industrial power to direct political ends.

June 5 was a brilliant summer's day – good demo' weather. The militants – Communists, Trotskyists, the young anti's (anti-war in Vietnam, anti-war in Biafra, anti-South Africa, anti-Ian Smith, anti-Harold Wilson and, on this day, anti- *In Place of Strife*), together with some ordinary sensible trade unionists, coach loads of shop stewards up for the cup, were gathered in force with their banners and placards outside the Fairfield Hall, Croydon. "Hang Harold Wilson" was one of the less moderate thoughts for this festive day. "No fines on the workers" was the more general theme. The leading figures attending the one-day special Congress ran the gauntlet of cheers and jeers – a rough guide to their place in the spectrum of Labour Movement politics – as they entered the building by avenues mapped out in policemen's blue. The vultures, the cranks, the political litter bugs who thrust obscure pamphlets into unwanting hands, the dedicated undeterrable comrades who sell the *Morning Star*, the unmotivated goofers and loiterers, one or two representatives of the Special Branch no doubt, and the vendors of the early racing editions – all were gathered to honour this great political event.

Inside the hall, where last I had seen a Chekhov play, there was none of the atmosphere of history in the making. The modernity of this theatre, a hygienic laboratory for music, drama and the dance, was unbecoming to the representatives of nine million workers. This hall at Croydon, once a respectable suburb now a thrusting, sprouting concrete patch – a business and shopping centre, almost a city in its own right – had been adopted by the TUC for its annual conference of executives. At this new event in the calendar the professionals set the economic framework for the year's wage bargaining. Croydon thus was the theatre of the new TUC, in contrast, say, with the Opera House, Blackpool, a music hall – home of Ken Dodd, rude diddyman of the north – and the true home of the old TUC. But now Croydon was seeing for the first time the whole Congress, that conglomeration of occupational fiefs, the industrial revolution personified in the assembled presence of twisters and turners, bevellers and beamers, sorters and sawyers, glaziers and grinders, plasterers and polishers, trimmers and tenters, warpdressers and wirepullers. Here in the Fairfield Hall, a place more suitable for a convention of advertising executives – nothing beery about it, the sort of place for "No smoking" – it did not seem very likely that we would witness some great proletarian drama, rather – as in Chekhov – a crumbling, a decay, some nostalgia perhaps.

The silver bell of Congress, the hardwood gavel, the lectern, the bound reports of one hundred Congresses and the thirty-nine members of the General Council were set out on the platform. (A room had also been set aside for their use backstage but not the one whose door was labelled "Quick Change Artistes".) "British trade unionism is once again defending the right of working men and women to work out their own destiny", said John Newton, chairman of the General Council, leader of the tailors and garment workers. "May God and the card vote lead you on the path of righteousness" was his prayer. The card vote was a foregone conclusion. The great unions had already spoken their intentions, a vast majority was arranged – nine votes to one in favour of the General Council and against the Government. And there was very little left to say. It was all over bar the voting before it ever began. Observers from the DEP were present, instructed by Number 10 to report to the Prime Minister on the spirit of the occasion. At lunchtime they returned to town, before the vote was taken, causing TUC leaders to comment that the Government was determined to be unimpressed by the solidarity demonstrated when the cards were counted. They cannot have told Harold Wilson much of use concerning the atmosphere. The Congress was as inspiring as the thud of a rubber stamp.

The General Council's recommendations were neatly capsulised by Victor Feather: "The first expresses our unalterable opposition to statutory financial penalties on work people or on trade unions. The second says that some of the other White Paper proposals could in principle help to improve industrial relations. The third asks you to empower the General Council to go ahead with their own proposals as outlined in the report." There were speeches, then there was lunch, then very soon – after an only brief digestion – there were cries for the vote and getting it over with. We were witnessing, Victor Feather told us, "not a step forward but a great leap forward". And with that the vote was taken. In support of the General Council's *Programme for Action* were 7,908,000 workers – or so said the keepers of their cards – and against were 846,000.

The Prime Minister, however, was not impressed.

8 *Mr. Solomon Binding saves the day*

WHILE the "great leap forward" was being made at Croydon our heroine was far away. Her exact whereabouts were a closely guarded State secret, which did not prevent them from being shortly revealed. She was cruising in the Mediterranean on a yacht loaned by Charles Forte the restaurateur. Among the party was Richard Crossman. On June 5 somebody (could it have been the mischievous Dick?) had turned off the master switch of the generator which operated the ship-to-shore radio telephone. From ship Barbara Castle was trying to get through to her department in London to discover what was going on. From shore Roy Hattersley, the Parliamentary Under-Secretary at the DEP, was trying to reach her in order to stop the press statement which the Government was proposing to issue following the special Trades Union Congress. No communication was effected.

The press statement came as a shock to the TUC leaders and Labour backbenchers. Its tone was quite uncompromising. It was issued by the DEP, but was effectively the work of Number 10. Later, at a party meeting, the Prime Minister took full responsibility for it. It said:

"As the Government have made clear in their exchanges over the past weeks with the TUC, they recognise that the General Council's proposals are a major advance and in particular those for dealing with inter-union disputes now seem broadly satisfactory. But the Government have considerable reservations about the effectiveness of the General Council's proposals for dealing with unconstitutional strikes and, in particular, about the proposed arrangements for ensuring that awards and recommendations made after a TUC inquiry into such disputes are implemented by unions and their members."

Here was not a calory of additional warmth. Hopes that a stirring display of trade union determination and responsibility at Croydon would give the Prime Minister the opportunity to begin lifting himself gently from the hook were now dashed. The message was clear: Harold Wilson intended to press on regardless.

In fact he had decided upon this before the Croydon Congress had even taken place. He had been much affected by a top secret conclave which had taken place the previous week-end at Chequers, the Prime Minister's country residence. Barbara Castle broke her Mediterranean holiday. A deputy secretary from her department, Conrad Heron, and her private secretary, Douglas Smith, made assignation with her in a café in Naples and spirited her home. Hugh Scanlon was addressing a meeting in the Midlands. "The time for talking is over" he declared and then climbed into the car which bore him to Chequers for what were perhaps the most consequential talks in the whole affair. The exclusive company consisted of Harold Wilson, Barbara Castle, Victor Feather, Jack Jones and Scanlon. No officials were present. The meeting took place at Feather's initiative. He hoped that an intimate and frank encounter with Jones and Scanlon would convince the Prime Minister that there was no possibility of the TUC going beyond its *Programme for Action.* Therefore he hoped that the confrontation would persuade the Prime Minister to use the occasion of the Croydon conference to abandon the penal clauses. This turned out to be Feather's one major miscalculation: the confrontation had exactly the opposite effect on the Prime Minister. Wilson was enraged at the intransigence and arrogance of the two union leaders. One of the exchanges went like this:

Scanlon: "Prime Minister, we don't want you to become another Ramsay Macdonald."

Wilson: "I have no intention of becoming another Ramsay Macdonald. Nor do I intend to be another Dubcek. Get your tanks off my lawn Hughie!"

The meeting at Chequers convinced the Prime Minister that no undertaking by the TUC would be worth the paper it was written on unless Jones and Scanlon could be pinned down. It determined him to put them in their place if he could. The next morning, after Hugh Scanlon had graciously recorded his appreciation of Chequers in the visitors' book, the Prime Minister sat on the lawn fulminating against the arrogance of these powerful men. The result was that at 8.30 p.m. on Tuesday, June 3, Feather received a letter from the DEP which he took to be a deliberate attempt to sabotage the Congress at Croydon two days later. The conclave at Chequers was also the cause of the unfriendly press statement which on the Thursday was the Government's answer to Feather's "great leap forward".

The letter contained another list of detailed points which the Government would want to discuss again with the General Council after the Croydon meeting. It repeated the Government's "considerable reservations" about the TUC's *Programme for Action.* It struck Feather as being a petty, spiteful and wilfully ignorant document. He feared that if he communicated its contents to the General Council Jack Jones and Hugh Scanlon might seize the opportunity to withdraw their support for the TUC's *Programme for Action.* And he suspected that this was exactly what the Government intended. Therefore, he indicated only that he had received a letter from the First Secretary, the contents of which he need not at that moment put before them. It was not until after the vote at Croydon when the General Council met back stage that he read out extracts from the offensive letter.

Hopes that a compromise was on the way were thus quickly dashed. The letter from the DEP and the press statement of June 5 indicated that Croydon had solved nothing, that the battle would go on. Hopes of a compromise had been excited by the very fact that the Government had postponed its decision on legislation until after the Congress. It was hardly conceivable that having once received the endorsement of Congress for its programme the General Council would agree to further amendments of substance. The vote at the Congress could hardly have been more impressive. Moreover, the parliamentary session was running out. It seemed well-nigh impossible now for the Government to legislate in the current session. Opposition to the penal clauses from Labour backbenchers had reached a formidable proportion. Surely Harold Wilson would now beat his tactical retreat? But to the great alarm of MPs who had read the situation in this way the Prime Minister now proceeded to do the very opposite. He escalated the confrontation.

On the very night of the Croydon Congress he attended a dinner to celebrate the seventy-fifth birthday of Lord Thomson of Fleet, publisher of newspapers and printer of money, proprietor now of *The Times* among many other journals. The vulgar jollity of this occasion at which the attractions included bagpipes, a hilly-billy band, Lord Thomson cutting the cake with a claymore and the presence of Princess Margaret, was punctured by the Prime Minister's saying:

"It was a predecessor of mine, Stanley Baldwin, who referred to certain press lords who were exercising a certain degree of arrogance in political matters, that they were asserting their claim to power without responsibility. That claim is being reasserted now, not by press lords but by another estate of the realm. If that is the claim, it will get Baldwin's answer."

That was Harold Wilson's after dinner response to the "great leap forward". Power without responsibility, Baldwin had actually said, was "the prerogative of the harlot through the ages". No doubt the Prime Minister had Jones and Scanlon foremost in mind when he turned this contemptuous stricture onto the trade union movement, the Labour Party's lifelong partner. It may have been true but it was nevertheless insulting. (The Prime Minister might also have recalled the words of a more recent predecessor, Harold Macmillan, who at the time of the Profumo affair had declared that he was not going to be brought down "by a couple of tarts". Macmillan did not long survive.)

Parliament returned from its Whitsun Recess on the Monday after the Congress at Croydon. On the same day negotiations resumed between the Government and the TUC. In spite of their shock at the tone of the Prime Minister's response to the Congress, the resumption of talks with the TUC kept alive the hopes of MPs that Wilson was still playing for a draw, that after a decent show of purposiveness, and perhaps some face-saving gesture by the TUC, peace would break out within the Labour Movement. However, the week-end which intervened between Croydon and the return of the General Council to Downing Street served to harden still further Harold Wilson's resolve.

He spent it making a tour of the North-East. Ever since his days at the Board of Trade under the Attlee Government he had taken an intense interest in regional policy. An inveterate provincial, he had never throughout his political career come to love or admire, or perhaps even really to know, the metropolis. London, certainly Westminister – although he did love Parliament as an institution – was for him "the hot house", an unhealthy place in which flies in the form of political correspondents buzzed around the withering plants uprooted from their natural soil in the constituencies, the shires and the cities. His deep prejudice was for the sticks of the country against the smoke of the big city. An ancestor had been the founder of the *Manchester Guardian* and, according to his biographer, Leslie Smith, for succeeding generations of his family, it came "second only to the Bible in its influence". Harold Wilson continued to be a devoted reader of that newspaper although it too had gradually transplanted itself into the now more fertile south. Nevertheless, he remained strongly disposed towards the dictum, that what Manchester thinks today, London will think tomorrow. What

London thought today, city of pundits and opinion formers, was almost bound to be wrong. For many Londoners the north began at Hatfield, for Harold Wilson the people began at the River Trent. Moreover, the resurgence of regional life, the recovery of the regional economies was the aspect of his Government's progress in which he took the most confident pride. On practically every other score his policies were under fire, his record of accomplishment the subject of complaints, criticisms and sneers, but in the regions he at least could see the "New Britain" he had promised in 1964 beginning to take shape, in the new factories, the new motorways, the new theatres, galleries and civic centres. A walking Baedeker of the changing industrial north – his accent slipped the minute he crossed the Trent – he drew his inspiration from what he saw and heard there and from his mind's picture of it as he sat a lonely and, he often brooded, much maligned man in Number 10, Downing Street, London, S.W.1.

That weekend, before embarking on a fateful course, he consulted the North of England. He went first to Tyneside. He visited the head-quarters of the Amalgamated Society of Boilermakers, Shipwrights, Blacksmiths and Structural Workers, the chief union of the shipyards and, perhaps, of all the British unions the closest still in spirit to the industrial revolution and the exclusive, closed societies of Disraeli's "Coningsby". There he was greeted by Danny McGarvey, a Glaswegian whose voice was reputed to carry from the Tyne to the Clyde, although a good deal of what he said failed to carry from the nineteenth to the twentieth century. On the previous day McGarvey down at Croydon had accused Harold Wilson of destroying the Labour Movement, but now he was the courteous host to a Labour Prime Minister. The encounter was a reminder of the complacent bonds which united the Labour Movement, its political and its industrial wings, whatever the quarrels which took place in the family. Wilson trudged through the shipyards. He participated in a question and answer session with shop stewards. It was poorly attended and not a success, but imagine! – here was a Prime Minister, the leading citizen, successor of Pitt, Gladstone, Disraeli and Churchill, chatting away, one northerner to another, with real live shop stewards in a real clanking shipyard. The more cut off a public man becomes from the daily world the more he is moved and impressed by his contacts with it; no amount of political intelligence, reports and opinion polls, are substitute for a politician's personal encounters: for all the social science tools which assist them nowadays in their trade they remain impressionists – one opinion from an aproned housewife on a scrubbed and chalked doorstep is worth a thousand Dr. Gallups. As representatives of the people they claim some mystic communion with the will of the general populace. Harold Wilson underwent a revelatory experience of this kind the next day in Barnsley.

Barnsley is Yorkshire and Barnsley is coal mining. At no shrine could Harold Wilson's faith have received stronger succour. Yorkshire miners – they knew better than the cocktail party set in London. What is more he was there not to address the men of Barnsley, admirable folk that they were, but the people who really ran the world in those parts, their women. And from beyond Barnsley they came, from all over his beloved and true county, for a great rally of Yorkshire Labour Women. Harold Wilson was cheered and fêted in the streets; at the rally he received a tumultuous reception. In need of reassurance he was reinforced in his belief that the people, the real people of England, the Labour people, the wise, right, loyal, decent people of the North were with him.

The opinion polls were still confirming these personal impressions. The mood at Westminster on the trade union question was not representative of the country. Nor was it only the polls. The applause meter in his head at Barnsley confirmed the conclusions he had drawn from the daily postbag at Number 10. A Prime Minister receives a vast correspondence from the public. Throughout the row with the trade unions his mail, all carefully analysed – the cranks and the anonymous weeded out by his staff – had indicated an overwhelming support for the Government's policy. It probably did reflect the true state of opinion in the country. For Douglas Houghton's postbag told the same story – in his case 80 per cent of correspondents in favour of the Government's line, only 20 per cent against it. Transport House was picking up similar vibrations. The Labour Party general secretary, Harry Nicholas, a long-service official of the TGWU, started out not only a convinced opponent of *In Place of Strife* but convinced also that it would inflict tremendous damage upon the Labour Party in the country. But the more he travelled around the country that summer the more he became aware that the alarm at Westminster, the rows in the national executive and the battle stations at Congress House, did not accurately reflect the mood in the constituencies. Even some of the trade union leaders who were violently opposed to the Government's policy were prepared to concede, in private, that there was a great deal of support for it among their members. Jack Jones told me: "If you go around asking my members if they are in favour of something being done about unofficial strikes you will find large numbers of them in support, especially their womenfolk who are sick and tired of stoppages and lost wages. But you try fining a man, bringing in the law, and a different type of loyalty starts to operate. Then you'll see the old working class solidarity at work. Workpeople are in favour of doing something about unofficial strikes providing you don't actually do it to them when they are on strike for something they believe in. I don't claim that the Government's proposals are all that unpopular; I just know that they won't work".

In his speech at Barnsley, where he was so well received that Saturday, June 7, Harold Wilson began by stressing the "positive progress", already made in improving industrial relations. But, he added sternly, "one problem remains: the unconstitutional strike where perhaps a handful of wreckers can wreck a vital sector of our export trade. This has happened this week. (There was a strike going on at Leyland motors.) This problem must be solved. *It will not be solved by any abdication by the Government of its responsibilities, nor would it be solved by any threatened abdication by the TUC of theirs*".

And it was in this spirit of determination to govern and to be seen to be governing, fortified by the women of his native Yorkshire, that Harold Wilson acted the next day.

The Inner Cabinet met on the Sunday night and the next morning the Prime Minister told the General Council that he was not yet able to give the TUC a firm indication of what the Government would do following the Croydon Congress. But, the Cabinet would have to decide "in the next few days" whether to legislate and if so in what form. The TUC's proposals for dealing with unconstitutional strikes still lacked "credibility" he said. Since the discussions between the Government and the TUC had begun, he pointed out, there had been 241 unofficial strikes. He made the curious suggestion that the penal clauses might be included in Government legislation but "never applied". Consultations with the TUC could continue during the passage of the interim Bill through Parliament and it could be amended, or certain of its provisions dropped, as it went along. Alternatively the penal clauses could be amended or repealed when the major Bill was brought forward in the next session. He also said that the Cabinet would be looking at alternative forms of sanctions. It would look again at the Donovan Report, it might consider giving some form of statutory backing to the TUC's procedures for dealing with strikes. But on none of this was he specific. He continued to insist that the TUC should strengthen the *Programme for Action.* Those were his terms for dropping the penal clauses. Feather replied that the TUC would not enter into promises which it could not redeem.

They met again on Wednesday, June 11. "We are still a long way apart", said the Prime Minister. Before the penal clauses could be dropped the Government would have to be more satisfied than at present about the effectiveness, "and the saleability to the country", of the General Council's proposals. There were now, he said, three possibilities: the first was that the General Council agreed to strengthen its rule for dealing with unconstitutional strikes; the second was for the Government to legislate alternative sanctions based on the Donovan Report; and the third was for it to legislate the penal clauses but with delayed effect. If there was no agreement on either the first or second course then the third was the most likely decision of the Government. He went so far as to suggest that delaying the operation of the penal clauses until it was seen how the TUC's plan would work was as good as dropping them altogether.

Victor Feather claimed that the words "advice and guidance" which appeared in the Congress rule concerning strikes (Rule 11) were recognised trade union terminology which had the same force as the words "award or recommendation" – which appeared in the rule concerning inter-union disputes (Rule 12). If that was the case, said the Prime Minister, what was the objection to spelling it out in Rule 11? He didn't give advice and guidance to his officials if he wanted something done – he instructed them. The discussions continued between the Prime Minister, Barbara Castle and their officials and, a sub-committee of the General Council on which Hugh Scanlon and Jack Jones were included. The TUC offered to circularise unions explaining what would be expected of them under Rule 11. The Prime Minister said that he could not see why if the TUC was prepared to make what he assumed would be "a binding statement of intent" about the operation of Rule 11, it was not prepared to change the rule itself. He submitted to the TUC leaders the draft of a rule which would be satisfactory to the Government.

The next day they met again. The General Council first met alone, at 6.30 p.m. in Downing Street. It determined not to budge. It would not become the disciplinary body which Barbara Castle was demanding; it would not have *her* legislation in *its* rules. It rejected the rule change proposed by the Government. Then the whole Council met with Harold Wilson and Barbara Castle. The Prime Minister began by announcing that the Cabinet had given its full support to the rule change proposed by the Government and that that was the condition for dropping the penal clauses. What it boiled down to was, "If the General Council will agree to legislate the Government will agree not to legislate". If the General Council could not accept that then at the next meeting – arranged for the following Wednesday, June 18 – he would have to discuss with the TUC the form of the Government's legislation. There was "no possibility" of agreement, Harold Wilson emphasised, unless the TUC committed itself to a rule change. The meeting ended with him saying that the Government wanted to see definite rules, not pious intentions, and that the Government could not carry on credibly unless the country was satisfied that positive action had been taken. It was 11.35 p.m. when the talks broke down. Progress had been "virtually nil" said a gloomy Feather on the doorstep. "I thought there was more hope a week ago", he added. The TUC leaders went home that night believing that legislation by the Government was now inevitable.

The sight of the General Council trudging in and out of Number 10 during this week kept alive the hopes for a settlement at Westminster. The political correspondent of *The Times* reported that on the Wednesday night, "Very few Labour politicians doubted that a compromise is now nearly in reach. Indeed one or two cynical Labour MPs who are disenchanted with Mr. Wilson and Mrs. Castle were saying that the whole long drawn-out drama had been calculated from the beginning". The TUC leaders, however, formed a very different impression from their three days of protracted argument with the Prime Minister and First Secretary. They were convinced that Harold Wilson was negotiating for a breakdown. They believed that he was driven on to this by Barbara Castle sitting at his elbow. They did not believe that he was seriously interested in a compromise, but was merely preparing the political ground for legislation. After the first meeting one member of the General Council said, "Harold looked tired and drawn. There was something the matter with his right eye. It was drooping and showing too much white which is a sign of mental fatigue. At one point he said, 'Well, that sounds all right to me . . .' but Barbara nudged him. At another point he said, 'I'm bewildered by all this'. He looked to me like a man under her spell".

Victor Feather stayed behind and drank some brandy with the Prime Minister after one of these meetings. Late at night Harold Wilson accused him of placing the Government in a serious position, one which threatened its survival. "You would have given more to the Tories than you are giving to me", accused Wilson angrily. "If I was playing the Tories I would have called for the new ball by now", replied the captain of Yorkshire.

What was Harold Wilson really after? No longer by this time something "equally effective and urgent" as the Government's proposed legislation but something which could be made to look equally effective and urgent. This was apparent from what he actually said to the General Council. He was worried about "saleability to the country" – he used that very expression. He was ready to consider other forms of legislation providing the Government could be seen to be legislating in some form on the trade union question. He was offering, in effect, to legislate the penal clauses now but to remove them from the statute book later on the grounds that the TUC's endeavours had made them no longer necessary. He was offering not to legislate at all if the TUC would legislate through its rules. But only "legislation" by the TUC would be credible as a substitute for legislation by the Government – "a binding declaration of intent" would not do. Harold Wilson *did* want a compromise but it had to be a saleable compromise. And that meant that the authority which the TUC would exercise over such as Jones and Scanlon had to be credible.

Did he think he would get a compromise? By then probably not. Certainly Barbara Castle did not believe so. She remained convinced that there would have to be legislation and that it would have to contain penal clauses. She said as much at the final meeting. For the Government to drop the penal clauses, she told the TUC, would be interpreted as "capitulation". The Government was prepared to face that only if the TUC was willing to take equally effective action. By then she knew there was no chance of it doing so. In all the semantic contortions of the three long encounters one fact stood out: the TUC would not after Croydon make further changes in its rules, it would not "legislate", it would not do the only thing which could get Harold Wilson and Barbara Castle off the hook. Therefore, she and the Prime Minister were all the time preparing their fall-back position. They would be able to report to the Cabinet that they had tried everything, literally everything. They had offered to drop the penal clauses. All they had demanded in exchange was that a form of words, all of which were already to be found in the TUC's document and which were no different in essence from those contained in the circular which the TUC was offering to send out to unions, should be incorporated in the TUC's rules. Surely that was not unreasonable. They had offered to put the penal clauses in deep freeze; they had hinted that they might be left for ever on ice. They had leant over backwards to find some alternative form of sanctions, but the TUC was interested in none. They had delayed decision beyond the eleventh hour and parliamentary time was running out. Could they do more? The credibility of the Government was at issue. The trades unions were refusing to help the Government in its predicament. The Government could not in these circumstances afford to "capitulate" whatever the merits now of the arguments about how best to deal with strikes.

There is no doubt that Barbara Castle was prepared to resign on this issue. She too had been recently fortified in her belief that the country and many rank-and-file trade unionists were behind her. On the Wednesday morning she had dashed down to Brighton where she had made what she believed was probably the best speech of her career. She was addressing the annual conference of the National and Local Government Officers' Association. Hostile resolutions were down against *In Place of Strife*. Yet her passionate explanation of her Socialist policy for industrial relations, for strengthening not weakening the unions, and for enabling them to play their part in a constructive partnership with a Labour Government, had won her a great standing ovation from the thousand delegates. The people were with her. She was also convinced that Harold Wilson was with her. She believed that he too would resign rather than accept a compromise which would destroy his credibility. He had stuck with her throughout. He had committed himself totally to her policy, sometimes, she thought, recklessly. After the Croydon Congress he had moved still further out onto the limb. This was not the behaviour of a man who was intending to sell out. She was convinced therefore that their suicide pact would stand the test. In any case how could he survive her own resignation? She could see the scene as she rose like Joan of Arc from below the gangway to make her resignation speech. Harold Wilson could never get away with a compromise which was branded by her as a sell-out. But she still could not believe it would come to this. Nor did the Prime Minister. The party in the past had always responded when it really came to the crunch and this was a crunch like none before. This time there would be no silly threats about dissolving Parliament. He would be saying calmly to the Cabinet, and to the party, that as far as he was concerned there remained no alternative: either the Government must exercise its authority or he could no longer lead it. He would go quietly if that was what they wished. But he and she continued to believe that if it came to this, neither the Cabinet nor the party would be ready to write their own writs of execution.

On Thursday, June 12, the night the talks with the TUC broke down, MPs were at Westminster in force waiting around for an all-night sitting on the Divorce Bill. Procedural questions delayed the opening of the debate until 1 a.m. The first to see the shocking news coming over the tapes just before midnight was John Horner, a Left-wing MP sponsored by the Fire Brigades Union. He dashed with the news to Douglas Houghton who was presiding over a meeting of the Liaison Committee. With so many Members in the House with nothing to do it was easy for the party officers quickly to take the temperature of the party. When they had done so a letter was sent through the night to Number 10 requesting an urgent meeting with the Prime Minister. The meeting took place at 11.30 the next morning. It was Friday the thirteenth. The party officers were informed of the TUC's readiness to send out a circular of clarification but of its refusal to make further changes to its rules. They were left with the impression that the Government would go ahead with legislation. Once again Houghton warned the Prime Minister of the feeling in the party that the difference between the Government and the TUC was not worth the political damage which would be caused by forcing the issue. Once more he warned the Government that a Bill could not be passed by Parliament in the current session.

For Victor Feather it had been a deeply depressing week. Until just before the Croydon Congress he had been optimistic about a settlement. Now he was deeply gloomy and, what was more, angry. He had been tempted during the Downing Street talks to break them off. The Government seemed to have no interest in a settlement. He was convinced that the penal clauses could not work. Why not let this obstinate and stupid Labour Government learn its lesson the hard way? Let it legislate its penal clauses; it would soon discover how useless they were. The first time the Government tried to impose fines on a determined body of strongly organised workers it would quickly discover how penal clauses made industrial relations worse not better. But another voice in Feather's head told him that he must go on talking. If the law was brought into disrepute in this way the trade unions, who live under the hostile gaze of the press, would be brought into greater disrepute. Inevitably the unions would get the blame for the failure of the law and the stupidity of the Government. Then the cry would go up for still more draconian measures against the unions. It was the TUC's duty to keep trying. He tucked in his chin and determined to play a captain of

Yorkshire's innings.

After the breakdown on Thursday night he travelled by sleeper to the North. On Friday he spoke at the annual conference of the National Union of Tailors and Garment Workers. For the first time he warned of industrial disorder if the Government persisted. He said, "the legislation itself will cause protest strikes as a matter of principle and it will do nothing – literally nothing – to get at the real root causes of strikes". The next day he flew out to Geneva for a weekend of conferences. He was a worried man now, bruised a little by the Prime Minister's late night wigging. For the first time in the whole affair Feather now took the initiative in contacting Douglas Houghton. Houghton had in any case been trying to track him down but did not know that he was in Geneva. They spoke on the telephone. Houghton was more confident than Feather. He was convinced by now that Wilson could not carry the party and he had begun to doubt whether he could carry the Cabinet. Moreover, he informed Feather, the Liaison Committee was active.

The decisive step was taken by the Liaison Committee on the Monday. The fateful meeting of the Cabinet had been fixed for the next day, June 17. Wilson was down in Eastbourne making a speech to the conference of the Socialist International. The Liaison Committee, or at least its four elected representatives, had for some while been discussing how they could make a more positive impact on the Government. They felt that the Government regarded them merely as errand boys for delivering messages to the party, they felt that their side of the story was not getting through to the Government. They considered trying to by-pass the Prime Minister by addressing a letter on behalf of the party to each member of the Cabinet individually. This was rejected on grounds of constitutional impropriety. But a letter to the Prime Minister was drawn up and despatched to him in the hope that he would lay it before the Cabinet – although he is believed not to have done so. There was nothing very new in its contents – there was not anything very new to say by now. The letter once more drew attention to the state of opinion in the party, it expressed the desire for unity, it argued that the gap between the Government and the TUC was too small to justify splitting the movement. It emphasised that these sentiments were widely held in the party and shared by many of the Government's most consistently loyal supporters. However, the importance of the letter lay in not what it said but the authority it carried. It was a formal communication from the party to the Prime Minister. For the first time in the affair the Liaison Committee was acting officially and collectively, not simply leaving its chairman to report its views verbally to the Prime Minister. And most important of all, Robert Mellish, the Government Chief Whip, was present at the meeting and endorsed the decision to send the letter and its contents. Harold Wilson received it in the early hours of the Tuesday morning on which his Cabinet was to meet.

The timetable of Tuesday, June 17, was as follows:

9.30 – 10.30	Meeting of the Inner Cabinet.
10.30 – 1.10	Cabinet meeting at Number 10, Downing Street.
3.15 – 3.30	Prime Minister's Questions in the House of Commons.
4.30 – 7.15	Cabinet Meeting at the House of Commons.
7.30 – 9.15	Prime Minister attends meeting of trade union group of MPs.

At question time Harold Wilson said, "If the Government, having regard to the tremendous advance the TUC has made, should drop the idea of legislation in that form (i.e., penal clauses), it would be necessary for the TUC themselves to legislate through their rules". The Government's position apparently remained unchanged. Yet by that time, as he appeared coolly at the Despatch Box, Harold Wilson was fighting for his political life.

The Inner Cabinet that morning had quickly disposed of the possibilities of alternative sanctions. The suggestion for removing the legal immunity from unofficial strikers so that they could be sued in the civil courts was rejected as it had been when Donovan first proposed it. The senior Ministers felt it was far too late in the day to propose new schemes. The disqualification of unofficial strikers from social security benefits or entitlement to redundancy pay – which had been canvassed in the press – was not even discussed. The Inner Cabinet agreed that the Prime Minister should be authorised to inform the TUC that unless it was prepared to make the changes in rule proposed by the Government, the Government would be obliged either to legislate the conciliation pause on a reserve basis (according to the jargon, in "deep freeze") or would legislate so that fines fell upon trade unions instead of upon their members.

The meeting of the full Cabinet began with the Prime Minister reporting on all that had passed with the TUC. He gave it as his judgement that the credibility of the Government required it to legislate if the TUC would not legislate through its own rules. He proposed that he should inform the TUC of the Cabinet's decision to this effect the next day. Barbara Castle followed in total support for this line. The Prime Minister then moved to consult his Cabinet colleagues in the usual fashion. But for once he was cut short. The Chief Whip is not a member of the Cabinet although he attends its meetings. Normally he does not speak unless spoken to or requested by the Prime Minister to make a contribution. But Robert Mellish is not a man to stand on constitutional formality. The scene now resembled the interruption of the preacher in the dockyard church when, in the words of the old seamen's song, "Up jumped Jack, in the third row back" and mouthed some dreadful obscenity. Bob Mellish, the dockers' friend from Bermondsey, now intervened, uninvited, beginning with words to this effect: "Prime Minister, before you consult your colleagues of the Cabinet I feel you and they should hear what your Chief Whip has to say. . . ." He went on to speak the blunt truth as he saw it. There was not a hope of this measure passing, the party would not stand for it, the loyalists were in revolt, there was hardly a supporter left for the penal clauses. He could not get a Bill upstairs to committee; he could take no responsibility for what might happen if it was taken on the floor of the House like the Parliament Bill. There was no hope of passing the Bill this session now that it had been left so late. The split in the movement was fundamental and serious. MPs could no longer see any important difference between the Government and the TUC. Croydon had convinced them that the fight was no longer worthwhile. In short the penal clauses should be dropped.

Mellish's unscheduled contribution had a powerful effect on the Cabinet. Here was the Government's Chief Whip, the Prime Minister's appointed agent, an experienced party man speaking within his own area of knowledge and responsibility and laying the unpleasant facts on the line. Amazingly Harold Wilson in appointing him had never once inquired about his views on the union question. Mellish from the beginning had regarded the penal clauses as nonsense; he knew what would happen if the Government tried to fine his dockers down in Bermondsey. He had taken on the Whip's job, at a drop in salary, because the Prime Minister had asked him to do a job for the party. Harold Wilson was the Prime Minister and Mellish would serve him loyally and honourably, but that did not change his opinion of him. He was in a strong position: having sacked one Chief Whip Wilson could not sack another. So Mellish now gave it him straight in the presence of the Cabinet.

His unscheduled intervention had a powerful effect. Several

Ministers began their contributions: "In view of what the Chief Whip has said. . . ." Harold Wilson watched his Cabinet crumble before his eyes. Ted Short, a former Chief Whip, endorsed Mellish's judgement. Peter Shore, his closest protégé, deserted him. Judith Hart, recently promoted, gave the impression that she would resign. Roy Mason, the only *bona fide* manual trade unionist in the Cabinet, played an influential part in the argument. Cledwyn Hughes, the Minister of Agriculture, was another to desert his Master. Wilson acidly reminded them that none would be sitting where they were if it wasn't for him; but he could not stop the retreat. These Ministers and others swung over to support James Callaghan, Richard Crossman, Anthony Crosland and Richard Marsh – all of whom had long opposed the Wilson-Castle policy. Crossman having been the leading exponent of the "let's get it over with" school in April was now talkingly alarmedly about a "1931 situation" Finally, Roy Jenkins broke from his concordat with Barbara Castle. The Cabinet was putting the Prime Minister in an impossible position, the Chancellor conceded, but he could no longer support them. As one colleague put it later, "Roy slid elegantly onto the fence". At the end Wilson and Castle were virtually isolated.

Harold Wilson was quiet in the way that he is when he is really angry. The Cabinet was refusing to authorise him to threaten the TUC with legislation. It wanted him to settle on whatever terms he could obtain from the General Council the next day. Wilson refused to be so instructed. "You can go and tell them Jim" he said. To each suggested recipe for appeasement he replied obstinately, "All right, but you'll have to send somebody else. I'm not going on that basis". Callaghan, for his part, sought to assure Wilson of his complete loyalty if he consented to drop the penal clauses – the leadership question would be closed. And that was how it remained at the end – a failure to agree between Prime Minister and Cabinet. The Prime Minister would not consent to meet the General Council under orders to settle: the Cabinet would not authorise him to inform the General Council that unless they agreed the rule change there would be legislation. If he returned to the Cabinet the next day without a settlement he could expect to be defeated. James Callaghan stood to become Prime Minister.

Deserted in this manner by his colleagues, a Prime Minister with the support neither of his Cabinet nor his party, Harold Wilson went straight to a meeting of the trade union group of MPs. He spoke to them for forty minutes, without saying anything, and he answered questions for another hour, without giving anything away. If any doubt remained in his mind about the state of opinion in the party this meeting should have dispelled it. It bore out every word that Mellish had said at Cabinet. At question time earlier Jack Ashley had declared, "Some of us who supported the White Paper on industrial relations believe an entirely new situation exists. The Government have persuaded the TUC to take action on unofficial strikes". Now at the meeting of the trade union group Ken Lomas dropped out, so did John Hynd. These three trade union MPs had been among the very few who had been prepared to speak up for the Wilson-Castle policy. Now there was nobody.

Back at Number 10 Wilson let off steam. The word got round that night, "Don't worry. The little man's not going to go". His lusty determination to wreak retribution on his enemies did not suggest that he intended to lay down the power of patronage and punishment.

The news of the Prime Minister's position spread fast that night along the grapevine which linked the Cabinet Room with Congress House. Houghton met secretly with Victor Feather as they had arranged on the telephone from Geneva. He warned him that in the morning the TUC would probably be presented with proposals which it would not spend more than ten minutes upon. (That was the choice between the conciliation pause in deep freeze or fines on unions as an alternative to fines against strikers.) Feather gathered how weak the Prime Minister's position was. Houghton appealed to him to do all he could to reunite the Movement and save the Government, for Houghton believed that the Prime Minister might be forced to resign the next evening. People began to rush round wondering how to stop Callaghan. There was talk of drafting Denis Healey as a compromise candidate around whom the party might unite, but the Defence Secretary was far away in Asia. Barbara Castle went to bed that night wondering if it might not be for the last time as Her Majesty's First Secretary of State and Secretary of State for Employment and Productivity. She still believed that it might be Harold Wilson's last night as the tenant of Number 10, Downing Street.

At 10.30 the next morning the General Council came into the State dining room at Number 10 for the last time. The insiders had a pretty good idea of the Prime Minister's position. The ones who knew said nothing. He knew that they knew, they knew that he knew that they knew. But Harold Wilson gave no clue to his predicament. In Aneurin Bevan's famous phrase he had come "naked into the conference chamber", but nobody noticed the Emperor's new clothes; he was as bouncy as ever and still smoking the specially large pipe. He opened boldly: If the situation which had been reached the previous Thursday night represented the TUC's last work, he said, then a very serious situation would arise. If the General Council could not agree in any circumstances to any change in Rule 11 the Government had to consider what form their legislation would take. There were two possibilities but before he mentioned them he wished to discuss once more the situation which had arisen at their last meeting. If that marked the end of the road it meant a deep split in the Movement, running from top to bottom. One certain consequence would be to put the Tories in a strong position just as there was the prospect of the situation improving for the Government. The Government was prepared to drop the penal clauses if the General Council would agree to make a change in Rule 11. The proposed rule change did no more than give effect to what was already stated in the *Programme for Action*. The General Council had offered to circularise a note of clarification but he had said that this was not sufficient. That remained the Government's position. But before he indicated the two possible forms of legislation he wished to ask the General Council once more to consider changing the rule.

Feather knew that he had no need to budge. He repeated the offer of a circular. Harold Wilson repeated firmly that the Government would drop the penal clauses if the rule was changed but not otherwise. Feather once more tried to explain that what mattered was Congress policy; rules were incidental, he said. He cited the Bridlington Principles which governed disputes between unions over members. The Bridlington agreement did not have the status of a rule and the TUC's *Programme for Action* would be just as binding on unions as the Bridlington Principles. The Prime Minister suggested a further amendment to the Government's draft of Rule 11. This was designed to make it clear that the TUC would not be expected to order an unconditional return to work if it thought that to do so was unreasonable. Then he and Barbara Castle retired while the General Council considered its position again.

The General Council decided, in the words of Hugh Scanlon, to "stick". The sub-committee of seven went back to the Prime Minister. They informed him that they had little quarrel with the form of words suggested by the Government but still could not agree to give it the status of a rule. They also wanted him to amplify his pledge to drop the penal clauses. Was he simply talking about dropping them from the interim legislation? Wilson replied that he was giving a firm indication that if agreement was reached there would be no question of introducing the penal clauses or alternative sanctions during the lifetime of his

Government. There would be no interim Bill. But, said the Prime Minister, he would only be in the position to give these pledges, which went far beyond any he had made the previous week, if he had something to demonstrate the TUC's commitment. This needed to be enshrined in TUC rules. "A piece of paper is not sufficient," he declared.

Feather again said that he could not understand why the Government believed that a statement of principles would be any less binding than a change of rule. Would it not be more politically advantageous to the Government to settle than to accept the consequences of a failure to agree? No, said Harold Wilson; if there was no binding undertaking from the TUC the Tories would be able successfully to conduct the next election campaign on a basis of union bashing. If the TUC would agree to a rule change the Government could present the agreement to Parliament and the public as the Government dropping legislation because the TUC was itself legislating. That would make all the difference. Feather could not see that this would make any difference in political terms. But industrially it made a great difference. Trade unions would lose confidence in the TUC if they saw the Government writing its rules for it.

It was nearly lunchtime. The Prime Minister had held out for more than two hours. The General Council had gone on calling his bluff. Before they broke for lunch Wilson said that he was prepared to admit that he had learned a lot from the recent discussions but he could not agree to a formula which it would be impossible for him to defend publicly.

He was prepared now to accept defeat but not humiliation. Over their lunch he and Barbara Castle decided to save themselves. Victor Feather had thrown them the lifebelt when he had mentioned the Bridlington Principles. The Bridlington Declaration of 1939 set out a code of behaviour for unions competing to recruit members. It was not a rule but it was something more than a mere declaration of intent. It had not stopped the unions poaching but in nearly all cases they accepted the rulings of the gamekeeper when they were caught at it. A Downing Street Declaration with the same status as the Bridlington Declaration would save some of the Government's face. Whether Wilson was at any time prepared to break off with the TUC and face his Cabinet again we cannot know. If it was the choice between that and humiliation he would probably have done so, believing that the deserters would return to him when their nerve was really tested. He may still have hoped to carry his party in a situation in which the Government had reached the edge of collapse.

But Victor Feather was not seeking to humiliate the Prime Minister but to save him if he could. He had seen his opponent's cards and therefore he knew that he needed to make no concession of substance. In any case he could not, for Hugh Scanlon and Jack Jones continued to prescribe the limits of what the TUC could undertake, as they had done throughout the affair. Nor was it in Feather's interest to destroy the Prime Minister even had he wished to. In the first place he could not have been sure of doing so, for there would be the risk that the Prime Minister might carry his Cabinet on the second attempt. Then there would be legislation and Feather's one and only objective was to prevent that. But in any case it would be immensely damaging to the TUC to be seen to bring down a Prime Minister and perhaps a Government. The art of negotiation lies in knowing when to stop. Wilson was a skilled and brave exponent, as he had shown that morning; Feather also knew when to let the opponent off the hook.

After the lunch interval, and after a brief private meeting with Victor Feather, Harold Wilson announced to the General Council that on his own initiative, and with Barbara Castle's agreement, he was prepared to discuss with them "a solemn and binding undertaking" which would be entered into unanimously by the General Council and which would embody the words which the Government had proposed as a rule change. Such a solemn and binding undertaking would in the annals of Congress be comparable in standing to the Bridlington Declaration.

The rest was formality. The afternoon was spent drafting the "solemn and binding undertaking". "Solemn and binding", it sounds like a character out of George Eliot said one of the officials afterwards. The Attorney General was brought in to assist with the wording. The text of the declaration was laid before the whole General Council. Victor Feather declared it accepted unanimously, for he was not going to risk a vote at that stage. The Prime Minister reported to the waiting Cabinet at 5.15. There is said to have been applause. The Cabinet took only a few moments to endorse the action he had taken. Harold Wilson and Barbara Castle returned from the Cabinet to the General Council. Wilson said, "I hope that the outcome will not be regarded as a victory for either side, but as a victory for good industrial relations". With that, those who felt there was something to celebrate stayed for a drink. The others went home.

Later the Prime Minister addressed a packed meeting of the

Parliamentary Labour Party. Backbenchers were jubilant – the battle fleet had turned back, the missiles had been removed, the confrontation was over. Harold Wilson presented himself to his supporters as the author of a considerable coup. "Even last night", he said dramatically, "when I met the trade union group, we were still far from satisfied that the powers were there. With the negotiations still in progress there was very little I could say, but at least I think I might claim that the dire warnings of last night have proved to be wide of the mark. I was told last night with great authority that the TUC could not move further and that Croydon was the end. Today, in fact, they have. . . . Our requirements have been met today".

The next day Harold Wilson was given one of the roughest handlings he had ever received in the House of Commons. But with the Conservatives baying for his blood his party was once more united behind him. The Speaker was obliged to intervene: "I must insist that the Prime Minister be heard". Edward Heath badgered him to answer one single question, "What will happen when unofficial strikers ignore the trade union leaders and go on striking?" It was a question Wilson had himself put a score of times to the leaders of the TUC. Now his own reply from the Despatch Box was as imprecise as the answer he each time had received from the TUC and was as unsatisfactory to the Opposition as the TUC's answer had for so long been unsatisfactory to Harold Wilson.

That night Wilson addressed the public on television. Had there not been a satisfactory settlement there would have been legislation, he asserted. He went on: "In view of the tripe I read in some of this morning's papers let me make it clear that we were utterly resolved to do this by law – no matter what the political repercussions, no matter what the opposition in my own party or anywhere else".*

The next evening Edward Heath replied. He said, "He knows, you know, the world knows after last Wednesday, that although they may still wear the trappings of office, the power resides elsewhere".

* * * * *

The "Solemn and Binding Undertaking" entered into at Number 10, Downing Street on June 18 did not involve any substantial movement by the TUC. On June 11 it had been prepared to circularise

---

*I was among the tripe merchants. I had reported in *The Guardian*: "Mr. Wilson fought to the last ditch for his policy of union reform but at Tuesday's protracted Cabinet Meeting it became evident that a majority of his colleagues was not prepared to support the hard line."

affiliated unions with what was already described as "a binding statement of intent". The form of words adopted did not go beyond what had been stated in the *Programme for Action* agreed at Croydon. At question time on June 17 the Prime Minister had publicly stated once more that the Government's condition for not legislating was the TUC legislating through its rules. The terms of the "Solemn and Binding Undertaking" made it clear that the TUC would only place an "*obligation on trade unions to take energetic steps to obtain an immediate resumption of work including action within their rules*" in cases where the TUC deemed the strikers to be at fault. Where the TUC considered it "*unreasonable to order an unconditional return to work*" the General Council would merely tender its "*considered opinion and advice*". With this the TUC had won its essential point: it was going to judge disputes on their merits; it had not committed itself to automatic action. In this way the purpose of the conciliation pause was lost. The Government's objective throughout was not to adjudicate in disputes, according to their merits, but to achieve a resumption of work pending negotiation or inquiry. Barbara Castle had spelt this out over and over again. As for Bridlington, the point had been made often enough that policy decisions of Congress were as binding (or as unbinding) as its rules. However, the Bridlington analogy did make the piece of paper signed at Number 10, Downing Street slightly more credible. Victor Feather did not consider that he had moved in any essential beyond the position established at Croydon. But the Prime Minister, as he had frankly told the TUC, needed something he could "defend to the public", something "saleable". What had been agreed was really a solemn and binding face saver for the Prime Minister and Barbara Castle.

In terms of industrial relations the outcome was probably the best that could be obtained. It would probably not have made very much practical difference if the TUC had altered its rules to suit the Government. Its ability to deal with unofficial and unconstitutional strikes depended neither on rules nor the wording of declarations but on the strength of its will and the voluntary cooperation of unions. Jack Jones and Hugh Scanlon effectively set the limits on that. Probably it would have made little difference either if the penal clauses had reached the statute book. For the success of Barbara Castle's scheme would have depended no less upon the willingness of unions and their members to observe the law in letter and in spirit. In the long run they might have done so, but that would have required a profound change in social attitudes and success in the slow, complex programme of shop floor reform advocated by the Royal Commission. In the absence of a voluntary compliance the law would more likely have been brought into disrepute.

It was true the trade unions had moved a long way and they had done so under the pressure of Government intervention. Until legislation was threatened progress had been minimal. The advance represented by the Croydon Congress can be measured against the Douglas, Isle of Man, Congress of 1960. In that year there was a great fuss about a bromide of a report on disputes by the General Council. It had said that where strike action was taken or prolonged contrary to the general policy or specific advice of unions they "should take some form of disciplinary action against the members concerned". Even this caused great alarm and it was necessary for the General Council's spokesman to assure delegates, "If the union does not want to exercise any discipline, the TUC cannot force it to do so and does not intend to". The General Council's study of the strike problem petered out the next year and after that nothing more was heard of it. Now in 1969 the problem was at last recognised, a responsibility accepted and the General Council determined to do its limited best to prevent and settle disputes and to stop unjustified strikes. For the new general secretary of the TUC, Victor Feather, this would be the chief task during his term of office. He had not promised to do more than be believed he could; he intended fully to do what he had said. By publicly declaring its intentions in a specific fashion the TUC has subjected itself to the pressure of public opinion. That too might make for some progress. But the central question remained unanswered. What can society do when its bad labour relations result in destructive strikes? There appeared to be no answer – except to patiently improve its labour relations and its trade unions.

Politically the Wilson Government could take some credit for prodding the trade unions into action. But that would depend on the action they actually took. In the words of Barbara Castle, the Government had "gone nap", on the will and the ability of the TUC. From now on irresponsible, damaging strikes of the Girling variety could do greater than ever political harm to the Government and the Labour Party. In the meanwhile, however, the public was entitled to judge the Government's performance by the criteria set by the Government itself. Harold Wilson had made many rash assertions, the chief of which was that the Industrial Relations Bill was essential to the Government's economic success and its continuance in office. He had said many times that the only alternative to Government legislation was TUC legislation. Now there was to be no Government legislation and the TUC had refused to legislate. Within the terms of reference prescribed for himself by himself the Prime Minister suffered a defeat at the hands of the trade unions.

Yet it was not trade union power which prevented the Government from legislating. Harold Wilson and Barbara Castle were held back by their own supporters in Parliament and, ultimately, by the Cabinet itself. The TUC operated effectively as a pressure group; it was skilfully led by Victor Feather; the left and the right wings of the General Council came together in remarkable unity; MPs were kept supplied with simple, strong practical arguments against what the Government was proposing. The TUC fought the case on its merits, arguing that the Government's plan would worsen industrial relations while the TUC's plan was the best means for improving them. But the hysteria in the Parliamentary Labour Party was caused not so much by these industrial arguments as by the symbolic political implications of Barbara Castle's proposals. It seemed to a steadily increasing number of MPs that an internecine war was being fought for no good cause. The party was by no means united against the principle of State intervention in industrial relations. It was not even united on principle against the penal clauses. If it had been a clear question of whether the Labour Party should be a trade union party or a broadly based radical alliance there would have been a majority for the latter choice. Therefore the situation was not at all like the earlier party quarrels over public ownership or defence, for both these controversies were essentially about whether the Labour Party would remain a party of protest or become a viable party of government. When it was suggested that Clause Four of the Party's 1918 socialist constitution should be rewritten, the trade union dominated Centre of the party had sided with the Left. When it was proposed to ban the bomb the trade union Centre had sided with the Right. But for the majority of MPs the industrial relations question was not an ideological controversy. The Right, the Left and the Centre of the party united not on principle but in doubting the wisdom and practicality of the Government's policy, in doubting the Government's competence, authority and judgement for pursuing it, and in questioning the leadership of the Prime Minister.

When *In Place of Strife* was published as a White Paper in January there were few passionate feelings about it and with few exceptions nobody predicted the full extent of the trouble it would cause. It was the April decision to legislate as a matter of urgency which provoked the hysteria. By then the morale of the party had reached rock bottom and respect for the authority of the Prime Minister was at its lowest ebb. This was the result of the Government's continuing record of failure and of dispiriting muddles unconnected with the trade union question. In other circumstances the Government could have carried its policy, as governments almost invariably do. For example, the prices and incomes legislation had been forced upon the party in spite of offending just as many principles, sentiments and interests. Parliament had grown no stronger in the meanwhile and "backbench power" was a phenomenon confined to the unique procedural circumstances of the Parliament Bill. What had happened was simply that the authority of the Government and the Prime Minister had declined to the point at which it was much more difficult, if not impossible, to impose an unpopular and unconvincing policy on an unwilling party. In these unusual circumstances the TUC proved an unusually effective lobby on Government but the affair proves nothing about the power of the trade unions as a pressure group on Government. For the trade unions had failed to resist a statutory incomes policy. Again, the only change was the decline in the Wilson Government's authority, particularly as a result of the failure of its economic policies hitherto.

Even in these circumstances the Prime Minister could not be removed. But on two occasions he was vulnerable. He was not seriously threatened by the attempted backbench coup in May but dissatisfaction with his leadership reached an unprecedented level. The reasons why in the end the coup was not attempted were chiefly because there was insufficient support for either James Callaghan or Roy Jenkins, and because the Prime Minister's opponents came to believe that he would beat a tactical retreat on the trade union question. On June 18 Harold Wilson came more dangerously close to deposition by his Cabinet but then he did beat a tactical retreat and saved himself. The "power of the Prime Minister" was thus sufficient for him to remain in office, but insufficient for him to remain in office *and* have his way. The explanation was not that his formal powers, *vis-à-vis* the Cabinet, Parliament or his party, had been in any way reduced but that his standing with his colleagues, his party and the country was at that time greatly diminished by the failures of his Government. The same applied to the Inner Cabinet. It had been assumed that any course of action agreed by the most powerful group of Ministers in the Government and, in particular, by the Prime Minister, Chancellor and First Secretary operating in informal unison, was bound to prevail in the Cabinet as a whole. In the unusual conditions of the summer of 1969 that was no longer so. The authority of a Government directorate is no more and no less than the authority of the Government as a whole and of the Prime Minister.

Harold Wilson was trying to prove that Labour could govern. But the proof was to be found in the ultimate success or failure of the Government's policies, notably in the economic field. By making the strike question the test of Labour's competence as a party of government he succeeded in the end in demonstrating the opposite of what he intended. For at the end of the affair the Labour Party was more vulnerable on the trade union question than it had been at the beginning. As measured by the Gallup Poll, opinion on which party was best able to deal with the strike problem moved as follows:

	Oct. '68	Jan. '69	April '69	June '69	Aug. '69
Labour	33	25	25	31	26
Conservatives	30	37	42	31	33

Apart from in June 1969 when the Government's confrontation with TUC was reaching its climax the Government's emphasis on the strike problem had the effect of advertising the claims of the Conservative Party as the one which would be toughest with the trade unions. The Tories had struck this posture with their policy statement of 1968. The public was clearly becoming increasingly impatient with strikes. Yet there was no evidence since the war to suggest that trade unionism or strikes had on any occasion been a leading election issue. By linking the strike problem so closely with the country's economic problems Wilson risked making it into an election issue which would rebound against Labour in any other than the unlikely circumstances of industrial peace.

In addition to trying to demonstrate Labour's competence to govern Harold Wilson was attempting to establish his party as a national party. For Labour to replace or compete equally with the Conservatives as the "ruling party" (the party which people expect to hold power more often than not) he had to build a permanent alliance between progressive middle and working class voters. By the time he embarked on the reform of industrial relations the middle class support he had won in the 1966 election had drained away in large quantity. And traditional Labour voters, who were abstaining in huge numbers in by-elections and local government elections, were becoming more and more irritated by strikes which threw them out of work or ate into their pay packets. The loyalists had to be won back – that was the precondition of victory. But in order to win and hold the vital centre ground the Labour Government needed to show that its programme for reforming the major institutions of society did not exclude the main vested sectional interest within the Labour Movement.

It was assumed, although it is not self-evident, that reforming the trade unions and doing something about strikes required direct State intervention in industrial relations. By that standard, the standard set by the Government for itself when it adopted Barbara Castle's dirigiste policy, the Government failed. But the failure cannot be attributed simply to the nature of the Labour Movement. It had more to do with the inadequacy of the policy adopted, the intractability of the problem and the diminished authority of the Government at the time when it embarked upon the attempt. It was trying for quick results in unfavourable circumstances; and it was too late in its term of office to initiate a policy which depended chiefly for its success not on the devices for restraining and punishing strikers but on their, largely symbolic and exemplary, contribution to an underlying change in social attitudes. The problem was to make the two sides of industry more accountable to the public and one way of doing it was to begin constructing a framework of law so as to gradually break down the outlaw mentality of the trade unions and the short-sighted autocracy of many employers. It will be surprising if the State does not eventually discover means of exercising its responsibilities in the matter of industrial relations. However, this longer-term objective – implicit in the original White Paper – gave way to the short-term objective of appearing to be "doing something" urgently about unofficial strikes. The obsession with the immediate condition of the economy, which had for so long gripped the country and the Government, prevented a calm consideration of the complexity of the human problems in industry. Again, the Government was in part to blame for encouraging a simpliste view – problem: strikes; answer: fines. These mistakes reflect on the competence of the Wilson Government at that time, perhaps of Labour Government in general, but they do not much affect Labour's claims to be a national party, or the allegation that it remains predominately a sectional or class party. Indeed, it could be argued that the Government would have made a better job of reforming the trade unions had its industrial base been stronger. It suffered grievously from the absence of a trade union statesman in the Cabinet itself. The three leading proponents of the policy in the Government – Castle, Wilson and Jenkins – were none of them trade unionists, all of them Oxford educated politicians with no industrial experience. There was no one in a Cabinet of twenty-three approaching Ernest Bevin's statute.

Whether incompetence is endemic in Labour Government is a different and more difficult question. The story of the attempt to reform industrial relations does not suggest that the quality of the Government's decision-making was directly affected by the structure and nature of the Labour Movement. However, it does illustrate how the credibility of a Labour Government was undermined by the style in which the Labour Party apparently has to be led, or at least by the style in which Harold Wilson chose to lead it. There are too many horses in the "bloody circus". The leader of the Labour Party has to embrace within his rhetoric the socialist ideologues who inhabit a party which purports to be the competent manager of a modern mixed economy, the powerful conservative forces contained within a radical party of the left, and the unsatisfied material expectations of its mass supporters which increase rather than diminish with prosperity and which mostly conflict with the vague idealism of Social Democracy. What above all went wrong was that the importance of the Government's proposals for dealing with strikes became exaggerated out of all proportion. To the extent that unrealistic expectations were aroused in the minds of the public, unjustified fears built up in the minds of trade union leaders and MPs. On the one hand, the Government claimed to be "strengthening the trade unions"; on the other hand it was advertising its willingness to fine trade unionists. The result was that the eventual outcome lacked credibility. For the same reasons the legislation, had it gone through, would also have lacked credibility, and this was one of the chief reasons why it did not go through. The Social Democratic dilemma – how to contain the interests of organised labour within a broadly-based political party, and how to combine free trade unionism with the efficient management of a mixed economy – remained unsolved. Perhaps one of the troubles with Labour Government is that it noisily asks itself such awkward questions in public instead of getting on quietly with doing the best it can.

Harold Wilson's chief mistake was to lose touch with his party. He ventured further than Hugh Gaitskell had ever dared in offending the beliefs and sentiments of his party in a bid to establish it as a national party and a governing party. A better display of sound judgement in the handling of the affair might have been more impressive than his undoubted determination to tackle the problem. The decision to bring forward the short Bill as a matter of urgency was the first fatal error for it closed all the options and brought about a confrontation. However grave the dangers of allowing the controversy to fester on, there was room for manoeuvre until that moment. That error was the collective error of the Government. The escalation of the confrontation after Croydon was the Prime Minister's own. He recklessly doubled his stakes at the one moment when he could have withdrawn most gracefully from the game. But whatever he proved or did not prove about his Government and his party he proved his own political virility. He looked political death in the eye. He proceeded honourably out of conviction until he could proceed no further. He acted according to principle not expediency and put country – the national interest as he saw it – before party. He showed courage bordering on the foolhardy and determination bordering on pig-headedness. At the end he did not climb down, he was dragged down. In the course of losing the great battle of Downing Street he perhaps was the victor of some private battle with himself.

Epilogue

On June 18, 1969 the Harold Wilson Government abandoned its plan to legislate trade union reforms, notably penalties against unconstitutional strikers in certain circumstances. On the previous day the Prime Minister had failed to carry his Cabinet in support of the policy he was pursuing in close co-operation with his Secretary for Employment and Productivity, Barbara Castle. At Number 10 Downing Street on June 18, 1969 a compromise – of a somewhat face-saving kind – was reached with the General Council of the Trades Union Congress. The TUC entered into a "solemn and binding" declaration of its intention to take firm and effective action itself to deal with unconstitutional strikes. There was no doubting, however, that this represented a defeat for the Government which had frequently stated that the only substitute for legislation by Parliament was legislation by the TUC itself through its rules. A year later to the very day the Labour Government was rejected by the voters in a General Election.

The Wilson Government failed (as the election on June 18, 1970 showed) to recover fully from the crisis which overwhelmed it in the spring of 1969. Its failure to do something effective about industrial relations, and in particular unofficial strikes, and the angering or alienation of some of its own supporters by the proposals contained in *In Place of Strife* or by the incompetence of the attempt to carry out its policy, all probably contributed in some part to Labour's defeat. However, these were not the chief causes of it. The chief cause was the Labour Government's failure to meet sufficiently people's expectations of higher living standards. But that failure was in large part the failure to reconcile the practice of free collective bargaining between numerous and autonomous trade unions and employers and employers' associations with policies for full employment and faster economic growth. It can be argued that had not the exchange rate of the currency for so long been given absolute priority the Government would have turned in a better performance in promoting growth. Even so, at any given rate of exchange, the tendency for wages and costs to be pushed up faster than the increase in national productivity is a problem which no government can ignore. Labour's failure to get the measure of the problem, either by a policy for prices and incomes or by reform of the institutions and procedures of collective bargaining, was a part – and an important part – of the central failure in economic management. That was what the "Battle of Downing Street" was about.

A year later and industrial relations were no better as a result of the limited endeavours by the TUC to intervene in disputes in accordance with the undertakings given on June 18, 1969. Indeed the number of strikes and the number of working days lost through disputes has gone on increasing. Wage inflation, generated not by a too great demand for goods and labour but chiefly by trade union demands and institutional pressures on costs and prices, had gathered pace since the final demise of the incomes policy – for what was left of that baby went out with the bathwater of the policy for dealing with strikes. By mid-1970 the country was experiencing the twin evils of rapid inflation and near stagnant production, the so-called inflationary recession. Victor Feather, the TUC's general secretary, was doing his best to discharge the commitments entered into at 10 Downing Street but his best was clearly not good enough: his authority was circumscribed by the power of the greatest trade unions, by the refusal of groups of workers to accept the leadership of even their own unions, by the sheer volume of disputes and the intractability of many of the problems in the relationships between management and men. The problem of industrial relations is more serious than when the Battle of Downing Street was fought; a solution is no nearer.

It remains a problem for the Labour Party in opposition. For if Labour is one day and soon to form the government again it will have to restore its credibility as the party of growth and sound economic management. Therefore it will have to persuade the people once more of its will and capacity to govern the trade unions and not be governed by them. For that is how it must have looked to many when on June 18, 1969 Harold Wilson jettisoned a policy which he had previously stated to be "essential to our economic recovery, essential to our balance of payments, essential to full employment . . . essential to the Government's continuance in office." However, for the Labour Party it is more than a question of credibility as a party of government. The relationship between the Labour Party, as a party of social reform, and the trade unions, increasingly "instrumental" in their approach, is hardly satisfactory in modern conditions. Barbara Castle was surely correct in believing that a more constructive relationship between unions and a Labour Government, a changed balance of rights and responsibilities, was necessary for the successful achievement of Social Democracy. The more so if Labour in opposition discovers new radical purposes, for the trade unions are in many of their aspects forces of conservativism, slow moving and defensive organisations which cannot in their present form and with their present attitudes serve as effective and willing partners for a party of reform.

Now a Conservative Government will soon be in confrontation with the trade unions. It could be the making or breaking of Edward Heath: not only will it be a trial of strength, a test of governmental authority; the outcome will also help to determine the success or failure of the Heath Government in achieving an acceptable rate of increasing prosperity, the pre-condition of electoral success. For it is not only strikes – such as the seamen's strike of 1966 or the national dock strike which began in July 1970 – which can blow a government "off course"; the trade unions can by the denial of wage restraint oblige governments (unless they are prepared to follow the politically dangerous course of periodic devaluations) to defend the exchange rate with policies of deflation which bite upon the aspirations of the people. It is by no means certain that the proposals of the Conservative Government for reforming industrial relations – in essence the creation of a legal framework for the conduct of collective bargaining and in practice not dissimilar from what the Labour Government attempted – will either serve to reduce the economic damage caused by strikes or to promote greater industrial efficiency and less inflationary wage bargaining. However, there is nothing I can see in the experience of the Labour Government which suggests that a Conservative Government need fail to carry through its programme. The reader is likely to conclude that it was not the implacable opposition of the TUC that denied Harold Wilson his way so much as the Government's failing authority at the time and the low morale and divided state of the Labour Party. The Heath Government has a clear mandate and a fresh one. It is tackling the trade union question at the beginning of its term and not, as Labour did, more than halfway through. And if the Conservative policies stand any chance of working it will not be through fining or locking up strikers but by gradually, over a period of years, breaking down the outlaw mentality of the unions and encouraging the development of more responsive institutions and responsible attitudes in the changed atmosphere of a legal framework. However, the story of the Labour Government's dealings with the unions as I tell it in this book offers small cause for hope that such changes can quickly or easily be brought about. The trade union question contributed importantly to the downfall of the Wilson Government. Edward Heath has yet to fight his battle of Downing Street.

July 20, 1970